The Hidden Heart

Other Five Star Titles
by Gayle Buck:

Lord Rathbone's Flirt

The Hidden Heart

Gayle Buck

Five Star • Waterville, Maine

Copyright © Gayle Buck, 1992

All rights reserved.

Published in 2004 in conjunction with Gayle Buck.

The text of this edition is unabridged.

Set in 11 pt. Plantin by Liana M. Walker.

Printed in the United States on permanent paper.

Library of Congress Cataloging-in-Publication Data

Buck, Gayle.
    The hidden heart / by Gayle Buck.
      p. cm.
    ISBN 1-59414-092-8 (hc : alk. paper)
    I. Title.
PS3552.U3326H53 2004
  813'.54—dc22   2003063104

The Hidden Heart

I

It was raining. The gray water hit the leaded windowpanes in a steady monotonous sheet. It looked cold outside, which made the warmth of the drawing room all the more congenial to its occupants. The room was ablaze with candlelight, only the farthest corners holding thin, wavering shadows, and a fire snapped cheerily in the fireplace behind the grate.

A footman silently and unobtrusively poured wine into the glasses that stood at the elbows of each of the fashionable gentlemen. The servant slipped quietly from the room without any of the four gentlemen having taken particular note of either his entrance or his exit.

The gentlemen's attention was focused on the playing cards in their hands. One gentleman's heavy brows were knit with the complexity of his thoughts. Another sprawled in a careless fashion in his chair, his thin lips curled in a lazy half-smile. Opposite them, the third gentleman sat with half-drooping lids, seemingly near asleep. The fourth, who was also the host of the impromptu card party, reached absently for his newly filled wineglass.

Lord Edward Heatherton, whose habitual expression of perpetual anxiety had deepened along with his concentration, broke the silence. "Dash it, Miles!"

The Earl of Walmesley set down his wineglass. He looked over the table at his frowning guest and gave a quiet laugh. "What, dicked again, Nana?" Lord Trilby asked, not unkindly.

"One should never bet against a man in his own house,"

7

intoned the third gentleman without opening his eyes.

Lord Heatherton, who was known affectionately to his closest cronies as "Nana" for his constant worrying, cast a fulminating glance at the sleepy-eyed gentleman. "All very well for you, Carey. You have lost but a pittance this night, whilst I . . . ! But how was one to know that Miles's wretched luck would do such a complete about-face? I ask you! It is quite unfathomable. And it is no good saying one shouldn't bet against a man under his own roof, for it ain't true. Why, not two days ago in this same room, Miles scribbled a fistful of his vowels to us all."

There was general laughter about the table.

"You are a fool, Nana," said the thin-lipped gentleman in a tolerant fashion. He picked up his glass and threw back the wine in a quick swallow.

Lord Heatherton appealed to the earl. "Well, one couldn't have known, could one, Miles?"

"No," agreed Lord Trilby.

"This is the last hand for me," Viscount Weemswood suddenly announced. He stared into his wineglass, not bothering to guard his cards.

Lord Heatherton turned his head sideways so that he could see the cards thus exposed. He puffed out his cheeks in dismay and shook his head. Mournfully he said, "I am all rolled up twice over."

Upon the viscount's announcement, the sleepy-eyed gentleman abruptly sat up. Mr. Carey Underwood, now demonstrably wide-awake, demanded, "You're never going to attempt it in this weather, Sinjin."

The gentleman addressed raised his gaze to meet his friend's alarmed eyes. His sardonic half-smile widened. "Why? Have you laid your ready on me, Carey?"

Mr. Underwood swore. "You know very well that I have!

And I don't wish to see my investment thrown away during the course of one of your freakish starts, my lord."

The Earl of Walmesley, who had remained silent, listening, eased his shoulders against the back of his chair. He yawned lazily before saying, "Come, Carey, Sinjin will hardly be so unconscionable as all that."

"There you are out, Miles. Sinjin cares for nothing while in the throes of one of his black tempers. Aye, nothing suits his lordship better than to set us all on our ears," Mr. Underwood said bitterly.

"You don't mean to set out in this storm, do you, Sinjin? The horses will do no good in it," Lord Heatherton said, his heavy brows puckered low over his soulful brown eyes. He sighed. "I've plunked down a pony on you myself, you know."

Viscount Weemswood glanced at the Earl of Walmesley. "And you, Miles?" he asked softly. "Do you also add your persuasions to those of our companions?"

Lord Trilby shrugged. He riffled his cards through his long fingers. "You may go to the devil for all that I care about the matter, Sinjin. You'll do as you wish in any event, whatever the rest of us may say."

"Well, if that ain't just like you, Miles! All unconcern and disinterest, even though you yourself bet sharply in Sinjin's favor," Mr. Underwood exclaimed.

Viscount Weemswood cracked a laugh. The expression in his cold eyes warmed as he said, "I am flattered, indeed. Your faith in me surpasses all understanding, my lord."

Lord Trilby lifted his brows. "Do you think so? I had thought that I expressed just the right dash of indifference. I am forced to conclude that I am losing my touch."

The viscount swung lithely out of his chair, casting down his cards as he did so. "So you are, my friend. Nana, you may claim my winnings from the last hand. I should not wish you to leave tonight with your pockets completely to let—not after you have expressed such touching concern for my cattle. Place it on my chances, if you wish. As for my racing to-night"—he threw a mocking glance in Mr. Underwood's direction—"I am not so damnable a fool as all that." His lordship made a careless salute that encompassed them all before sauntering to the door and opening it.

"I say, mighty handsome of you, Sinjin. You don't often make the kingly gesture," Lord Heatherton said, gratified. He began counting his gratis winnings.

Mr. Underwood stared after the viscount as his lordship disappeared through the open door. "No, it isn't like him at all." He glanced at the Earl of Walmesley. "I think that I shall go after his lordship, just to tag along a bit and perhaps share a cab."

"Sinjin will not turn a kindly eye on uninvited company," Lord Trilby said quietly.

"Don't I know it," Mr. Underwood agreed feelingly. He rose from his chair. "I've felt the sting of his damnable cutting tongue before this. All the same, his lordship is acting in a queer mood even for him. Well, see what he has tossed to Nana as coolly as you please, as though we don't know he is four quarters to the wind since the old gentleman up and married that mistress of his because she was increasing. Dash it, Miles, where's the justice in it?"

Lord Trilby fingered his wineglass. "One learns early enough that justice is blind, my idealistic friend."

Mr. Underwood was affronted. "I am no more an idealist than yourself, Miles! If I choose to ensure that Sinjin makes his way safely to his door, it is because I wish to protect my investment in this race." Mr. Underwood stared at the earl, daring his lordship to challenge his statement. When the earl only smiled, Mr. Underwood gave a sharp nod of satisfaction. He left the room, and the remaining gentlemen could hear his raised voice. "Weemswood! Wait a moment, for I've a notion to share that cab."

"I shall be taking my leave also, Miles," Lord Heatherton said as he finished collecting his winnings. He swept them into the capacious pockets of his frock coat.

The earl cast a glance at the clock on the mantel. "It is not above two-thirty in the morning and I am to be entirely deserted," Lord Trilby complained.

Lord Heatherton paused to look at his host, wearing his most anxious expression. "I hope you are not offended? The thing of it is, Miles, m'mother is in town and I promised that I would meet her tomorrow—today!—for breakfast, and I need to make myself presentable."

Lord Trilby was too familiar with the terror with which Lord Heatherton regarded his mother's infrequent London visits not to feel sympathy for his friend. "Then you must go, indeed. No, Nana, not another word of explanation is necessary. Females of any persuasion have a natural bent for making us poor fellows as uncomfortable as possible."

"That's it in a nutshell," Lord Heatherton said, relieved that the earl understood his predicament so well.

The Earl of Walmesley pulled the bell rope and when the footman appeared requested that Lord Heatherton's driver be notified of his lordship's desire to depart. The footman left. Lord Trilby picked up the more-than-half-emptied bottle of wine from the table and splashed a measure into Lord Heatherton's glass. He handed the glass to his friend. "Here, Nana, fortify yourself against the coming ordeal."

"Don't mind if I do," Lord Heatherton said, seizing on the wineglass. He was not usually given to excessive drink, preferring to sip appreciatively at a good brandy such as the earl served, but this time he downed the wine without hesitation. He coughed a little as he returned the glass to the table. "Thank you, my lord. You are a true friend," he said hoarsely.

"I am happy that you think so, Nana," Lord Trilby said, amused.

He walked with his last guest from the drawing room to the front door. "Pray give my regards to your mother, my lord," Lord Trilby said, speaking in a more formal fashion than was his wont for the sake of the servants' presence. He gestured for the footman to open the door and signal Lord Heatherton's driver.

"I shall be certain to do so, my lord. M'mother approves of you more than all the rest," Lord Heatherton said. At the earl's expression of mild surprise, he confided, "She once told me that you at least are respectable, not like Carey with his preference for the petticoats or Sinjin with his taste for hardened gaming."

"Indeed!"

Lord Heatherton's face split in a rare grin as he stepped out into the rain. He was delighted to have shaken even by a hair the Earl of Walmesley's famous and unshakable self-possession. With a wave, he dashed down the steps to his waiting carriage.

The door was closed by the footman, but Lord Trilby remained fixed where his friend had left him. He stood a moment more in reflection.

"Good God, I am become respectable. What an intolerable bore," he murmured. Then he shrugged and went upstairs to his bed, leaving the butler and the footman to straighten up the drawing room, put out the candles, and bank the fire.

2

Lord Trilby was attired in a chintz dressing gown over his shirt and pantaloons. He had just finished breakfast before he had been waylaid by his secretary and drawn into the study. Sprawled in an easy chair, he cracked a huge yawn. Immediately he apologized for his rudeness. "Forgive me, Weston. It was a long evening last night and I did not sleep well afterward, owing to the storm. My ceiling unaccountably leaks, you see, and directly over my pillow. Now, what is it that has so excited your interest that it cannot wait until I am come back from my morning calls?"

"This, my lord," Mr. Weston said. He handed a set of closely written sheets to the earl.

Lord Trilby glanced at the elegant spidery handwriting. "Ah, the venerable grandduchess." With resignation he said, "What new direction has the old tartar conjured up for my painful perusal?"

Mr. Weston did not answer, knowing a rhetorical question when it was asked, and indeed, the earl had already begun to read the letter.

Lord Trilby read swiftly, but at one point he stopped completely, to back up and reread a particular page, before he continued on to finish the letter. He looked up, saying blankly, "Good God."

"Just so, my lord," Mr. Weston said. The flicker of a sympathetic smile touched his lips at his lordship's expression of stunned disbelief.

The Earl of Walmesley looked at his secretary. He said in a

13

hollow voice, "I am undone, Weston, quite undone."

"I hope not, my lord."

Lord Trilby shook his head. "Oh, but I am, my good man. You will naturally recall the last letter I directed you to send to my great-aunt. It would appear that your strenuous advice to me on that occasion was most sound, Weston. I should have listened to you, of course. You have never steered me aground, as far as I can recall. Have you. Weston?"

"I should hope not, indeed, my lord!" Mr. Weston said, appalled at the very idea that he could ever allow himself to give his illustrious employer any but the most well-thought-out advice.

"No. Well, then, I trust that you have some words of encouragement to offer me in this dark hour?"

Mr. Weston reluctantly shook his head. His expression was pained. "I fear not. I am most sorry to fail you in this instance, my lord."

The earl laughed quietly. He got to his feet. "Do not flagellate yourself, Weston. I had not actually expected you to come forth with an instant solution." Lord Trilby clapped his hand against his secretary's shoulder. "I am to blame for this contretempts. If I had listened to you, I would never have given the Grandduchess of Schaffenzeits to understand that I was engaged in the first place. But it seemed such a perfect solution to her grace's last letter, in which she told me so forcibly that I was too nice in my requirements. Do you recall the letter that precipitated that reaction, Weston?"

"Indeed, my lord. You gave the grandduchess to understand that there was no one in all of England whom you would consider suitable for your bride," Mr. Weston said.

"Yes, so then I was obliged to tell her grace that I had found someone after all and that we had agreed upon a lengthy engagement owing to some vague family considerations." Lord Trilby eyed his secretary and suggested, "Perhaps I was a bit too vague, Weston?"

Mr. Weston pursed his lips. "Indeed, I feared so at the time, my lord."

The Earl of Walmesley sighed. "And so it has proved. Now only look at what has come of it." He slapped the sheets of the letter with his free hand. "She means to see me firmly wedded this time, and to some chit I have never met, to boot! Listen to this, Weston. 'Marie is a good, biddable girl who will do as I tell her. She will make you an admirable wife.' Then there is some rubbish about the girl's proper manners and delicate beauty and sweet quiet nature, before we get to the core of the matter, which I shall quote: 'Marie will make you a father many times over. Her family has the reputation of breeding like rabbits, and it is true—I have myself investigated the genealogy. I am satisfied that you will find Marie acceptable in every way.' "

Lord Trilby looked over the sheets at his secretary. His brows were raised in incredulous amazement. "Can you believe it, Weston? I am to marry this girl, if you please, because she will breed like a damned rabbit."

Mr. Weston had difficulty swallowing the disrespectful laugh that unexpectedly rose to his lips. He changed it hastily to a cough. "The Grandduchess of Schaffenzeits is inordinately fond of you, my lord, and of her connection to you."

"Aye," the earl agreed gloomily. " 'Tis a pity I am the last of the English line. If there was another, I would not now be in this awkward position." He reflected a moment. "Perhaps I should go into the army. It is pretty warm going in the Peninsular, so one hears, so I should probably find it lively enough. One could not very well leave a new bride behind, so there would be no question of marrying until the war was done. Of course, there is always the possibility of one's luck turning at just the wrong moment; but there is the other side of that, as well. If I was killed, the Grandduchess of Schaffenzeits could not very well marry some rabbity chit to me, could she? What think you, Weston? Shall it be the army?"

"No, my lord," Mr. Weston said firmly.

The earl sighed. "You are probably in the right of it. The grandduchess would follow me to hell itself, my unwanted bride in tow, and see that we were joined together over the fires of the pits whilst all of Satan's dominions looked on."

"My lord!" Mr. Weston was shocked by such blasphemous ramblings, even though he thought he knew the earl's teasing character too well to take his lordship seriously.

"Have I shaken you with my nonsense, Weston?" Lord Trilby asked. He sighed a little. "I am so completely at point non plus that I cannot think what to do."

"If I may suggest, my lord, that perhaps this once you might explain the matter clearly to the grandduchess and she will relent," Mr. Weston said.

"Lay my cards on the table, do you mean?" The earl shook his head. "It won't do, Weston. I have attempted it on several occasions in the past, all to naught; hence these later abortive maneuvers. Nothing will move the grandduchess from her determination to see me safely wedded. Dash it, Weston! I am but eight-and-twenty. I am not ready to saddle myself with a wife and a growing nursery. I know that my line dies with me, but why must the grandduchess insist that I wed just now?"

"I believe it is often so with the elderly, my lord. They feel great anxiety to have everything wrapped up and tidied," Mr. Weston said.

"Oh, I realize that her gace is more than four-score years and she feels herself increasingly mortal. But is that good enough reason to hurry myself into leg shackles? I cannot believe that it is," Lord Trilby said.

"The Grandduchess of Schaffenzeits is inordinately fond of you, my lord," Mr. Weston said gently.

Lord Trilby sighed. "As I am of her grace, or otherwise I should have told her to go to the devil long since." He reflected a moment. "Well, stands to reason, doesn't it? I have not seen my German cousins upwards of half a dozen times in my life; but when I was a boy, and even later, the grandduchess spent nearly every summer with my parents and me here in England. I have many fond memories of the old lady. She is a grand lady in every sense of the words."

He waved his hand, deliberately dismissing such sentimentality. "But that is neither here nor there. The matter at hand is how I am to extricate myself from this trap of my own making. Any notions, Weston?"

Mr. Weston spread his hands in a helpless fashion. "I am sorry, my lord, but nothing immediately comes to mind."

Lord Trilby sighed again. "Quite all right, Weston. I suppose that I rely upon you too heavily at times."

"It is a pity that your lordship does not at least have a tentative understanding with some lady," Mr. Weston said regretfully.

Lord Trilby's head whipped up, an arrested expression on his face. "What was that, Weston?"

Mr. Weston was thrown off-balance. "Why . . . why, I was but thinking aloud, my lord."

"And an inspired thought it was, Weston!" Dawning light entered the earl's eyes. "I have only to present a *fiancée* to the grandduchess and she will have no choice but to take her rabbit back to the duchy with her."

Mr. Weston stared at his employer in confusion. He faltered. "Your intended, my lord? But . . . you do not have an intended."

The earl seemed not to hear him. "I do not know why I did not think of it before. It is the answer, Weston, I am certain of it. I have only to do the thing right, and with any luck at all the Grandduchess of Schaffenzeits can be cajoled out of this rut of wishing to marry me off to some chit or other."

"But, my lord! You cannot be serious. Surely I need not recall to you that you have not got an intended and, what's more, you do not want one," Mr. Weston said.

"Quite right, Weston." There was a bright gleam in the earl's eyes. He sat down at his desk and pulled a sheet of paper to him. "But the first matter can be easily remedied, I fancy."

Mr. Weston was thoroughly bewildered. "But you said not a moment since that you do not wish to wed, my lord."

"Nor do I. But what is that to the purpose?" Lord Trilby asked, dipping a pen in the inkwell. He began writing rapidly on the sheet of paper. "I shall call on the lady immediately to see whether I am able to arrange it."

"My lord, you cannot mean to offer for a lady under false pretenses!" Mr. Weston exclaimed, horrified.

"No such thing. I hope I have a better notion of what is due my honor than that. No, I mean to cast myself upon the lady's mercy and enlist her help in putting into motion a grand deception," Lord Trilby said, still writing.

Mr. Weston's facile brain instantly grasped the truth. "Lady Caroline!"

Lord Trilby glanced up at his secretary. "Weston, your percipience fills me with admiration. Yes, I hope to enlist Lady Caroline in this dark hour to enter into my little plot."

"My lord, pray reconsider!" Mr. Weston was beside himself with alarm. "You cannot possibly ask such a thing of Lady Caroline. 'Tis rank folly!"

"Do not look so appalled, Weston. Lady Caroline knows

me better than anyone. She will not allow me to get in over my head, I assure you. She don't want to marry me any more than I wish to marry her. We'll do the thing between us, I am certain," Lord Trilby said. He put aside his pen and perused the closely written sheet. Satisfied, he sanded it and handed the missive to his secretary, who had been rendered utterly speechless. "These are my instructions while I am gone, Weston. You must cancel my engagements for the next several days, of course. I shall keep you apprised of my progress with Lady Caroline, so that you will know what to do when the Grandduchess of Schaffenzeits and the rabbity chit arrive."

As the earl was speaking, he had risen from his desk and sauntered across the study toward the door. A queer sound was uttered behind him, and he paused to glance back at his secretary, who stood statuelike with half-parted lips and a shocked expression. "Well, Weston?"

Mr. Weston appeared to gather himself. He held up the sheet that had been entrusted to him. The paper shook in his hand. "My lord, what exactly am I to tell the Grandduchess of Schaffenzeits?"

"As little as possible," Lord Trilby said easily. "Now I'm off. Convey my regards to my great-aunt whenever she and her entourage should arrive. If you have not had word from me before my great-aunt descends upon the house, put her grace off as best you can until I am able to communicate with you in regard to my success with Lady Caroline."

Before he went out the door, Lord Trilby regarded his secretary's odd color and starting eyes. "You look damned queer, man. Weston, perhaps you should have a physician in to see you." He left the study and the door closed gently behind him.

For several moments Mr. Weston stared at the spot vacated by his lordship. Then he roused himself with a shake. He went with stilted steps to the sideboard to pour himself a small amount of brandy from the decanter. He regarded the level in the glass and recklessly splashed in another measure. It was an unusual liberty, but he felt this one instance could be fully justified. Before touching the glass to his lips, he said morosely, "Disaster shall come of it, I shouldn't wonder."

He tossed back the brandy in a single swallow. Unaccustomed as he was to such reckless action, he immediately fell into a whooping, coughing fit. When he at last recovered, his eyes continued to water. Somehow the sheet of instructions had fluttered to the carpet, and it lay there in mute testimony of his failure in his duty, for he had been unable to sway the Earl of Walmesley from his mad course.

The Grandduchess of Schaffenzeits was undoubtedly already on the way to England. Brooding upon that, Mr. Weston felt strong pity for himself.

Naturally, Lord Trilby was to be pitied for the horrible situation in which he found himself, but, Mr. Weston thought, the earl would not be the one who must greet the formidable grandduchess upon her arrival. Mr. Weston had had occasion to meet the Grandduchess of Schaffenzeits once before, and the event was most vividly imprinted upon his memory. His ears still rang with her grace's strongly worded opinion regarding the qualifications required in one so privileged as to be the Earl of Walmesley's secretary.

It occurred to Mr. Weston that perhaps the individual to be most pitied was the lady who was expected to provide a shield for the Earl of Walmesley.

3

The object of Mr. Weston's pity, Lady Caroline Eddington, was at that moment herself wondering at the vagaries of life.

The morning had begun auspiciously enough, having dawned bright and clear after the previous night's thunderstorm. Lady Caroline had perforce risen early and in possession of a mild mood that perfectly matched the splendor of the day. She had gone downstairs to enjoy a solitary breakfast, a common occurrence, since only she and her maternal aunt presently shared the house, and Mrs. Burlington preferred to take her daily chocolate and toast in bed.

Lady Caroline skimmed the morning papers for the war news over her coffee, as was her habit, before she went to the study to begin the day's labors on the stack of paperwork that awaited her attention. Halfway through the morning, the groundskeeper requested a few moments' speech with her ladyship to discuss a small estate problem. The groundskeeper was gratified by Lady Caroline's attentive and knowledgeable questions and eventually he went away satisfied that the matter would be adequately resolved. The housekeeper was waiting to bring in the household accounts for the upcoming quarter, and she and Lady Caroline dealt with them together to their mutual satisfaction.

When luncheon was announced, Lady Caroline felt the personal gratification common to all who have accomplished much. Lady Caroline smiled as she rose from the desk. "You come in good time, Simpson. I am famished. There is nothing so like worthwhile employment to make one appreciate a good luncheon."

"It has been a productive morning, then, my lady," Simpson said, making of it a statement.

"Indeed it has. I shall finish up the most pressing items this afternoon, I feel certain. His lordship shall have nothing to complain of upon his return," Lady Caroline said as she allowed herself to be ushered out of the study.

"His lordship naturally placed every confidence in you, my lady," Simpson said. There was the faintest note of censure in his tone.

Lady Caroline turned to the butler with a laughing look in her eyes. She was well aware of the butler's disapproval of the arrangement that existed between herself and her brother. Lady Caroline's brother, Lord Eddington, now the Earl of Berwicke, had always preferred the amusements and pleasures of London over the estate in Sussex and its attendant responsibilities. Since the death of their father, the old earl, Lord Eddington's tastes had not changed and he had been content enough to leave the running of the estate in his sister's capable hands.

"Indeed, and as always. But we shall not speak of that, if you please," she said in gentle reproof. "Has my aunt come downstairs?"

"Yes, my lady." The butler's face became, if possible, a shade more expressionless. He coughed delicately. "It is my understanding that Mrs. Burlington spent an indifferent night."

Outside the closed door to the dining room, Lady Caroline paused. She threw the butler a glance in which dismay mingled with resignation. "I see. My aunt's indifferent nights have become all too frequent of late. Unfortunately, one cannot cry craven, can one?" It was at that moment that she wondered about the vagaries of life and how one was unwill-ingly compelled to see them through.

She sighed and nodded to the butler. "Thank you, Simpson." The butler executed the briefest of bows as he opened the door for her. Lady Caroline entered the dining room with a firm step. Her countenance was serene and an amiable smile curved her lips. However, the expression in her deep blue eyes, though friendly enough, was cool. "Good af-ternoon, Amaris. It is a lovely day, is it not? A pity that it is still so damp, or otherwise one might have enjoyed a leisurely walk after luncheon," she said cheerfully as she seated herself across the table from her maternal aunt.

Mrs. Burlington eyed her niece with disapprobation. "That is so like you, Lady Caroline. You blithely assume that everyone about you holds the same opinion. Walk, indeed! Only peasants resort to such unhealthy exercise. What is wrong with ordering out the carriage, pray?"

Lady Caroline quietly indicated to the footman that he might serve her before she replied, saying evenly, "The car-riage is naturally at your disposal if you should wish it, Amaris."

"Well, I do not wish it! Pray do not put words into my mouth, my lady. It is a vastly unbecoming trait to presume to do so," Mrs. Burlington said waspishly. She irritatedly waved away the footman's attempts to serve her some barley soup. "Take away that ghastly concoction at once. I shall not touch it. Really, I do not know what the cook is about these days. One would expect to be better served at table in a house of this size. But one must not refine too much on it, for not every detail can be expected to be attended to with equal care whilst under *your* management, Lady Caroline." The last was said with a glittering glance and tight half-smile turned in her niece's direction.

Lady Caroline pretended not to hear the vitriol in her aunt's voice. With every appearance of continued amiability, she said, "I suppose at times it must seem so. However, I find the work both satisfying and stimulating."

Mrs. Burlington gave an angry titter. "Yes, so you have told me on numerous occasions. It is unnatural. A lady should never concern herself with figures and encumbrances and whatever else it is that you do when closed up in that stuffy study. Those matters are for the gentlemen to see to, my dear niece. They are far better equipped to it."

Uppermost in Lady Caroline's mind was the recollection that her aunt's late and unlamented husband had managed to squander his own and his wife's fortunes before he had died of a heart attack, very appropriately, at the gaming table. Ironically enough, his last hand had been a winning one, and if he had had time to play it, he might have recouped enough of his more recent losses that he could have left at least a small jointure for his wife.

As it was, Mrs. Burlington had found herself destitute without even a roof over her head, for the house was discovered to have been hopelessly mortgaged, and she had been forced to accept her sister's offer of a permanent home at Berwicke Keep.

The Countess of Berwicke, Lady Caroline's mother, had been a compassionate woman who seldom saw anything but the best in everyone. She had been universally liked by her acquaintances and her employees. If her ladyship had had any glaring fault, it was that she could at times deliberately blind herself to the most unfortunate circumstances.

Mrs. Burlington was from the first a difficult addition to the family circle, and matters had not improved with the years. The earl had learned not to disparage his sister-in-law to his wife, for if he ever did so, it was so upsetting to her ladyship's illusion of serendipity that she became miserable for days. Mrs. Burlington quickly seized the advantages inherent in such lack of criticism to usurp her sister's authority whenever it best suited her.

When the countess died, Lady Caroline was barely sixteen. It would have been natural for a young girl to turn to her nearest female relation for comfort over the loss of her gentle mother and her guidance into full womanhood, but such had not happened. Lady Caroline, who had inherited both her father's percipience and his practicality, had years before taken her maternal aunt's measure and had found her wanting. It was a measure of her judgement that she had never addressed Mrs. Burlington as "Aunt," for that would have connoted an affection between them that had never existed. Lady Caroline knew that it had greatly enraged Mrs. Burlington to be balked in her attempts to take on the role of mentor. Mrs. Burlington's unfailing attitude toward her ever since had been one of censure and thinly veiled dislike. However, on those days preceded by Mrs. Burlington's indifferent nights, her aunt habitually abandoned all but the most entrenched civilities. Indeed, Mrs. Burlington's insistence to address Lady Caroline with exaggerated formality but pointed up the lady's deliberate rancor.

As Lady Caroline coolly looked over at her aunt, she wondered why she even bothered to keep up the civilities with one who was so determined to wound her. Years before, she had determined to do so because she had not wished to burden her father with the open warfare that would have erupted between them. It had become habit thereafter, especially when her brother had come into the title and had proved to be much like their mother in his inability to deal with strife. But there were now just herself and the dreadful old woman in the house.

The thought spurred her own controlled temper to shake experimentally at its bonds. Her voice was deceptively calm. "And what would you have me do, Amaris? Shall I allow the estate to go to rack and ruin for want of proper attention? I do not think my brother would thank me for such careless administration of my responsibilities when he has entrusted me to handle all matters relating to the estate in his absence."

"Of course not! That is not at all what I meant. How you do take one up, Lady Caroline!" Mrs. Burlington said. "I merely wish to point out that it is most unbecoming in you not to at least consult with a knowledgeable gentleman before making any decision. That, surely, would be most unexceptionable even to one of your headstrong temperament."

Lady Caroline lifted shapely brows. "I apprehend that we at last approach the point of this exercise. Pray do tell me the name of this knowledgeable gentleman, Amaris. Or might I guess?" Her voice had become faintly mocking.

The footmen serving at table exchanged quick startled glances. Careful to remain as silent and unobtrusive as possible, they removed the soup bowls and began to serve the main course. They were unwilling to leave the dining room when such an unusual exchange was shaping up.

Mrs. Burlington stared at her niece through narrowed eyes. She could scarcely contain her annoyance. This niece of hers had always had the trick of setting her down without seeming to make the least push to do so. If she had been the girl's mother, she thought, then perhaps matters would have gone a bit differently through the years.

"Lord Hathaway is eminently suited to take such weighty matters upon his shoulders," Mrs. Burlington said.

"I do not doubt it in the least. However, I too am eminently suited to the task. My brother would not have left me in complete charge if that were not the case. So pray let us have no more about this, Amaris. I shall not welcome it, you see." Lady Caroline's words were gently said, but there was an underlying steel in her voice that would brook no argument. The expression in her eyes was as cool and as steadfast as her voice.

Lady Caroline signaled the footmen that they could begin clearing. Neither she nor her aunt had done justice to the excellent repast, but she found that her original appetite had dwindled with the unpleasant exchange. "We shall have coffee in the drawing room, I think." She turned to her aunt. "Shall we go to the drawing room, Amaris?"

If Lady Caroline hoped that her aunt would be angered to the point of refusing to remain in her company, she was disappointed. Mrs. Burlington acquiesced to the suggestion with a tight nod and also rose from the table.

In the drawing room the two ladies settled in their usual places. Lady Caroline seated herself in a wing chair situated so as to take full advantage of the sunlight glancing in the tall window. Beside the chair was a basket holding skeins of colorful threads and yarns and the embroidery pieces on which she was currently at work. She reached down to pick up the waiting embroidery hoop and began plying her needle.

Mrs. Burlington took the settee. She picked up the latest *Lady's Magazine* and flipped through the pages discontentedly while the butler set the tray on the low table that separated her seat from Lady Caroline's.

When the butler had left, closing the door softly behind him, Mrs. Burlington returned to the attack. "My dear niece, I do think that you should give heed to this much of what I have to say, at least. Lord Hathaway is a most worthy gentleman and he is absolutely devoted to you. You should be more encouraging of him."

Lady Caroline threw a glance at her aunt. This, too, was

an old argument, and she discovered that she had little patience for it that day. It seemed that after she had permitted herself the unusual luxury of snapping back at her aunt, it was now more difficult to control her temper. Setting aside her embroidery and picking up the coffeepot, she said shortly, "Lord Hathaway is all that you say, Amaris. He is also a dull dog."

"I do not find his lordship so," Mrs. Burlington said. "In any event, you are too nice in your requirements, my dear niece. The relationship between a gentleman and his lady is not one of spirited conversation or feeling, I assure you."

Lady Caroline did not answer. She poured coffee for her aunt, adding the milk and sugar for which Mrs. Burlington had a partiality, and offered the cup and saucer to her companion.

Mrs. Burlington took the cup and saucer with scarce thanks. It never failed to rankle her that it was her niece who served as hostess, even when they were alone.

Upon her sister's death, Mrs. Burlington had attempted to take possession of what she considered her rightful place as hostess for her brother-in-law and mistress of the household. But instead, those privileges had been seized by a sixteen-year-old miss just emerged out of the schoolroom, with what Mrs. Burlington had at the time realized was the full complicity of the servants.

When she had stridently remonstrated with the earl, his lordship had brushed aside her criticism with a fine disregard. "Let be, Amaris," he had said. "Lady Caroline must learn her future role as mistress of a grand house, and I can think of no better teacher than experience under my own roof."

Mrs. Burlington still seethed over that defeat. She had never forgiven the earl that slight, nor, indeed, the fact that she was at Berwicke Keep on sufferance.

Mrs. Burlington had always resented the turn of fate that had made her the object of her younger sister's largess—she, who had been the elder, the prettier, the wittier!—so that now she had become dependent upon her sister's daughter for those same courtesies.

"I should have been your mother. Then perhaps you would pay me the respect to which I am due," Mrs. Burlington said abruptly, as an extension of her thoughts. She set down the coffee cup sharply.

Lady Caroline looked over the rim of her cup at her aunt in startled surprise. In the complete stillness of Mrs. Burlington's unfriendly stare, Lady Caroline returned her cup to the table. She had never been one to quail before anticipated unpleasantness and she had long ago learned that her aunt's embittered nature led to festering of slights, imagined or otherwise, if the woman was not immediately challenged. "I see that you have something weighing on your mind, Amaris. Perhaps you should like to air it between us now," she said quietly.

Mrs. Burlington gave the slightest of shrugs. "It would hardly be of any interest to you, dear niece. Indeed, when have my opinions been sought out on anything these many years?"

Lady Caroline was not in the mood to retain the kid gloves that she was wont to use whenever her aunt was particularly provoking. She had worked diligently that morning and her exertions had left her pleasantly tired. Her patience had already been stretched to the utmost by Mrs. Burlington's spiteful utterances.

Lady Caroline's voice was cold. "I apprehend that you believe yourself ill-treated to have been given the home that you have enjoyed these many years since the demise of your wastrel husband."

Mrs. Burlington flushed with unpleasant surprise at her niece's unusual bluntness. "I am sure that I have never complained of my position in this house, such as it is," she said stiffly.

Lady Caroline's smile was faint at best and did not quite reach her eyes. "Indeed, that is undoubtedly true. However, I think that you would not have taken it amiss if my father had turned to you in the end. It would have justified your persistence in remaining here after my mother's death, would it not? After all, before he met my mother, my father was originally your suitor. And you thereafter envied your younger sister the fortune that you felt should have been your own."

4

Mrs. Burlington stared at her niece, aghast. It was all true, but that Lady Caroline should have guessed it was humiliation beyond bearing. "You are impertinent! You do not know what you are saying. What was once between your father and me has nothing at all to do with the matter!"

For the first time in her life, Lady Caroline pursued her aunt mercilessly. "On the contrary, it is the very crux. You harbored resentment and envy against my mother until the day that she died. I saw it and came to understand it. Unlike my dear lady mother, however, I did not close my eyes to it. When she died, you transferred those feelings to me. But I did not bow to them." She smiled, this time almost with amusement. "You always disapproved of the latitude my father allowed me, decrying it as shocking that I should become the mistress of the house upon my mother's death."

Lady Caroline stared a long moment at her aunt, who had apparently been rendered temporarily speechless, before she continued in a more moderate manner. "Pray allow me to remind you that I am my father's daughter and it was far more my right than yours to step into my mother's shoes. As for my brother making me his deputy, that also is not your concern. Nor is it your concern how I choose to receive Lord Hathaway. I am my own mistress, Amaris. Pray remember that from this day forward, for I do not wish to remind you again."

Rarely had Lady Caroline revealed the depth of her temper so completely. Mrs. Burlington felt herself to be scorched by the white heat of it. She said, with something less than her usual aggressive style and with an openly defensive note, "I have but attempted to guide you in what is considered to be the proper deportment of a young lady, which most certainly does not include acting the master of the house." She made a gesture of distaste. "I sometimes expect to find you attired in frock coat and breeches, so presumptuous have you become."

Genuine laughter was startled from Lady Caroline. Her anger was somewhat defused by her aunt's nonsensical revelation. "Really, Amaris! Such a picture you conjure up. I assure you that I have no intention of parading myself about in so ludicrous a fashion." She shook her head, the smile still lurking about her mouth as she picked up her embroidery again.

Mrs. Burlington perceived scorn in her niece's laughing rejoinder and she reacted accordingly. " 'Tis but the truth,"

When Lady Caroline merely sighed, Mrs. Burlington's increasing incensement rallied her to her former style. "I am sorry to wound your sensibilities, Lady Caroline, but since his lordship and his dear lady embarked upon their honeymoon, you have become quite the anecdote!"

"Have I? Then certainly my brother's return will set all straight again," Lady Caroline said. Her composure was again intact, as though the brief exercising of her temper had exorcised the worst of its heat.

"Oh, assuredly it will. You will have to give over precedence to the new countess at tea and elsewhere. You will no longer be mistress of this grand house. That will hardly suit you, will it, my dear niece?" Mrs. Burlington said, her narrowed eyes glittering once more with unmistakable malice.

Lady Caroline looked up quickly, renewed anger kindling in her eyes. The insult was not one to be lightly borne. A devastating retort trembled upon her lips, but at that instant the drawing-room door opened and she was forced to confine herself to an astringently delivered reproof. "My sister-in-law will naturally take precedence over us both. I am surprised that you did not realize it before now, Amaris."

While Mrs. Burlington sucked in air, Lady Caroline turned to the butler with almost palpable relief. "Yes, Simpson? Oh, it is the post. Thank you!" She sent a swift smile up at the butler as she took from the silver salver that he proffered to her several missives and a letter opener. The butler bowed and left the ladies alone once more.

Lady Caroline sifted quickly through the stack. There were several official-looking letters addressed to her and to her brother, which she set aside for later perusal in the study, and a number of personal letters as well. She extracted a few of the letters to hand to Mrs. Burlington. "Your mail, ma'am. I know that you will not mind if I open my own correspondence." She did not wait for an answer, but slit open the seal on one letter immediately and spread the sheets.

"No, indeed," Mrs. Burlington said with heavy sarcasm. She took up the letter opener in her turn and broke the seals of her correspondence. She was immediately riveted by the direction upon one, and with unusual eagerness unfolded the sheets. After a few moments' reading, a small satisfied half smile appeared on her lips. "Well, well. How vastly interesting, to be sure," she murmured softly.

At the sound of a chuckle from her niece's direction, Mrs. Burlington raised her eyes from her own correspondence. Her sharp glance took in Lady Caroline's softened expression. It was easy to guess that the source of Lady Caroline's amusement was the letter that she read so attentively. Mrs. Burlington caught a glimpse of the sprawling hand of the address on the back of the letter, and even across the distance that separated her from her niece, the scrawl was unmistakable. With deliberate spite she said, "I see that you have received another letter from Lord Trilby. How amusing that his lordship should still recall your existence these many years."

Lady Caroline raised her eyes. The warmth that had been kindled in her eyes by the contents of the letter cooled upon meeting her aunt's gaze. All of the amusement of the moment before vanished from her expression, but a trace of it remained in her voice. "Yes, isn't it? Lord Trilby and I have remained the best of friends. I suppose much of that has to do with our families having been neighbors for upwards of two generations."

She started to fold away the missive, and gathered up the rest of her correspondence, intending to finish reading all the letters later in privacy so that she would be able to fully enjoy them without her aunt's unpleasant interruptions.

"If you will excuse me, Amaris, I shall take the rest of these with me to the study. It is past time that I returned to my duties." She rose from her chair, letters in hand, and started toward the door.

"A pity that Lord Trilby was never brought properly up to scratch. It would have made an admirable match." Mrs. Burlington paused fractionally, her sharp eyes on her niece's retreating back. "Do you not think that you have outworn your hopes in that direction, my dear niece?"

Lady Caroline paused before she turned. Her eyes and her voice were extremely cold. "If you are implying that I have been setting my cap for Lord Trilby during his visits to the neighborhood, you are wide of the mark. His lordship and I have always enjoyed a neat, uncomplicated friendship. I am confident that we shall always do so."

Mrs. Burlington was delighted to have touched a nerve. "One may hope so, of course, for your sake. A lady needs gentlemanly companionship by inclination, and you have not precisely set yourself to capture the interest of any other eligible gentlemen."

"I have no great wish to excite anyone's interest, Amaris. Along with my unnatural headstrong independence, you may add that additional oddity of character to your mullings about me," Lady Caroline said. She reached for the brass doorknob and turned it.

"My dear niece! Such fortitude, I do swear! No female actually wishes to find herself on the shelf, but here you are at four-and-twenty with nary a gentleman in sight," Mrs. Burlington said.

Over her slender shoulder, Lady Caroline gave her aunt a slow, cool smile. "My dear Amaris, I suspect it is better never to wed than to wed mistakenly, as your own example has so eloquently proved to me." She exited the drawing room.

Mrs. Burlington gasped. "How dare you! You insolent . . ." Whatever else she might have said was lost as Lady Caroline pulled the door closed behind her in a decisive manner.

Lady Caroline spent the remainder of the afternoon in the study, finishing up the most pressing business awaiting her attention on the desk. She had requested that a cold collation he brought to her in the study in lieu of dinner, as she was unwilling to stop what she was doing or to spend another unpleasant hour in her aunt's company.

Later, when the butler brought in the tray of watercress sandwiches, thinly sliced slivers of beef and ham, cheeses, fruit, wine, and so on, she put down her pen with a thankful sigh. "You come in good time, Simpson. My eyes are beginning to swim in my head."

"I do not doubt it, my lady. It is going on dusk and you have not called for candles," the butler said in quiet reproof.

He arranged the collation on an occasional table against the wainscoted wall.

Lady Caroline looked about her in surprise. She had not realized it was so late, nor that the shadows had deepened in the room. "I shall need them, indeed, if I am not to go blind," she said humorously.

"I shall see to it at once, my lady. Will there be anything else?"

"No, that will be all, thank you, Simpson." Lady Caroline bent her head again to the figures on the page before her, her brows knitting again in concentration. She picked up the pen.

The butler bowed and went away. Shortly thereafter a footman entered and lighted a long taper from the fire in the hearth. He lighted the several bunches of candles gracing the study before he, too, left on silent feet.

Lady Caroline scarcely noticed; by that time she was properly engrossed in the tallying of the accounts.

A half-hour later, Lady Caroline stretched her arms above her head with bone-popping satisfaction. The columns of figures had tallied at last and she could turn her attention to other things. Her eyes alighted on the letter lying on top of the stack of correspondence she had tossed onto the desk earlier. She picked it up, wanting to reread the missive that had so unexpectedly excited such vitriolic attention from her aunt that afternoon.

As Lady Caroline read the letter again, a smile lighted her eyes. She sighed when she was done. "My aunt has the right of it in her own twisted fashion. I have indeed outworn my hopes. Dearest Miles. You have quite, quite spoiled me for any other gentleman," she said softly. She sat very still for several moments, her eyes not seeing the collation that awaited her or, indeed, anything at all in the study.

The families' estates had been close enough that she had

often met the youth who would one day ascend to the earldom of Walmesley. However, the future earl had gone away to Oxford and she herself had been sent to a seminary for young ladies and nearly forgot his existence.

It was during Lady Caroline's first Season in London that she was formally introduced to Miles, Lord Trilby, the Earl of Walmesley. She had been stunned, for this elegant lord who bowed over her hand was vastly different from the young sprig that she so vaguely remembered.

She had tumbled head over heels in love with his lordship and she had thought that he reciprocated her feelings. Certainly Lord Trilby had been extraordinarily attentive toward her, so much so that there had been widespread expectation in society that he meant to offer for her hand.

Lady Caroline recalled the dances, the whispered confidences, the shared laughter that they had enjoyed together even in the midst of the glittering round of entertainments. She could always depend upon Lord Trilby to be an amusing companion and, indeed, on occasion the trusted confidant. There had even been a few stolen kisses between them.

But it had all come to naught, after all. Lord Trilby never quite crossed the line that lay between his established position as intimate acquaintance and that of ardent lover.

Lady Caroline sighed again, a trifle wistfully. "It was such a lovely spring. Why ever did you not offer for me, Miles?"

Her father had known of her deep infatuation for Lord Trilby and he had not disapproved of a connection with such a noble house. The earl therefore had not pressed Lady Caroline to accept any of the proffered suits of a score of other admirers.

When the Season had ended without the hoped-for offer from Lord Trilby, the Earl of Berwicke had hoped that with time and a Season or two more his daughter would outgrow her first painful experience with love. But it had not proved to be so.

Six years later Lady Caroline remained unwedded, having spurned a dozen offers along the way, until she had settled quietly into her routine at Berwicke Keep as her brother's permanent hostess whenever he should take it into his head to invite several of his cronies into the country. Between these infrequent bouts of entertaining a roistering band of gentlemen, Lady Caroline saw to those things that the new earl declared to be a dead bore.

Lady Caroline knew it was of no use to dwell on what might have been. Indeed, she supposed she was content enough. She had tired of the round of London entertainments, especially so after she had come to be thought of as a permanently unattached female and it was assumed that she could always be depended upon to entertain the dullest or the most ineligible of gentlemen in a social gathering. Therein lay the reason for her quiet retreat into the country, but she had quickly discovered that idleness was not to her taste either, and it had come as a godsend when her brother had carelessly dumped the responsibilities for Berwicke Keep into her lap. Of course, by remaining at Berwicke Keep for the best part of the year, excluding the few visits she made to London to see friends, she had been compelled to tolerate her aunt's company.

Lady Caroline thought on the whole she had been rather fortunate. She must be thankful that Lord Trilby considered her still in the guise of one of his most intimate acquaintances. They corresponded regularly and she did not miss much about London doings because Lord Trilby kept her fully informed.

The years that had passed since their fateful meeting in London had but deepened an extraordinary friendship between them. Lady Caroline was confident that she could call upon Lord Trilby to render whatever assistance was within his power to give were she ever to find herself in need of aid, and she rather thought that his lordship could depend upon her to the same considerable degree.

Lady Caroline at last set aside the letter from Lord Trilby, rising from her chair at the same time. Without glancing at the untasted collation on the occasional table, she walked out of the study. Her thoughts still dwelled pleasantly on the Earl of Walmesley.

In the not-too-distant future she was to recall those same reflections with certain misgivings.

5

The following day Lady Caroline sustained a visit from Lord Hathaway, that same gentleman who was so highly recommended by Mrs. Burlington.

Lord Hathaway was a stocky gentleman of unimposing height and rather ordinary features. His slightly protuberant blue orbs and his rather heavy mouth lent him a habitual expression of mild surprise. Everything about Lord Hathaway, from his dress to his mannerisms to his opinions, could be summed up in one word—conservative.

Lord Hathaway himself would have been the first to agree that his person was not such as to inspire passion or dread or excitement in the female breast. Nor did he possess that flair of personality that seemed to characterize many of his peers. He was no Corinthian or reckless rake like a number of other gentlemen of his social standing. Not for Lord Hathaway the manly sports or skirt-chasing.

Lord Hathaway did, however, possess one quality almost unique to himself. He flattered himself with the belief that very few other gentlemen could lay claim to such a spotless reputation as his own.

Lord Hathaway had heard himself referred to as "The Worthy." He had passed over, as being of little consequence, the fact that the speaker had spoken in a derisive tone, but instead had accepted the sobriquet with all the gratification inherent of a gentleman secure in his position and positively certain of his own worth.

Some months previously, Lord Hathaway had concluded

after careful reflection that it had become time to cast about for an acceptable helpmate with whom to share his table. His deliberations upon the worth of several possible candidates were as studied as for any other decision he was called upon to make in the discharging of his duties and responsibilities.

One by one the candidates had fallen short of expectations as he discovered some previously unguessed-at fault or imperfection. At last his lordship made his choice, and it was to Lady Caroline Eddington that he had thrown his favor.

Lady Caroline was acceptable in every way. Her birth and her upbringing qualified her to preside at the foot of any of the grandest tables in England. Her ladyship's dowry was very respectable, especially when measured against Lord Hathaway's close-held ambition to deepen his already well-filled coffers. In addition, he considered that Lady Caroline's graciousness of manner and her beauty made her one of the true notables of the age.

The crowning point in Lady Caroline Eddington's favor had been her advanced age. Her ladyship was no longer a giddy young girl, but a woman seasoned and steady. Lord Hathaway of all things disliked unnecessary levity, and in Lady Caroline he thought that he had found a lady of settled nature who would be immune to the silly romantic notions so prevalent among young misses just presented into society.

Lord Hathaway was satisfied that he could not do better than place his ring upon Lady Caroline's slender finger. In the eighteen months that he had courted her, there had been nothing to sway him from that opinion.

While it was true that Lady Caroline on occasion displayed a breeziness of spirit that was foreign to one of his more temperate nature, and that she had an unfortunate knack for utterances of opinion that at times ran completely counter to his own considered words of wisdom, Lord

Hathaway was not deterred. These faults could, he believed, be laid straightaway at the door of an overindulgent father and a negligent brother. Lord Hathaway's opinion was formed and strengthened by certain delicate conversations he had conducted with Mrs. Burlington, who had given him to understand that as a young girl Lady Caroline had been so shamelessly spoiled that it had resulted in an unfortunate wayward tendency.

However, Lord Hathaway believed that by bringing the proper guidance and a firm hand to the matter, a gentleman could soon persuade Lady Caroline to a recognition of her faults, which would subsequently lead to her complete rehabilitation. Since Lord Hathaway was equally convinced that he was possessed of considerable powers of persuasion, he had every faith in himself as being the gentleman best qualified to take on the task of Lady Caroline's gentle reeducation.

Unfortunately, Lady Caroline had failed to recognize the same indisputable fact. She had consistently turned aside his measured proposals for her hand. However, her rejections were always couched in the friendliest of language, and Lord Hathaway dared to think that she was not as indifferent to the rightness of his offers as she would like him to believe. In turn, he was most civil in receiving her dear opinions of the matter, yet always ready to trundle forth whatever counter-argument seemed most appropriate. Their exchanges therefore did not satisfy his lordship, but neither did they deter him.

Now, as Lord Hathaway made his bows, he alluded to the crux of their long-standing cordial disagreement. "My lady, you are as stunning as ever. You must know it is still my hope that I may one day be gratified to have you at my side as my beautiful lady wife."

Lady Caroline, who had held out her hand to his lordship

upon his entering the drawing room, deliberately disengaged her fingers from his grasp. With a light laugh she said, "My answer is still the same, my lord. We shall continue better just as we are, as comfortable acquaintances. Pray be seated, Lord Hathaway. You must not stand on such ceremony with me, you know."

Lord Hathaway bowed slightly before he lifted his coat-tails and seated himself on the settee beside his hostess. "You are always most gracious, Lady Caroline. I have always held the opinion that it is one of your best qualities."

Lady Caroline acknowledged the compliment with only a wry smile. "I am sorry my aunt is not present at the moment, for I know that you are quite a favorite with her."

At once Lord Hathaway blew out his cheeks in a fashion designed to show the proper concern. He prided himself on his correctness at such times, though in this particular instance his solicitude was sincerely engaged. "I trust Mrs. Burlington has not taken ill? Such an estimable woman. One does not like to see such worthiness of character suffer."

As his lordship was speaking, the butler quietly entered carrying the tea tray. Simpson was followed by a footman who brought in the tea urn. The butler remained to offer a selection of biscuits and cakes on a salver in turn to Lady Caroline and Lord Hathaway.

Lady Caroline shook her head. "No, indeed. My aunt was finishing her correspondence when your name was announced. I am certain she will join us ere long." She declined the biscuits and cake quietly, saying that she preferred simply to take tea.

Lord Hathaway chose several biscuits, his penchant for sweets a healthy one. As he made his last selection, he said with an attempt at heavy humor, "Then certainly I must seize these few unchaperoned moments in order to persuade you to the advantages of my suit, my lady."

Lady Caroline choked on a laugh, Lord Hathaway's un-characteristic and exaggerated archness of expression having taken her by surprise. She quickly recovered, but her eyes continued to gleam. She poured tea for Lord Hathaway and gave it to him before filling her own cup. "Indeed, sir! I am, however, already well-versed in the advantages you speak of. You have labored mightily these last months to perfect my understanding of just those same advantages, after all. But I fear that despite your labors I shall continue to decline the honor you wish to bestow upon me."

Lord Hathaway smiled in his turn. He held up an index finger. "Ah! But I may yet surprise you this afternoon, my lady. I believe—no, I am certain—that I have hit upon a new approach that must persuade you to the validity of my argu-ments."

Lady Caroline set aside her unfinished tea and composed herself with resignation. She clasped her hands in her lap in an attentive attitude. "Then I am ready, my lord. But I must warn you that it will be a wasted effort on your part." She no-ticed that Lord Hathaway was steadily tucking away the bis-cuits in a concentrated manner, and a glimmer of hope entered her eyes. "Perhaps you would like a nice slice of sweet cake to accompany your tea, my lord? It is really quite good today. A rum poppyseed, which as I recall you commented fa-vorably upon on the occasion of your last visit."

Lord Hathaway hesitated, torn by his weakness for such a fine treat. He could always be assured of the most superlative concoctions at Berwicke Keep, which was in direct contrast to his own cook's glaring deficiency in that area. But staunchly he decided not to give way to temptation. "I most reluctantly shall pass on the cake this afternoon, Lady Caro-line. One must discipline oneself, you know." He complacently patted the rounded expanse of his waistcoat.

"Yes, indeed," Lady Caroline agreed, pronounced amusement in her eyes. "Perhaps, then, a bit more tea. Simpson, pray see to his lordship. We must not neglect our guest."

Lord Hathaway covered his cup with his hand to discourage the butler's attempt to serve him. "No, no. I am well-satisfied." He smiled, saying with ponderous playfulness, "If I did not know your gracious ways so well, my lady, I might suspect you of attempting to put me off."

"I am not one to fly in the face of the inevitable," Lady Caroline said with fine irony, well aware that it would go completely over his lordship's head.

True to form, Lord Hathaway bowed from the waist, acknowledging what he took to be a vast compliment to his determined character. "I am happy that you understand me so well, Lady Caroline."

Lady Caroline sighed, knowing from old that there was little point in delaying Lord Hathaway from his purpose. His lordship would but stay longer so that he could fully expound his arguments. "That will be all for the moment, Simpson. I shall ring when I require you again. Pray remind my aunt that Lord Hathaway has called upon us. I am certain that she will not want to miss his lordship's visit."

"Very good, my lady," the butler said, his voice faintly threaded with the ghost of sympathy. He crossed to the drawing-room door and went out.

The door was not yet completely closed before Lord Hathaway launched the newest salvo of his campaign. "As I have informed you many times in the past, Lady Caroline, I have found you completely acceptable to me for a wife. Your illustrious birth, your beauteous countenance, your gracious—"

Lady Caroline threw up her hand. "Pray spare my blushes,

sir!" She had no wish to hear herself or her virtues cataloged in the ponderous fashion that Lord Hathaway inevitably employed. More gently she said, "I shall accept your compliments better if left unsaid, my lord."

Lord Hathaway inclined himself in another short bow. "Your modesty does you credit, my lady. It is but another of those numerous virtues that I so esteem in you." He began an oft-repeated discourse upon how well-matched he and Lady Caroline were.

Lady Caroline gave the tiniest sigh. She glanced at the clock on the mantel above the fireplace. She wondered where her aunt could possibly have got to. Even though she did not often see eye to eye with Mrs. Burlington, she could at least rely upon her aunt to appropriate a measure of Lord Hathaway's gallantries. His lordship was too well-bred not to direct a few of his compliments to Mrs. Burlington, and, too, when her aunt was present, Lord Hathaway felt compelled to restrain some of his dry ardor.

It occurred to Lady Caroline suddenly that perhaps her aunt was deliberately not making an appearance. In the past, Mrs. Burlington had always tended to practice a stifling chaperonage. It was, then, rather odd that she had not already acted upon the knowledge that Lord Hathaway had come to call.

Upon the suspicion, Lady Caroline took advantage of Lord Hathaway's having paused to draw breath to say, "You are most kind, my lord. Do you know, I have but this moment realized that my aunt has not put in an appearance for tea. I shall go at once to find her, for I know that she will not wish to let you go without saying good-bye."

Lady Caroline rose from the settee, but found to her astonishment that Lord Hathaway detained her by the simple expedient of taking hold of her wrist. She looked at him in considerable surprise. "My lord, whatever are you about?"

Lord Hathaway also stood. He wore an unusually determined expression. His brows had lowered over his rather prominent orbs and his full mouth was half-pursed, which served to give a fishy effect to his countenance. "I had not planned to put into effect my newest form of persuasion so soon, my lady, but you bear all the appearance of haring off before I am ready."

"Whatever can you possibly mean?" Lady Caroline asked in growing astonishment.

His lordship portentously cleared his throat. "My dear Lady Caroline, it occurred to me sometime previous that those gentlemen who could have been most expected to exert some influence upon you were singularly inept in doing so. However, I am made of sterner stuff, as you will quickly gather."

Lady Caroline stared at his lordship in continued astonishment, but a gathering of anger as well. "This is unlike you, my lord! I am not used to insult from you. I shall not continue to suffer it kindly, and so I warn you. Unhand me at once."

Instead of heeding her icy command and proffering a profuse apology, as she had expected him to do, Lord Hathaway pulled her clumsily into his arms.

"My lord!"

Her shocked tone fell on deaf ears. Lord Hathaway was determined to present his case. "You are in need of a firm hand, Lady Caroline. I have thought so for some time. I am the master for you, my dear lady, as you shall agree before I leave here this day!"

With this grand declaration, Lord Hathaway lowered his face toward hers. Lady Caroline realized his intent and quickly turned her head. His lordship's dry lips slid over her cheek. At the same time, Lady Caroline brought her hand up smartly against his face.

Her eyes blazed up at his stunned expression. "Let me go this instant or I shall scream!"

"A pretty scene, I swear," an amused voice drawled.

6

As one, Lady Caroline and Lord Hathaway realized with equal measures of horror that the drawing room door stood open and they were being regarded by the stunned Simpson and a tall gentleman dressed with a negligent elegance that bespoke the Corinthian.

Lady Caroline flushed to the roots of her hair. "Miles!" she uttered in mingled disbelief and laughter.

Lord Trilby advanced leisurely into the drawing room. "Yes, it is definitely I," he agreed. He turned his cool gray gaze on Lady Caroline's companion, who had begun to sport an interesting shade of purple about his face and neck. "Lord Hathaway, good day to you. I apologize for interrupting your tea with Lady Caroline. Simpson did not inform me that it was a private party, or I would have sent in my card first."

Lord Hathaway breathed heavily with his embarrassment. "Not at all, my lord." He realized that he was still clasping Lady Caroline about the waist, albeit quite loosely, and he removed his arms hastily. "Not at all what it appears, you know."

"Isn't it?"

Lord Hathaway, goaded by that gentle ironic voice, snapped, "No, it is not. I hold her ladyship in the upmost regard—"

He stopped abruptly as the Earl of Walmesley's brows rose. Renewed red crawled up his neck from under his cravat. He well knew that if he had chanced on such a scene he would have thought exactly what Lord Trilby's stiffnecked manner appeared to convey. He had privately always considered the earl to be something of a fashionable fribble compared to himself, and it cut him to the quick to be the object of the gentleman's censure. "I assure you, I meant no disrespect to the lady."

"Indeed?" Lord Trilby made of it a derisive question.

Lord Hathaway blew out his cheeks. There was no reasoning with the fellow, he thought. His perception of himself had been badly shaken and he resented the author of that discomfiture. He made a stiff bow to Lady Caroline but completely ignored the Earl of Walmesley as he stalked from the room.

With grim satisfaction Simpson closed the door, leaving his mistress with one who he thought could be better trusted to toe the line with her ladyship.

"That is a most pompous donkey," Lord Trilby observed. "I don't know why ever you receive him, my dear."

Lady Caroline laughed, her embarrassment vanished. She went to him with outstretched hands. "For shame, Miles! You must know that his lordship means to make me his wife. I am of half a mind to accept him."

Lord Trilby caught her fingers and carried them to his lips. Without releasing her hands, he shook his head. "Much better not to. His lordship is such a stiff stick that he'll bore you to distraction in a fortnight. Either that or you will drive him to apoplexy."

Lady Caroline's lips quivered with amusement. She said demurely, "Lord Hathaway said that I am in need of a firm hand."

"That is indisputably true. I have known it for ages. It is why I never made an offer for you myself. I am too easy a fellow for us ever to have suited," Lord Trilby said, smiling down at her.

Lady Caroline's own smile faltered. She gently pulled her

hands free of his warm, easy clasp. "You will have tea, I expect."

Lord Trilby regarded the remains of the previous tea with disapprobation. "Good God, rum-and-poppyseed cake." He grimaced. "Thank you, my lady, but I shall decline tea."

Lady Caroline laughed as she went to pull the bell rope. Before she had done more than give a short tug, the drawing-room door opened and Simpson came in carrying a tea tray.

"I have taken the liberty of bringing up a fresh pot of tea and sandwiches for his lordship, my lady," the butler said.

Lord Trilby's eyes lit up at sight of the stacked sandwiches. "Good man, Simpson! I shall recommend you for a bonus in your wages."

The butler merely smiled. After placing the tea tray on the side table, he cleared away the old tray with its remnants of cake and biscuits.

Lady Caroline saw that the earl was settled with tea and a plate of sandwiches before she said, "Your sudden appearance came as quite a shock, my lord."

"So I gathered when I so ineptly interrupted that charming *tête-à-tête*," Lord Trilby said dryly.

Lady Caroline laughed, even as a tinge of color stole back into her face. "You know very well I meant nothing of the kind by my statement, my lord! I must own, however, I was glad to see you at just that moment. I was never more shocked in my life than I was at Lord Hathaway's strange behavior."

The Earl of Walmesley cast over her an encompassing glance. She was looking particularly fetching in an afternoon dress of cerulean blue trimmed lavishly with lace at the bosom. Her hair was swept up in masses of glorious chestnut curls, held in place by copper and inlaid combs. "My dear Caroline, you malign your own charms. I would have been more surprised to learn that you did *not* excite such behavior."

Lady Caroline thought she knew better than to place any deep underlying construction upon his compliment, and she accepted the accolade with a gracious nod. "Thank you, my lord. But what I meant was that I received your last letter not above a day ago and you made not one mention of surprising me in this fashion, wretch that you are."

Lord Trilby had been making rapid inroads into the sandwiches, but at this he set aside the last one, unfinished. His former easy humor disappeared from his manner and his voice had of a sudden lost its lazy, half-amused drawl. "A few days ago I did not know that I would be visiting you, my lady."

Lady Caroline's mildly surprised gaze had followed the banishment of the sandwich plate. When she heard the change in his lordship's voice, her eyes lifted swiftly to his. "My lord! What is it? Something has happened. You must tell me at once."

Lord Trilby's sudden smile was one of self-mockery. "I came to Berwicke for that express purpose, my dear. I am caught fast in a coil, one of my own making, I confess, and I harbor the hope that you will be able to aid me in extricating myself."

"You know that you may call upon me, Miles," Lady Caroline said quietly. Her heart was beating uncomfortably hard. She could not imagine what sort of difficulty the earl could possibly be in, but that it was of a serious nature was patently obvious to her. Lord Trilby's uncharacteristic seriousness greatly alarmed her.

Lord Trilby was not given over excessively to any vice that she was aware of. He was wealthy enough that any losses at the gaming table would hardly be noticed, so she was easily able to dismiss the outrageous thought that he had come to beg a loan of her. She knew also that Lord Trilby was too even-tempered and moderate in drink to indulge in dueling or anything of that nature, even if provoked.

That left only the possibility that his lordship was having some difficulty with a woman.

At the thought, Lady Caroline's fingers momentarily curled in her lap. The Earl of Walmesley was no saint, of course. There had naturally been the odd mistress or two that she had been told about by well-meaning friends, and each time she had died a little death. But she had not realized before how thoroughly she had dreaded the day that Lord Trilby would come to tell her that he had become seriously involved with someone.

"It is a female," she stated, with what she thought was creditable calm in consideration of how violently she was shaking inside.

Lord Trilby looked at his companion with surprise and a heightened degree of respect. "Your percipience amazes, Caroline. You are exactly right, however it is that you fathomed it."

Lady Caroline rose swiftly from the settee in order to put distance between herself and the earl, fearing that he might read her vulnerability in her expression. She went to the side table in pretense of wanting to freshen her cup of tea from the urn. Her hand shook as she poured. "What is it that you wish me to do?"

Lord Trilby studied her profile, faintly startled by a glimpse of something that he could not quite put a name to. "Are you not interested in the round tale, my lady?"

Lady Caroline gestured dismissively with her free hand. "I doubt it is much consequence to me. I am more interested in discovering how it is I may help you."

"You are accommodating, indeed. But I suspect that in all fairness you should hear the whole before you commit yourself in any fashion," Lord Trilby said.

Lady Caroline glanced swiftly back at him. "Tea, my lord? No? Very well, then." She gracefully returned to the settee, her own cup in hand. Sinking down in her former place, she said with the glimmer of a smile, "I perceive that you are determined to tell me all, so proceed."

It was Lord Trilby's turn to rise, in testimony to his slight discomfiture. He took a quick turn about the room with his hands clasped behind his back. He frowned as he composed his thoughts. "The thing of it is, I am not all that certain that I have the right to call upon you," he said at last, turning to regard her. "When I was in London and thought of you, I saw instantly how you might aid me. We are such good friends that it never entered my head at that time that what I meant to ask of you borders on the preposterous. Now, of course, I have had ample time for reflection, and it is not as simple as I originally believed."

"Why do you not let me be the judge, my lord?"

Lord Trilby half-smiled in acknowledgment of her willingness to give him a hearing. "You are a rare one, Caroline. Very well. I suppose that you recall my occasional mention of my great-aunt, the Grandduchess of Schaffenzeits."

"Yes, indeed. I believe her grace is the only personage that you have ever admitted to a dread of," Lady Caroline said, smiling.

Lord Trilby laughed. "Yes. In any event, Grandduchess Wilhelmina Hildebrande has written to me that she will shortly descend upon me for a lengthy visit."

Lady Caroline regarded her companion with mild surprise and some bewilderment. This was not at all the confidence she had expected to hear. "I do not quite understand the difficulty, my lord, for if I am not mistaken, I seem to recall that you have always spoken of the grandduchess with enormous affection."

"True enough; I do hold the grand old lady in the fondest regard. However, her grace is a regular tartar, making a career of ordering others' lives for them. She is quite determined to arrange mine to her satisfaction while she is in England," Lord Trilby said, his eyes glinting with rueful humor.

"Oh, dear, I begin to see," Lady Caroline said with a curious lightening of her spirits. The earl's difficulty had nothing to do with a young and nubile female, after all. "But I still do not understand what it is you believe I may do to help you. I should be most willing to do my part in entertaining the Grandduchess of Schaffenzeits, if that is what you are hoping. I am, however, fixed here at Berwicke until Lord Eddington's return, which of course you know. I assume, then, that you intend to bring her grace down to Walmesley?"

"Yes, I shall have her grace down to Walmesley for the entire length of her stay, she and her whole entourage. She never travels without being accompanied by at least a dozen servants, her secretary, and her pet pugs, all of which are loaded into four or five coaches drawn by large showy teams with liveried attendants," Lord Trilby said.

Lady Caroline was amused. "Grandduchess Wilhelmina Hildebrande sounds a character of the first water."

"You may well say so. I could never fit them all comfortably into the town house, nor would I wish to make the attempt. The grandduchess detests London. She has informed me so on numerous occasions," Lord Trilby said.

He leaned one shoulder against the mantel and regarded Lady Caroline with anticipation. "She has also advised me many times to give up my frivolous London life. She wishes me to settle at Walmesley with a good wife and an increasing nursery. I am to have no fewer than six children and at least half of those should be sons so that there will be a better-than-even chance that the family name will be carried on after my demise. It is my duty to marry and procreate, since I am the last of the British line. My honor is at stake, et cetera, et cetera."

"Dear Lord," Lady Caroline murmured, stunned.

Lord Trilby laughed at her bemused expression. "As you have gathered, the Grandduchess of Schaffenzeits is a lady of formidable opinions, with which she is very vocal and very generous."

"I can readily believe it." Lady Caroline regarded his lordship with ready sympathy. "You fear that her grace's visit will be one of vexation and discomfort, do you not? I know that you dislike excessively such situations. It will be very bad, indeed, if you are to be subjected to such strictures for weeks. The only thing to do, of course, is to provide enough entertainments so that the grandduchess's attention is diverted from your bachelor state. It is rather a problem, since her grace so dislikes London, particularly since most of our neighbors are themselves away in London for the Little Season. But I think that even so we may stir up a few activities in our quiet county that might be relied upon to engage an elderly lady's interest."

Lady Caroline smiled reassuringly at the earl. "Leave it to me, Miles. I am certain that I can manage a few respectable parties, at the very least."

"That is not quite what I had in mind, actually," Lord Trilby said slowly.

The slightest lift of Lady Caroline's brows indicated her surprise. "Is it not?"

Lord Trilby crossed to sit down beside her on the settee. He took her hands, to hold them loosely between his own. "Caroline, I have come to ask you to help me deceive the Grandduchess of Schaffenzeits—by pretending that there is an understanding between us."

7

Lady Caroline stared at the earl in speechless astonishment for several heartbeats. She regained her voice, at the same time attempting to free her hands. "Are you *mad,* Miles?"

Lord Trilby tightened his hold on her hands, refusing to allow her to withdraw from him. "I told you it was a ludicrous notion, Caro. But now that I have said it, at least allow me to explain more fully before you reject it out of hand. Will you grant me that, Caro?"

Lady Caroline looked at his lordship. He so rarely addressed her by that intimate diminution of her name, doing so only in moments of great feeling. She nodded warily. "Very well; I shall hear you out. But I should give you fair warning that, at best, I suspect you mad, and at worst, disguised."

"Foxed at teatime? You know me better than that, I hope," Lord Trilby said, not at all offended at the aspersion she had cast upon his sobriety.

"Then you are mad," Lady Caroline said decisively.

"Perhaps I am," Lord Trilby admitted. "But you will listen, will you not?"

"I suppose I must, if I am ever to understand what has knocked loose your senses," Lady Caroline said on a sigh. She glanced thoughtfully down at her entrapped hands. "Or even if I am to regain possession of my hands."

Lord Trilby let go of her then with a laugh. He leaned back against the cushions of the settee. "I shall give it to you quickly, then. Several months ago the Grandduchess Wilhelmina Hildebrande tired of my polite assurances that I would one day fulfill my duty and wed. She wrote to me that she wished to have me firmly committed to matrimony before she died, so that she could rest easily in her grave. Such dramatic rot I have never read before or since, I assure you. I thought I was very clever in conveying the reply that I had entered upon an engagement with a suitable young lady, just thinking to put her off a bit longer, you see. It was to be a lengthy engagement, of course, out of deference to the lady's family situation. Later, I meant to inform her grace that the lady in question and I had agreed that the understanding between us be quietly dissolved, for reasons which by honor I naturally could not reveal."

"Oh, Miles," Lady Caroline said in quiet dismay. She was beginning to see at last the magnitude of his lordship's difficulty.

Lord Trilby gave a self-mocking smile. "Caught myself finely, did I not? You have already divined it, of course. Weston warned me at the time how it would be, but foolishly I did not heed him. The upshot of it all is that the Grandduchess of Schaffenzeits does not believe that my engagement exists. Moreover, since I have not seen fit to provide myself with a bride, she has decided to select a suitable helpmate for me."

"Oh, my word! It is no wonder you pitched such a corkbrained suggestion to me," Lady Caroline said, disgusted.

Lord Trilby laughed quietly. "You do not yet know the real facer, my dear. The Grandduchess of Schaffenzeits will be accompanied by the young lady of her choice, so that I may meet her formally before we are whisked to the church altar." He expected that his last revelation would come as something of a shocking climax, but his companion's reaction was not quite what he had anticipated.

After an astonished second, Lady Caroline threw back her

head and pealed with laughter. She whooped so hardily that the tears began to roll down her cheeks. Still caught in the throes of her amusement, she made a helpless gesture that his lordship understood.

Lord Trilby obligingly offered his linen handkerchief to her.

Lady Caroline snatched it. She mopped her eyes, but they were still brimful with laughter when she looked over at him. At his pained expression, she bit her lip, suppressing a fresh outburst. She cleared her throat experimentally before she dared speak. "That is better. I can see your dear foolish face again," she said. There was an unmistakable wobbling in her voice. "You *have* done it, haven't you, Miles?"

"And for no better purpose than to provide you with such unholy amusement," Lord Trilby said gravely.

That nearly set her off again. Lady Caroline gurgled protest, throwing up her hand in appeal. "Do not tease me, pray! I will be good, I promise." She straightened her shoulders and clasped her hands in her lap in an attitude of grave attention. "There, you see? I have put on my most sober frown. I am ready to make all sorts of sympathetic noises and to offer well-meaning advice." Despite her declaration to the contrary, an irreverent chuckle escaped her.

"I appreciate the massive effort, my lady," Lord Trilby said, his eyes reflecting his own pronounced amusement.

Lady Caroline's eyes danced irrepressibly. "My poor witless friend. What will you do?"

"I still harbor hopes that you will step into the breach, my dear," Lord Trilby said lazily.

At once her high appreciation of his imbroglio was at an end. Lady Caroline shook her head quickly. "Not I! I value your friendship, my lord, but not to the point of ruining my reputation and yours. The risk of taking part in such a grand deception makes my faint heart flutter with fear. Lord, but think of the gossip and the scandal."

"You said but a moment ago that most of the neighborhood has taken up residence in London for the Little Season. As there is no reason why any of our neighbors should ever hear of the arrangement, I begin to think that the possibility of a scandal is very nearly nonexistent," Lord Trilby said.

Lady Caroline was taken aback by his calm assertion. "You cannot possibly be serious, my lord!" She saw by his thoughtful expression that he was indeed quite earnest. She raised a further objection, one which she was certain must weigh heavily. "You have forgotten my aunt. Amaris would of a certainly tumble to something being in the air if you were suddenly to pay assiduous court to me in the company of the grandduchess."

Lord Trilby nodded, but slowly. His brows were slightly knit while he reflected. "Mrs. Burlington is a formidable hurdle, I agree, but I think not unapproachable. She need never hear of the arrangement. I shall not call upon you here with the Grandduchess Wilhelmina Hildebrande. Instead, you may ride over to visit with my great-aunt over tea. Mrs. Burlington will not cavil at your paying a neighborly visit or two while I am known to be at Walmesley, and I do not anticipate that it will take more than a few appearances on your part before her grace is fully convinced of our 'understanding.' As soon as the grand old lady comes to accept it, I shall pack her off as speedily as possible, and then we may be comfortable again."

Lady Caroline felt as though she was caught up in the unreal plot of the most lurid popular romance. "My aunt would never countenance my going to Walmesley without her chaperonage. Oh, I know that I have ridden over countless times in the past with only my groom in attendance, but I certainly cannot be expected to greet the Grandduchess of Schaffenzeits in my riding dress. Really, Miles! I should have to come in the carriage, which would be certain to arouse my aunt's suspicions. And if Amaris should hear even a whisper that such a grand personage is in residence at Walmesley, she will be bent upon inserting herself into the grandduchess's presence."

She paused, seeing that the frown had deepened on his lordship's face, and when she spoke again, the thread of amusement had returned to her voice. "You know well enough that it is impossible, my lord. Do give it over, for it won't do, you know! Just see, such a tiny consideration as Amaris' wishing to present herself to the Grandduchess Wilhelmina Hildebrande throws it all into a cocked hat."

"Then don't tell her anything," Lord Trilby said simply. "Let Mrs. Burlington exclaim to her heart's content at your frightful manifestation of independence. I'll wager that there is not a personage in the county that gives serious attention any longer to that lady's malicious utterances."

Lady Caroline stared at him. She shook her head, marveling. "You have made it all sound altogether too simple, my lord."

"I merely see that my original instinct was correct. The notion is not as ludicrous or as impossible as I had begun to fear," Lord Trilby said, agreeing with her.

"But it *is* impossible!" Lady Caroline explained. "Quite, quite impossible."

Lord Trilby leaned toward her and took hold of her unresisting hands. "My dear lady, will you not change your mind?" he asked in a persuasive voice. "Pray, will you not do me the honor of pretending to be engaged to me in order to foil the grandduchess's horrid scheme to marry me off to some chit I have never laid eyes on before in my life? I shall be quite, quite rolled up otherwise, you know."

With his lordship's nonsense, the interview was once more placed upon the plain of the ludicrous. Lady Caroline couldn't stop the smile that trembled to her lips. She shook her head. "My dear lord, you make it difficult indeed to deny you."

Lord Trilby smiled at her in turn. "Dare I to hope, then?"

Lady Caroline did not immediately reply. She glanced down at their clasped hands.

The scheme was mad. It was ludicrous. It was fraught with pitfalls, not the least of which were her own well-hidden feelings. That, of course, was precisely the fascination of the idea. Such a pretense would be all too poignant a reminder of her once-close-held hopes that Lord Trilby would ask for her hand. Under such dangerous disguise, her heart might betray itself to him. But the temptation to agree to the deception was there, in the fast beat of her pulse and in the seduction of her fantasy that, once entered into, a pretended understanding might become one in truth. She felt her better sense wavering, even though she knew that she should not entertain the idea for even a moment.

"What is the verdict to be, my best of friends?"

The words were the final catalyst. Lady Caroline raised thoughtful eyes to the earl's expectant expression. His audacity in asking of her such a favor had initially stunned her. His easy assumption that their friendship should stretch so far had struck her as extremely telling. They were intimate but casual friends, and would remain so. In fact, his lordship seemed to look upon her much as he would a male colleague.

Despite knowing all that, she might have agreed.

She might have acquiesced if Lord Trilby had remained silent.

But Lord Trilby had spoken. With humor in his voice, he had addressed her as his "best of friends." Best of friends! It cut her to the quick. Abruptly all fantasies of being able to mold the pretended understanding into one of permanence were dashed as though they had never been.

Lady Caroline rose precipitately, leaving his lordship behind on the settee as she went to the window. She looked through it with blind eyes. "What you would ask of me is ludicrous. I am more sorry than I can say."

When Lady Caroline left him so suddenly, Lord Trilby caught a glimpse of a peculiar bleakness in her eyes. He gathered that he had gravely offended her. At once he stood up and moved to stand close beside her. He said quietly, "Caroline, you and I have been such good friends. You know that the notion would never have crossed my mind otherwise."

She made a small dismissive gesture that he interpreted as reproof.

Lord Trilby said even more quietly, "I would not have you think that I hold our relationship trivial or insignificant. That has never been the case, and what's more, never shall be."

Lady Caroline turned her head to glance over her shoulder at him. Her large eyes were somber. "I do not think it, Miles. I, too, treasure what we have—more than you know. I would do anything in my power to help you. But to pretend to be your intended . . ." She shook her head.

The shadow of her former smile returned to her eyes. "Why, the temptation to hold you to the deception could have proved irresistible, my lord."

She spoke only half in jest. As soon as she had done so, she feared that he might sense the underlying truth in her bantering tone. She was relieved when he laughed.

Lady Caroline turned fully toward him, saying decisively, "Definitely that would not do."

A full smile now graced her lips, though it did not entirely dispel the shadows in her eyes. "You shall simply have to work your devious escape in another fashion. If the war were not on, I would suggest that you assume another name and take up residence abroad. I suppose that you have thought of making a clean breast of the matter to the Grandduchess of Schaffenzeits and discarded it—yes, I thought that you must have. Well, then, I suspect that I shall shortly read of your upcoming nuptials in the *Gazette*."

"I am overpowered with apprehension at the mere thought," Lord Trilby declared. There was a certain quizzical light in his eyes as he watched her face.

Lady Caroline felt the alertness of his regard and instantly her defenses went up against him. Lord Trilby knew her perhaps better than anyone else. Not wishing him to see more than she wanted him to, she moved away. "I shall inform Simpson that you are staying the weekend, shall I? If you have no other engagements?"

"No, none at all. I did not send word to my staff at Walmesley to expect me before setting out from London. I posted directly down to Berwicke with but one errand in mind," Lord Trilby said, with the faintest twist of his lips.

Lady Caroline paused before she had reached the door. She said sympathetically, "I *am* sorry your trip has been in vain."

"Ah, well, it was a gamble, and a madder one than most," he said with a shrug and a smile.

Lady Caroline shook her head and turned once more to the door. She was reaching for the knob, when suddenly the door was flung open. She stepped backward swiftly to avoid being knocked aside.

Mrs. Burlington stood framed by the doorway, while behind her was the hovering figure of the butler.

Lady Caroline recovered herself almost at once, laughing at herself for her moment of fright. "Amaris! How you startled me."

8

Mrs. Burlington looked at her niece without a hint of apology in her visage. She did not enter the drawing room, but stood on the threshold with her hand still on the knob. The door shielded most of the drawing room from her view. Unsmiling and without preamble, she demanded imperatively, "What is this I have heard from Simpson that Lord Hathaway has gone away very hurriedly?"

Lady Caroline glanced swiftly at the butler, whose expression was one of appalled anxiety. She sighed and returned her attention to her aunt. "I am certain that his lordship regretted being unable to pay his respects to you, but Lord Hathaway felt that he had overstayed his welcome."

"Pah! You have sent his lordship away with a bug in his ear! Have you so little sense? Why, the gentleman is positively your last hope of wedding and becoming mistress of your own house. I cannot imagine any female so lost to her senses that she would turn down such an acceptable offer as Lord Hathaway has repeatedly made to you," Mrs. Burlington said.

From the corner of her eye Lady Caroline was painfully aware of Lord Trilby's interested expression. The half-open door still hid his presence from her aunt, and she could not imagine why he had not already made himself known, unless he was quite simply struck immobile by the ghastly *faux pas*.

Lady Caroline saw that her aunt was drawing breath to deliver another denunciation and she hurried to deter Mrs. Burlington's embarrassing diatribe. Not for worlds would she have wanted the Earl of Walmesley to know what wretched dealings she endured from her aunt. "Amaris, please. This is neither the time nor the place. Lord—"

Mrs. Burlington pounced. "Lord Hathaway! Yes, he is whistled down the lane for the last time, I'll warrant, which you will doubtless regret—and much sooner than you could ever anticipate."

Lord Trilby thought he had heard enough. He had already crossed the room in response to Lady Caroline's rather wild glance in his direction, and now he stepped around the edge of the door into sight.

Mrs. Burlington gasped and fell back in astonishment. "My lord! I had no idea! I had no notion whatsoever that you were present."

"So I gathered. It is perhaps unfortunate that I was unable to bring myself immediately to your attention." Lord Trilby's voice was austere. His gray eyes rested thoughtfully on Mrs. Burlington's face. She flushed under his cool assessment.

Lady Caroline trembled with anger and mortification. She held her hands clasped tightly together, fearing that in her vexation she might slap her aunt. She maintained, however, a carefully neutral voice. "Lord Trilby arrived just as Lord Hathaway was taking his leave."

"As I fear that I now must," Lord Trilby said. He caught Lady Caroline's fleeting glance before her eyes fell from his. He knew her character well enough to ascertain that the flush of color blooming in her face owed more to the seething fury that he had glimpsed in her eyes than to the embarrassment she must have felt that he had been made witness of her aunt's abominable treatment of her.

Lady Caroline offered her hand to the earl. "I am glad that you came, my lord."

Lord Trilby carried her fingers to his lips. "As am I. I shall be fixed at Walmesley for an indefinite time, as I told you. I will call on you again, Lady Caroline."

She understood then that he would not be remaining for the weekend at Berwicke. It was an example of his exquisite discretion, and the anger burned brighter in her eyes for the humiliating moments just past. "I will be most happy to receive you, my lord," she said formally.

Lord Trilby slanted a smile down at her. Then, with a nod and a long cool look for Mrs. Burlington, he sauntered past the ladies. He was met in the entry hall by Simpson, who stood ready with his greatcoat, beaver, and gloves. "Thank you, Simpson."

He left by the front door, and it was as though the sound of the closing door set free the two immobilized and silent ladies.

Mrs. Burlington at once stepped fully into the drawing room and sharply shut the door. "I was never more mortified in my life! How dared you let me go on when all the time his lordship was behind the door!"

"It is quite your own fault, Amaris. As I recall, I did make some attempt to warn you, but you were absolutely bent on speaking your mind," Lady Caroline said coolly. She brushed past her aunt without another word or glance, not trusting herself to retain her civility.

Mrs. Burlington's strident voice followed her. "Pray do not think that you may so easily push me aside, niece! I have had a letter from Lady Eddington, advising me of her and Lord Eddington's own early return."

Lady Caroline paused in the act of opening the door. Making an immense effort to ignore her aunt's spiteful tone, she said, "Their return? But I have heard nothing of this."

"Perhaps you would like to be apprised of the whole, then," Mrs. Burlington said.

There was a short silence while the two ladies exchanged stares. Lady Caroline said quietly, "How is it that Lady Eddington has written to you, Amaris? I had no inkling that you and she were on such friendly terms."

Mrs. Burlington smiled with a certain satisfaction. "Lady Eddington and I became quite close in those short weeks that she, whilst in company with her stepmother, was visiting Berwicke before her marriage to your brother, the earl. Surely you must recall that Lady Eddington was often to be found in my company."

"Yes, indeed. It became something of a joke with my brother that he always knew where to look whenever he had misplaced his prospective bride," Lady Caroline said, deliberately deflating her aunt's pretensions. She was still in a flaming temper, and if it were not for the information that Mrs. Burlington claimed to hold, she would not have willingly chosen to stand about bandying words with the disagreeable woman a moment longer than necessary.

Mrs. Burlington's eyes flashed at the set-down, and she snapped, "I found Lady Eddington to be just as she ought to be, most respectful and accommodating to one who must by age and experience be thought to be wiser than she in her own tender years."

The implication was plain, but Lady Caroline did not react to it. "When are my brother and his lady returning, Amaris?"

"The letter was postmarked nearly three weeks before I received it, so they must already have set out. I expect that Lord and Lady Eddington will be returned to Berwicke in less than a fortnight," Mrs. Burlington said shortly. She paused a moment, then added, "Lady Eddington and I are as one in our agreement that your continued presence here at Berwicke would be a matter of considerable upset to Lord Eddington."

There was a short silence.

"I beg your pardon?" Lady Caroline's voice was at its most controlled, quiet and yet not at all retiring.

Mrs. Burlington was unheeding of the danger signals telegraphed by Lady Caroline's eyes. Her own eyes were bright with triumph. "Lord Eddington will naturally wish to indulge his new bride in all her little whims. And I do not think it at all unusual. After all, a newly wedded couple should not be required to divert their attentions from one another to accommodate the awkward presence of a family relation. His lordship will also wish Lady Eddington to take on the responsibilities of her new position, which she cannot easily do under the present circumstances, as even you must agree."

Lady Caroline stared at her aunt for a long moment. Her delicate brows had lifted slightly as Mrs. Burlington had spoken, and now there also came an unmistakable curl to her lips. "I see. What of your own presence, Amaris? I should think that if mine was *de trop*, yours must be equally so."

Mrs. Burlington was momentarily taken aback. Her surprised expression quickly smoothed, however. "My dear, it is hardly the same thing. I am an old woman and unlikely to demand much either in the way of entertainment or lavish civilities. In addition, Lady Eddington has most graciously assured me that she does not regard my presence at Berwicke as inhibiting in any way. To the contrary, I believe she thinks of me mostly in the guise of an amiable aunt."

"And what has Lord Eddington said?"

Mrs. Burlington's eyes slid away. She smoothed her sleeve. "As to that, I couldn't say."

"What you mean is that my brother has not been consulted one way or the other, but that you have taken it upon yourself to make every attempt to eject me from my home before ever he arrives, so that you will be firmly ensconced as mistress of the house," Lady Caroline said. "Pray allow me to inform you, Amaris, that I have no intention of packing my bags and bidding leave to Berwicke Keep in accordance with your opinion, nor on the basis of what you say are Lady Eddington's wishes. When I leave Berwicke, it will be when I wish it or at my brother's express request. I hope that I have made myself understood."

"Perfectly," Mrs. Burlington said through stiffened lips. "However, I think you should know that the matter does not end here, with you and me."

"No, I should rather think not," Lady Caroline said. Before she went through the door, she glanced once more back at her aunt. Cold anger shone out of her eyes. She was past caring that servants had begun to linger curiously in the entry hall.

"I do not think I have ever told you before, out of respect for my mother's memory, Amaris, what I have always thought of you. But now I feel compelled to do so. I have always found you to be ill-bred, patronizing, and quite mean-spirited, to boot." With that, she flung shut the door behind her and walked swiftly away.

9

The sky was lowering and sullen, threatening snow.

Lord Trilby cast a calculating look up at the heavy gray clouds overhead. His breath frosted the air as he said, "Ugly weather shaping up, John."

The bag bearer knowledgeably eyed the sky in his turn. He sniffed the air experimentally, much like the tired spaniel at his feet was doing. "Aye, m'lord. I can scent the new snow. A right nasty spell we're in for, I'll warrant."

"Yes," Lord Trilby agreed thoughtfully. He had left the manor house early, with his hunting gun over his shoulder, dressed warmly in hunting togs, a spaniel cavorting at his heels, and accompanied by his bag carrier.

The sport had been indifferent and resulted in a disappointing brace of hares and a pheasant or two, when what Lord Trilby had hoped for was a haunch of fresh venison for his dinner that evening.

The weather and the cold seemed somewhat ominous to him. He decided suddenly that he had had enough tramping about the fields and woods. "Let's go in, John."

"Aye, m'lord," The bag bearer threw a sympathetic glance at his master as they started back the few miles to the manor house. The earl had started out in good spirits, but the exercise and the disappointment of not even catching sight of a likely stag had brought a deep frown to his lordship's face. The bag bearer shrugged philosophically, reflecting that the next time his lordship took his gun out, the sport would likely be more to his taste.

Lord Trilby would have been amused at the construction that his servant had put upon his frowning expression. Actually he had a prescience of something impending. Perhaps his restlessness was brought on by the threatening weather, but more likely it was owing in large part to the lack of word from his secretary.

Lord Trilby had sent to Mr. Weston by messenger word that his meeting with Lady Caroline Eddington had been unsuccessful, along with a query whether the Grandduchess of Schaffenzeits had arrived. The messenger had returned with only a short acknowledgment of the earl's message, which had left Lord Trilby dangling in mild suspense. He still had no notion when, or even if, the grandduchess had yet arrived in London. It was very unlike Weston not to think of including some indication of the situation, Lord Trilby thought, and not for the first time.

When Lord Trilby got back to the manor house, he was greeted by the intelligence that a personage had arrived. The young manservant, who had not been with the household more than two years, appeared uncharacteristically flustered as he led the earl to understand that the personage was demanding his lordship's immediate attendance.

Lord Trilby raised his brows as he continued to give over into the trust of the footman his gun, his hat, and his gloves. "Indeed!"

As he walked rapidly in the direction of the drawing room, his keen ears picked up an unmistakable voice raised in imperious query. Servants bearing unfamiliar and innumerable pieces of baggage scurred past him with scarcely a murmured recognition. The very air seemed to crackle with energy. Lord Trilby grinned to himself, recognizing without ever having heard a name that the personage who was the cause of such a stir of activity could be none other than the Grandduchess Wilhelmina Hildebrande of Schaffenzeits.

Lord Trilby stepped into the drawing room.

The earl's entrance was at once noted. The diminutive and aged lady who was beleaguering the butler at once laid off with her demands and questions. She brushed past the butler as though the man had ceased to exist. She stretched out one withered hand, wielding a finely polished walking stick with the other. "My dearest Miles." Her greeting was heavy with the guttural accents of her country.

Lord Trilby took his great-aunt's hand and bent down, avoiding the brim of her bonnet, so that he could place a fond salute on her powdered and wrinkled cheek. "Your grace."

The Grandduchess Wilhelmina Hildebrande stepped back so that she could look at her grandnephew. The pleasure that had lightened her sharp visage lessened as she looked him over. Her guttural voice deepened with disapproval. "Why have you attired yourself in such a mode? I do not find it at all appropriate that you should receive me in your dirty boots."

"Forgive me, your grace. I have but this moment returned from hunting. When I was informed of your arrival, I so much forgot myself in my eager wish to greet you that I did not go upstairs to make myself presentable first," Lord Trilby said with a half-smile.

The Grandduchess Wilhelmina Hildebrande nodded, accepting the necessity of his lapse in proper manners as a form of compliment to herself and to the esteem in which he held her. "It is understood, of course. You were not to know in advance of my arrival. Your secretary is a worthy and loyal man, Miles. He was not easily persuaded to permit me to indulge my wish to come upon Walmesley all unexpected."

Lord Trilby's brows rose in surprised understanding. This was the explanation, then, for his secretary's odd omission regarding any mention of the grandduchess. "If I had known of your intentions, I could have better prepared for your arrival, your grace."

The grandduchess flashed a thin smile. "I think we each have an understanding of why I should wish to do so," she said, watching with satisfaction the sudden wariness that entered the Earl of Walmesley's expression.

She turned her head and gestured imperiously to a small voluminously cloaked figure who had stood apart during the conversation. When the young lady appeared to hesitate, the grandduchess reached out for her hand and firmly drew her forward. "Come, Marie. Do not be so shy with us. Lord Trilby, I wish you to meet my protégé, Fräulein Gutenberg. Fräulein, this fine English gentleman is the one whom I have told you so much about. Lord Miles Trilby, the Earl of Walmesley."

Lord Trilby shot the Grandduchess of Schaffenzeits a keen glance. As she met it, an expression of amused malice lit her heavy-lidded eyes. Lord Trilby thought his great-aunt knew very well what she was doing in pushing forward the young woman, and his thoughts were not charitable toward the grandduchess. He was reluctant to enter even so far into her schemings as to acknowledge the bride she had chosen for him. However, he was too well-mannered to parade his feelings.

The Earl of Walmesley gathered himself to carry out his obligation with noble fortitude. With the politest of expressions he took Fräulein Gutenberg's small gloved hand. She cast up a single glance at his face before lowering her eyes. The brim of her bonnet so shaded her face that he could not have studied her features even if he had wanted to do so.

Instead of raising the Fräulein's hand to his lips as he would assuredly have done with any other lady whom he had just met, Lord Trilby shook her hand in the most civil manner of which he was capable. This most impersonal of salutations was calculated to convey to his great-aunt that he was not as amenable to her plans for him as she might wish. His verbal greeting, too, was worded in such a way that the Grandduchess of Schaffenzeits could not mistake his stand. "Welcome to Walmesley, Fräulein. I hope your stay here is pleasant. I hope also that you will always retain fond memories of your visit to England."

The Grandduchess Wilhelmina Hildebrande gave a delighted cackle. The lines were now well and truly drawn. She liked nothing better than the struggle of wills and the maneuverings that came with such skirmishes. It was, after all, how she had managed to keep her own duchy intact for so long when all about her others were forced to fall in with the usurper Bonaparte. For now, however, she would let go the earl's open challenge. There would shortly come a better time to demonstrate her strength and to engage forces.

"My lord, I suggest that Marie and I repair to our rooms to put off our cloaks and make ourselves presentable for dinner," the grandduchess said. She glanced significantly at the earl's soiled hunting attire. "You shall make the required adjustments before rejoining us, of course."

Lord Trilby bowed, a faint smile on his face for the imperious command and the raising of the grandduchess's brows as her sharp eyes swept his disheveled figure and muddied boots. "Of course, your grace. The footman will show you to your rooms."

The Grandduchess Wilhelmina Hildebrande nodded her

satisfaction. "Come, Marie. You shall attend your toilette at once. We do not wish to keep his lordship waiting for us." She started for the drawing-room door, her walking stick tapping dully against the carpet. The silent young Fräulein resembled a cutter in the tow of a competent old barge as she obediently accompanied the grandduchess.

The Grandduchess Wilhelmina Hildebrande suddenly swept around on the earl. "We do not keep town hours while I am in residence at Walmesley, as you will no doubt recall. I am an old woman. I do not like to wait until the small hours for dinner, when it is time to seek to the comforts of my bed."

"I often observe country hours when at Walmesley," Lord Trilby said without betraying even by a flicker of his eyelids the untruth.

The grandduchess's thin lips stretched once more in a satisfied smile. "Good. I detest unpunctuality of any sort, whether in my meals or in my companions." She sailed regally out of the room.

Fräulein Gutenberg glanced briefly back at the earl before hurrying in her mistress's wake.

Lord Trilby waited a moment before he, too, left the drawing room. He stopped in the entry hall to inform the butler that the dinner hour was to be advanced before he continued up the stairs to seek the ministrations of his valet.

Though he could not see or hear the reaction of the household upon receiving the news that country hours were to be observed, he could well imagine the consternation in the kitchen when it was realized that dinner had to be served two hours earlier than had been anticipated. He laughed quietly to himself. The Grandduchess of Schaffenzeits had just begun to make her firm presence felt, as he well knew. He shrugged. The grandduchess's visits had always been stimulating.

When Lord Trilby entered his bedroom, his valet was setting out attire for the evening. The earl indicated the knee breeches that were laid over the back of a chair. "You have anticipated me, Wims."

The valet came forward to divest the earl of his hunting coat and, when the earl sat down on the chair, to begin the task of pulling off his lordship's muddy boots. "Indeed, my lord. I had heard that her grace, the Grandduchess of Schaffenzeits, had arrived."

Lord Trilby smiled. "The word travels quickly. I suppose that the rest of the household must also recall that her grace is a stickler for the old dictates."

The valet nodded, rising, the boots in his hands. "It is vividly recalled, my lord." He set the boots carefully aside on paper that had been previously spread to receive them, where they would remain until his lordship had gone downstairs to dinner and he would be free to clean them.

The earl laughed. He whipped off his neckcloth and carelessly dropped it to the carpet. In short order he discarded waistcoat and shirt, dispensing with them in the same manner. "So they should, after her grace's last descent upon the house. All had to be rearranged and regimented according to even her grace's most eccentric wishes, and there was the devil to pay if something was not quite up to snuff. It is to be hoped that this visit will proceed a bit more smoothly." Lord Trilby grimaced ruefully, his thoughts veering to the grandduchess's express purpose in coming to England. "I myself shall toe as fine a line as I may, but I fear that it will likely all be in vain."

The valet cocked his head, pausing in the task of gathering up the discarded clothing. "Shall you be wishing powder for your hair, my lord?"

Lord Trilby stopped in the act of shedding his breeches. He stared at his manservant, revolted. "Good God, no! One goes only so far in humoring the grandduchess's preferences."

The valet permitted himself a small smile. "Very good, my lord. The bath is prepared, my lord."

10

In a little over an hour, Lord Trilby returned downstairs. The butler quietly said a few words to him upon his descent of the last step, and Lord Trilby nodded. When he entered the drawing room, he found that the Grandduchess of Schaffenzeits and Fräulein Gutenberg had already preceded him. He was interested and amused to note that his great-aunt had chosen to attire herself in a round robe, high-waisted and very full, with a neckline filled in with a fichu, which, however faintly, resembled the old court gown of days past. The Grandduchess of Schaffenzeit's headdress was also on formal lines, being a toque of lamé trimmed with a fine plume.

Lord Trilby transferred his gaze to Fräulein Gutenberg in expectation of seeing the same formality of dress, but he was surprised. The Fräulein was robed in a simple round dress that set off an admirable figure. The low décolletage of the gown was trimmed lavishly with lace, adding piquancy to the swell of her firm bosom. Her dark hair had been dressed so that it appeared to be a fine cloud about her small, neatly formed head, and set off her dark brown eyes.

Fräulein Gutenberg was a beauty.

Lord Trilby was still grappling with the discovery as he advanced on his guests.

The ladies watched the Earl of Walmesley's approach with varying degrees of interest. He could read nothing in the Fräulein's expression, but he had no difficulty in deciphering the knowing look in the Grandduchess of Schaffenzeit's eyes.

She had anticipated his shock at discovering that the prospective bride she had brought to him was undeniably and devastatingly beautiful.

Lord Trilby had recovered his equilibrium enough to be able to greet the ladies with an easy manner. "Your grace, Fräulein. I am honored that I am to have such fair company this evening."

The grandduchess looked over her grandnephew with a critical gaze.

The earl was handsomely turned out. His dark, curly hair was brushed forward from the crown in the fashionable style. Lord Trilby's brows quirked over the amused expression in his eyes as he good-naturedly withstood the scrutiny. The dark blue coat set his broad shoulders to perfection. The embroidered silk waistcoat that he sported was left open but for the last few buttons so that the frilled shirt beneath it was revealed. The old-fashioned knee breeches were lighter in color than the coat and admirably drew the gaze down to the muscular calves sheathed in gray stockings and the black pumps on his feet.

The Grandduchess Wilhelmina Hildebrande nodded in approval. "You are a distinguished gentleman when you wish it, Miles."

Lord Trilby again bowed over her hand. "I shall take the rare compliment to heart, your grace."

The grandduchess cackled and snapped her fan sticks against his knuckles. "Now, make your pretty leg to Marie. A young woman has far greater appreciation for such nice accomplishments than does an old crone such as myself."

Lord Trilby did as he was bidden. He raised Fräulein Gutenberg's hand and gave a light pressure to her small fingers. He said in a polite form, "Fräulein Gutenberg, I welcome you again to Walmesley, and this time in proper form."

"*Danke*, my lord." Fräulein Gutenberg's voice was pitched low, and underscored, not unattractively, her own heavy accent.

The Grandduchess Wilhelmina Hildebrande directed an imperious query at her grandnephew with a lifting of her scant brows. "I hope that we are soon to go in to dinner, Miles. The hour is already well-advanced, as may be seen by the mantel clock, and I do not like to be kept dangling by inept servants."

Lord Trilby glanced in the direction of the drawing-room door, where at that moment the butler had appeared. He lifted his own brow, and the butler nodded. "Yes, I believe it is time. Allow me to escort you, your grace." He aided the Grandduchess of Schaffenzeits to her feet and then drew her withered hand through his arm. He smiled down at her sharp features. "Your company greatly honors me, your grace."

The Grandduchess Wilhelmina Hildebrande pinched his sleeve with her clawed fingers. "Ah, you have ever had the smooth tongue in your head. In that, you closely resemble your father. I recall quite clearly that his lordship was a stubborn man, as well. We shall see whether that quality is so forthcoming and as ingrained in his son." The grandduchess gave one of her short cackles. Abruptly her mood changed. She rapped her cane on the floor. "We shall proceed, if you please, my lord! " Without glancing around, she ordered, "Marie, you shall follow."

Lord Trilby escorted the grandduchess to the dining room, where he saw that she was comfortably seated. It was a mild relief to him that one of the footmen leapt forward to perform the same office for Fräulein Gutenberg. He rather thought that the less attention he was forced to dispense, even in terms of the simplest civilities, to the quiet Fräulein, the better it would be for the preservation of his position.

As Lord Trilby took his place at the head of the table, with the ladies placed at either hand, he glanced in Fräulein Gutenberg's direction. Her gaze was lowered, and so whatever feelings might have been revealed in her eyes were hidden from him. He studied her features again, marveling once more at her unexpected beauty. Her face was heart-shaped and very lovely. However, not once had he detected even a spark of animation in either her expression or her manner, which, for him, detracted considerably from her natural charms.

Lord Trilby thought there must surely be something lying behind Fräulein Gutenberg's apparent passivity. He wondered what her thoughts were on being brought to England to wed a man that she knew next to nothing about. Surely she felt something. Had she agreed wholeheartedly to the proposed match or did she harbor private and thus far inarticulated reservations?

An appalling possibility that had not previously occurred to him reared its head. Lord Trilby shot a narrowed look at the Grandduchess of Schaffenzeits, who was impervious to his sudden scrutiny as she directed the footman how she wished to be served her soup.

The earl pursued his incredible thought. It was not entirely improbable that Fräulein Gutenberg had been left completely in the dark. She could be ignorant of the grandduchess's purpose in introducing her to himself. She might have been told that she was being brought along to England to serve in the capacity of a companion to the grandduchess, which surmise fitted exactly the fashion in which the Fräulein had been treated.

Perhaps the explanation had been given to her that her inclination on the journey had been granted as a sort of favor to the young lady's family in order to broaden her horizons. The future of a young and well-bred daughter of a noble family exiled from their own homeland was uncertain, at best, and an opportunity to expose her to the well-bred society of Britain would be looked upon with favor, especially if it resulted in a creditable marriage with a gentleman of name and means. Fräulein Gutenberg could be hoping to marry an English gentleman, but not necessarily himself, Lord Trilby thought. In short, the Fräulein might not know anything at all about the outrageous scheme that the Grandduchess of Schaffenzeits was determined to force upon him.

Lord Trilby's jaw tightened as he weighed the possibility and its ramifications. If it was as he speculated and the Fräulein knew nothing, then his cold manners toward her could only have wounded and offended. It was not in his nature to willfully inflict hurt or dispense deliberate insult, and yet that was the position he must already occupy if Fräulein Gutenberg was indeed not in the grandduchess's confidence. It was an intolerable position.

However, if he alluded in any way to the match proposed by the Grandduchess of Schaffenzeits, such intelligence could only come as a decided shock to the Fräulein. It might also serve as an unfortunate catalyst in crystallizing Fräulein Gutenberg's previous unformed and nebulous ambitions. In that circumstance, he would himself have created the very atmosphere that he had hoped to discourage with his stiffly formal manner toward the young lady.

On the other hand, if Fräulein Gutenberg was indeed aware of the role that the Grandduchess of Schaffenzeits intended for her, then he could not afford to change his manner. Anything other than the most correct protocol would erode his defenses, for a more friendly manner must inevitably lead the young lady to expect, in short order, some sort of declaration from him.

Good God, what a convoluted coil.

"My lord, do you not find the beef to your taste?"

Lord Trilby was startled out of his reverie. He glanced up at the footman standing at his shoulder, then around the table, to discover that the soup had been removed in favor of the main course. "I have discovered little appetite in myself this evening," he said shortly.

"I have frequently observed that one's private reflections often make for poor company without additional stimulation. Although our intellect always assumes itself to be clear and certain, our mind still often feels itself to be beleaguered by uncertainty," the Grandduchess Wilhelmina Hildebrande said obliquely. She regarded the earl with a thin smile on her lips, as though willing him to question her meaning.

Lord Trilby did not succumb to the temptation. He did not need to ask for translation. He knew of old the devious ways of the Grandduchess of Schaffenzeits. She was toying with him, attempting to draw him into further uncertainty of his position.

The way to circumvent the old lady's scheming was readily seen, and that was to present the staunchest of defenses while at the same time rendering himself so disagreeable to Fräulein Gutenberg that she would refuse to comply with the Grandduchess of Schaffenzeit's wishes. His dilemma was that he did not know enough about Fräulein Gutenberg's situation, nor her place in the ludicrous game.

He knew where stood the grandduchess on the board and how well fortified was his own position, but he had not as yet a clue to Fräulein Gutenberg's position. She had been represented to him by the grandduchess as a free player, much akin to a knight or bishop who could at any moment put him into check. But the Fräulein could as easily be a pawn, and as such would require a modified approach.

Lord Trilby inwardly groaned. It was a pretty dilemma, indeed, and he had a strong suspicion that it had not been brought about by accident. The Grandduchess of Schaffenzeits was a past master of manipulation and deceptive position. She had managed far longer than anyone thought possible the diplomatic dance with Napoleon Bonaparte, giving lip service to the self-styled French emperor without giving up the actual autonomy of her small duchy. When that had become no longer possible, she had gone into self-exile in St. Petersburg, with all her court in train, rather than bend the knee in allegiance to French rule.

When the earl had written to her grace in placation, fabricating the existence of an intended bride, he had not given proper thought to the grandduchess's character, nor to her most probable reaction. She had come to England to call his bluff, and thus far she was succeeding on all counts. He had been unable to properly regain his balance, which had begun to annoy him, for he knew that such was the grandduchess's intention.

Lord Trilby knew that he had to wrest the upper hand to himself or he was as good as lost. Attrition, if nothing else, would gradually grind away at his defenses. The Grandduchess of Schaffenzeits was famous for her persistence and her obstinancy in gaining her own way. The grand old lady would not easily be persuaded to leave England without gaining her object, and that object was his own firm commitment to an acceptable lady.

Lord Trilby looked at Fräulein Gutenberg. She was gazing at him with an expression of polite interest. There was a void in her eyes, but he did not think that she was unintelligent. No, there was something waiting just behind those luminous brown eyes that he could not quite put a name to, but which he knew with certainty was not what he wished for himself.

"I am quite certain of my own mind. My intellect does not lead me far astray, not in this instance, at least," Lord Trilby said slowly.

The Grandduchess Wilhelmina Hildebrande cackled. Her finger slipped around her wineglass. "Indeed, my lord! How odd it is that I can find no fault at all in the beef, whilst you have pushed away your unfinished portion. When one becomes as ancient as myself, one sees far more than one is given credit for." She lifted the wineglass and touched it to her lips, tasting the wine with appreciation. As she set down the glass, she said quietly, "Though I eschew London, I have always the greatest curiosity about all that is encompassed by your life in that hideous city. Perhaps while I am in England I shall have the singular honor of meeting a few of your friends and . . . intimates, Miles."

Lord Trilby met the implacability in the grandduchess's eyes. She was of course referring to his nonexistent intended. It was a thousand times a pity that Lady Caroline had refused him. He deliberately brought a lazy half-smile to his lips. "As to that, I suppose it is a matter that can be arranged." He saw the instant of startlement in her eyes before her expression smoothed to one of polite incredulity. He knew that she had expected him to parade excuses out for her inspection, but he had taken her by surprise with his agreeableness, which had also effectively cut the ground out from under her.

At all costs he must avoid entangling himself in any more lies and deceits. The Grandduchess of Schaffenzeits was too skilled at verbal dueling not to recognize his weakness, and certainly the fabrication of an engagement must qualify as his greatest weakness. Damn Caro's eyes, he thought with a flash of frustration. Now he must dodge whilst on the run, and would very likely run his neck into the noose before he became aware of it.

Lord Trilby reached leisurely for his own wineglass and drank from it. "An excellent vintage, do you not agree, Fräulein?" It was the proper question of a host, but it was also a lowering of his defenses.

Fräulein Gutenberg smiled ever so faintly. Her lovely dark eyes shone. "Indeed, my lord."

Though Lord Trilby gave every appearance of ease—his posture relaxed, his lips touched by a smile—within he was taut as a bowstring. Steadily, and without a sound escaping from between his teeth, he cursed.

II

For several days a state of suspended hostilities existed between Lady Caroline and Mrs. Burlington. They avoided one another's company as nearly as possible, Lady Caroline doing so by the simple expedient of closeting herself in the study or the library for lengthy periods of estate work or reading.

Soon after the heated clash between the ladies, the first vestiges of winter had made their appearance in the form of icy rain and sleet. The sullen weather discouraged either lady from visiting with their neighbors still in residence; nor could they look forward to the unfriendly atmosphere of Berwicke being alleviated overmuch by callers of their own.

Lady Caroline, made restive by the enforced inactivity and the tension between herself and her aunt, would have been particularly delighted to have received Lord Trilby. The earl had a trick of making her laugh, which she felt in sore need of these days. In addition, her curiosity had been engaged by his plight, and several times since his visit she had wondered what had happened. But there was no word from Lord Trilby and she could only surmise that his lordship's situation was not as desperate as he had made it out to be.

As the dismal days dragged by, there was but one caller, and that was Lord Hathaway. Lady Caroline was not informed until much later of his lordship's visit, since Lord Hathaway had, strangely enough, specifically requested to see only Mrs. Burlington. Simpson informed Lady Caroline that the two had been closeted together for a little better than three hours.

Lady Caroline had put up her brows in surprise. A speculative expression had entered her fine eyes. "Indeed! I wonder whatever it was all about?"

"That I could not tell you, my lady," Simpson said regretfully.

Lady Caroline had shrugged and put it out of her head. It was of little consequence, after all. If Lord Hathaway chose to seek out her aunt, perhaps even to complain of how his overtures to herself had been received, it was certainly better to let the matter be brought to her attention. She was not so curious that she wanted to deliberately seek out Mrs. Burlington.

When Lady Caroline had almost despaired of ever seeing the sky again, it finally dawned a pale sun. The clear, albeit still gray, winter sky heralded more than the end of a week's bad weather, however, as she was to learn.

Lady Caroline was embroidering in the drawing room, having first checked to see that Mrs. Burlington was not already in residence. Outside in the entry hall she heard a bluff voice raised in good-natured question, and even as she quickly looked up and set aside her embroidery, the door opened to reveal her brother's familiar lanky figure.

Lady Caroline rose from the settee at once, her eyes lighting up with genuine affection. She went toward him with outstretched hands. "Ned! I *am* glad to see you home," she exclaimed, her spirits lighter than they had been for days.

Lord Eddington laughed. He brushed past Lady Caroline's hands to slip his arms about her trim waist and pulled her close for a quick brotherly buss on the cheek. "Dear Caroline! Have you preserved my inheritance for me in my absence?"

"Of course, and to the very letter of your instructions, I

might add," Lady Caroline said with a smile and mock salute.

Lord Eddington laughed again. "As though I don't know that compared to my man of business in London and you, I would make a very poor steward indeed." He spied his wife paused in the open doorway. "No need to stand on ceremony, my dearest. It is only Caroline, as you see."

Lady Eddington advanced then into the drawing room. She was pulling off her gloves, and as she freed one hand, she offered it to Lady Caroline. "Dear Lady Caroline. How nice that you are here to greet his lordship and me."

Lady Eddington was a fragile blond beauty whose oval face and small inches had endowed her with an ethereal appearance. Her limpid blue eyes held an expression that bordered on the wary when they met Lady Caroline's gaze, and her polite smile lacked genuine warmth.

"Wherever else would my sister be?" Lord Eddington asked rhetorically. He turned to the bell rope and gave it a vigorous tugging. "Where is Simpson? I requested tea to be sent in directly. I am famished for our good English tea and biscuits."

Lady Caroline observed the slightest tightening of her new sister-in-law's soft mouth at Lord Eddington's offhand rejoinder, and instantly the ugly assertion that Mrs. Burlington had thrown at her head not many days past was recalled. Perhaps Lady Eddington had indeed expressed the desire that Lady Caroline be removed from Berwicke Keep.

Lady Caroline cautioned herself not to leap to spurious conclusions. More likely, she thought, Lady Eddington was simply insecure and intimidated by her new position, and when she had voiced such timidities to Mrs. Burlington, the lady had grossly exaggerated them. The new countess was, after all, very young and untried, having been brought up in a somewhat straitened household under the tutelage of a not particularly affectionate stepmother.

With these thoughts in mind, Lady Caroline set herself to make her sister-in-law at ease. "I am happy that you and my brother have returned, Lady Eddington. Please sit with me so that we may more comfortably converse." She gestured invitingly toward the settee, and after the barest hesitation, Lady Eddington accepted with murmured thanks.

Lady Caroline seated herself and turned an interested expression to her companion. "Now, you must tell me all about your travels. I have never been out of England, though I have long wished to journey to the Mediterranean and especially to Athens, which I understand is very beautiful."

"Yes, it is beautiful. But I think that I prefer London over any other city," Lady Eddington said coolly.

"Too right!" Lord Eddington had joined the ladies by throwing himself into a wing chair opposite. He grimaced as he glanced across to meet his sister's amused glance. "No, Caroline, you have no notion. It was a jolly trip and all that, of course. But it is good to be home after all that traipsing about foreign parts. And all that incessant foreign gabbling too. I was never in my life gladder of anything than to hear plain honest English speech."

"Indeed, my lord, I never understood more than one word in ten. I was ever so happy to leave it all in your competent hands," Lady Eddington said, bestowing a warm smile on her husband.

Lord Eddington's flat chest expanded. "Aye, I was able to make myself fairly well understood in Cairo, was I not? I was made to study French as a lad, of course. Though I hated it at the time, I must confess that I was damned glad of it on more than one occasion. Once we got to Athens, though, the going was a bit rougher."

"How can you say so, my lord? Why, I do not recall that

you ever had the least difficulty," Lady Eddington said. She turned to Lady Caroline, her face at last showing some animation. "You will scarcely credit it, Lady Caroline, but his lordship spoke with magnificent fluency whatever outrageous language we chanced to encounter. I was never more astonished in my life. His lordship had not told me before that he was a linguist."

"I am impressed indeed. I had no notion of this hidden talent of yours, Ned," Lady Caroline said.

Lord Eddington had gone red with pleasure at his wife's extravagant praise. Now his flush deepened at the teasing note in his sister's voice. "No, nor had I. But do you know, all those tedious hours when old Tarrybone positively drilled the Latin into my head must have taken root, for I was able to catch on pretty quickly to the natives. Believe me, it made matters much smoother than they might have been in several instances. Caroline, you would not believe the roads. No, nor the lack of proper service that one is obliged to accept. It was nothing like one might expect whilst traveling in England."

"But that was only between the largest of cities, my lord. Surely you have not already forgotten the gracious reception with which we were greeted and the pleasures provided for our entertainment when we disembarked in the capitals," Lady Eddington said.

"By Jove, you're right! Now that I come to think on it, we could not have asked for a better time than what those foreigners provided us once we had visited our British embassies and made ourselves known," Lord Eddington said.

"I particularly liked Athens. I do not think that I have ever laughed and danced so much in my life as during the week that we remained there," Lady Eddington said. "I should like to go back sometime."

"Then we shall!" Lord Eddington declared. He smiled at

his lady. "You may have anything that your pretty heart desires of me, as you know."

Lady Eddington appeared properly pleased by this generous declaration, but Lady Caroline did not feel so sanguine. She glanced from one to the other of her companions, both of whom seemed to have forgotten where they were. She could not but feel somewhat left out in the cold when her beloved brother and her new sister-in-law gazed at one another so bemusedly and to the exclusion of all else. Once more the specter of Mrs. Burlington's allegation that Lady Eddington would be more than happy to see her take leave of Berwicke Keep surfaced.

She became angered at herself for succumbing to Mrs. Burlington's planting of doubt, but still she could not help feeling a measure of uncertainty.

Lady Caroline told herself not to be a nodcock. Even if it were true, she hoped that she would have sense enough to make a graceful departure without invoking Lady Eddington's ill will, for that would naturally affect the relationship between herself and her brother.

If it appeared that her presence did indeed prove to be a damper to the private cooings of the newly wedded pair, she would make the decision herself before anyone else could request it of her. That would be a trick, indeed, if she knew anything at all about her aunt's character and that particular lady's propensity to throw up a topic to discussion until one was heartily sick of the entire matter.

Lady Caroline was still chiding herself for the ungenerous thought when the door to the drawing room opened and Mrs. Burlington swept in. She was followed by Simpson and two of the footmen. The three menservants carried trays piled high with all the necessaries of a substantial tea.

"Well! You have returned safely, my lord, and none the

worse for wear," Mrs. Burlington said, giving her hand to Lord Eddington, who had risen from his chair to greet her.

"You are looking well, Aunt Amaris," Lord Eddington said. Some of his genial air had dissipated, which earned him the swiftest of glances from his new bride.

Mrs. Burlington did not wait for his lordship's reply, but at once turned her smile on Lady Eddington. "As for you, my dear child, anyone with eyes in her head can see that you are in fine fettle. Your countenance is positively glowing! How happy I am to see you again and to be able to renew our delightful acquaintance."

"And I, Mrs. Burlington. I much enjoyed our little talks before my marriage to his lordship," Lady Eddington said, smiling up in a friendly way at Mrs. Burlington.

"Oh, you must not stand upon such ceremony with me, my dear. After all, we are all family now, are we not? Pray address me as you would your own dear aunt," Mrs. Burlington said.

"Thank you, I am sure," Lady Eddington said with an engaging little laugh.

While this short interlude of exchanges had taken place, tea was set out and those who were standing settled into their places. Mrs. Burlington took the wing chair beyond Lord Eddington. It was not the seat she would have chosen for herself if she had come earlier to the drawing room, for she would have preferred to have been beside Lady Eddington. But that place had been usurped by her niece, naturally, and as she couldn't very well demand that she be given Lord Eddington's chair, so that she was sitting between the young couple, she was left with no choice but to smilingly seat herself at the outside corner of the small group.

"I was but a moment ago informed of your arrival, or I would have been present to greet you earlier," Mrs.

Burlington said. There was the slightest edge to her voice, and the glance that she tossed in the butler's direction spoke volumes. She composed a smile on her face as she turned once again to her young relatives. "I hope that I have not missed anything of interest by my tardiness."

"My brother and Lady Eddington were but enlightening me about some of their travels," Lady Caroline said, casting a smile at the two in question. "From all I have heard, I suspect that Ned would have made an excellent diplomat."

"Why, that is so very true!" Lady Eddington exclaimed. She bestowed her first uninhibited smile on Lady Caroline. Her eyes shone with approval. "You must be a fond sister indeed to so swiftly place your finger on the very thing that I have been attempting to put into words for weeks."

Mrs. Burlington did not like to see the friendliness of Lady Eddington's overture to her niece. It did not suit her plans in the least. She gave a brittle laugh. "Lord Eddington a diplomat! Why, what a perfectly novel idea. I am certain that such a notion never once crossed his lordship's mind, however. Lord Eddington could hardly wish for such a wandering life."

"Oh, I don't know. The notion does have its allure. We did rather enjoy the rounds of entertaining that those diplomatic fellows were always getting up in order to impress the foreigners," Lord Eddington said thoughtfully. He glanced at his wife with a lively, quizzical expression. "What do you say, Mary? Should you like knocking about from capital to capital in the diplomatic service?"

"If you should wish such a career, my lord, nothing could possibly make me happier," Lady Eddington said.

Lord Eddington reached for his lady's hand, and when she gave it into his care, he leaned over the arm of his chair to catch her fingers to his lips in brief salute. "I am the luckiest dog alive, I think," he said contentedly.

Mrs. Burlington looked from one to the other of them in complete astonishment and gathering dismay. "Surely you cannot be serious, my lord! Why, what of Berwicke Keep and your responsibilities here in England? What of Lady Eddington's place as mistress of this house? What of your places in society? You cannot simply throw it all over for some paltry career as a second secretary or some such thing!"

Lord Eddington flushed furiously.

Lady Eddington took up her lord's defense in her gentle voice, faintly chiding. "Of course my lord must do exactly as he thinks best. I have every confidence in his ultimate success, whatever course he chooses to pursue." Mrs. Burlington was unexpectedly silenced. Lady Eddington gently withdrew her hand from her husband's clasp and turned her attention to pouring of the tea. "Tea, Lady Caroline?"

"Yes, black, please," Lady Caroline said. She said nothing more, neither indicating her opinion of her brother's odd flight of fancy nor taking sides in the conversation. It was to her mind a most enlightening scene. Her brother's devotion to his new bride was obvious, as was hers to him, and she could not find it in her heart to envy their happiness. As for her aunt, Lady Caroline was beginning to suspect that Mrs. Burlington had counted too heavily on making of Lady Eddington a staunch ally and devotee.

As Lady Caroline accepted the cup and saucer from Lady Eddington's hands, that lady's gaze met hers. There was a speculative, measuring expression in Lady Eddington's eyes that startled Lady Caroline with its calculation. Then Lady Eddington turned away to graciously offer tea to the others.

Lady Caroline meditatively sipped her own tea. It was scalding hot, but she hardly noticed. She had just perceived that Lady Eddington was not quite the malleable and retiring young girl that she had opined her to be upon their previous short acquaintance. "Oh, Lord," she murmured ruefully.

"What was that, niece?" Mrs. Burlington inquired quickly.

But Lady Caroline merely shook her head and turned aside the query by beginning to tell a mildly humorous account to Lord Eddington about a minor estate problem that had cropped up in his absence.

12

If tea was not an unqualified success from Mrs. Burlington's point of view, it was also a rather mixed experience for Lady Caroline. She quickly gathered through her observations and the ordinary conversation one might expect to occur when travelers had returned that Lady Eddington, very quietly and quite unobtrusively, controlled Lord Eddington. Her ladyship often demurred to the Earl of Berwicke, yet somehow Lord Eddington's declarations always fell right in line with Lady Eddington's own gently voiced opinions.

Lady Caroline thought that her brother neither realized it yet nor was made unhappy by it. Indeed, she rather thought that Lord Eddington seemed steadier than she had ever known him to be in his life. Certainly he appeared content enough.

Lady Caroline only hoped that her brother was not destined for awful disillusionment. She knew very little about her new sister-in-law, except what she had been told of the young woman's background and what she recalled of the young woman's retiring, almost shy manner upon the occasion of her visit in the company of her stepmother to Berwicke Keep. There was also Mrs. Burlington's purported knowledge of Lady Eddington's opinion in regards to herself, but Lady Caroline thought that she could fairly well withhold judgment upon that.

On balance was Lady Eddington's open adoration of the Earl of Berwicke. Lady Caroline was inclined to believe that her ladyship's affection for Lord Eddington was sincere.

However, if it was not, Lady Caroline could only pity her brother, for she had observed enough to form the opinion that Lady Eddington could handle quite well those who presumed to counter her wishes. And that, Lady Caroline thought with an inward chuckle, might well come as a thoroughly unpleasant surprise to Mrs. Burlington.

During tea Mrs. Burlington had campaigned strenuously to stake her claim as Lady Eddington's mentor and confidante, but the young countess had slipped time and again out of her net. There had been nothing ungracious or even vaguely unfriendly in Lady Eddington's responses to Mrs. Burlington's overtures that one could point to, but still the impression was unmistakable that her ladyship preferred to retain a neutral position among her new relations.

Lady Caroline had been impressed by her new sister-in-law's adroit handling of Mrs. Burlington, but at the same time she recognized that if Lady Eddington did indeed choose to thrust her out of Berwicke Keep, and her brother's life, her ladyship would be a most formidable opponent indeed.

But that was for the future. In the meantime, Lady Caroline had another small problem that demanded a decision of her. She had received a communication from Lord Hathaway requesting a private interview of her. After their last *tête-à-tête,* Lady Caroline was not overly eager to see Lord Hathaway again so soon. However, she well knew the gentleman's obstinate nature and she was resigned that his lordship would present himself whether or not she acquiesced to his request.

It was with misgivings, therefore, that she returned a reply in the affirmative. Lord Hathaway could call upon her the following morning.

She had just sent off her message with a servant when

there was a light knock on the half-open door of the library and Lord Eddington entered. "Am I bothering you, Caroline?"

Still seated at the writing desk, Lady Caroline smiled up at him. "Of course you are not."

Lord Eddington closed the door. He stood a moment, seemingly irresolute, before he crossed to a wing chair positioned close to the desk. He looked at his sister with a somewhat distracted air. "I am in need of a spot of advice, Caroline, and as you are the only one that I feel able to come to, I hope that you can help me."

"Well, naturally I shall do whatever I can," Lady Caroline said. "What is the problem, Ned?"

Lord Eddington shook his head. A half-smile crossed his face. "The truth of the matter is, you are." He saw that he had stunned her, and he hurried on. "It is not just you, Caroline, but our aunt as well. I had not realized before what it meant to have everyone about. One becomes inured to it, you see. But now, being married and all . . . well, it will be a bit awkward at times. I know what you are going to say. We have but just arrived today and perhaps we should wait and see how things go on. But during tea I saw instantly how it was going to be. Mary mentioned it to me later, of course, being sensitive to such things herself. She is the dearest of creatures and would not wish to offend anyone, least of all anyone whom I hold in affection, and so I had to pry it out of her, but she, too, felt the uncomfortable tension among the four of us. Oh, don't you see, Caroline?"

"Indeed I do. When one weds, one naturally wishes privacy in order to adjust to one's new stature," Lady Caroline said, not allowing the hurt to cross her expression or tinge her voice.

"I knew that I could depend upon you to understand,

Caroline. But what do you advise me to do?" Lord Eddington asked.

She occupied herself with straightening the desk, putting away the inkwell and pens and sheets of paper, so that she would not have to meet her brother's anxious gaze straightaway. "I shall need some time to decide where I will go and, naturally, to set up my own household, but I think that I can manage to be in my own establishment in a month or so."

Lord Eddington's face reflected his initial surprise. "Well, it is awfully good of you to offer. I had not thought to ask if of you, meaning only to ask you to advise me whether Mary and I should not remove to London," he said doubtfully.

"Of course you and Lady Eddington must not remove to London just on account of myself and Amaris. I think my suggestion a far better plan," Lady Caroline said steadily.

"Well, naturally, if that is what you truly wish, I shall be more than glad to foot the bill for a town house in London or wherever," Lord Eddington said, a certain relief in his voice. He straightened in the chair and his smile broadened to one of more confidence. "But I should not like you to go quite as soon as all that, Caroline. I shall need your help in prying Aunt Amaris loose, you see. I should dislike the task myself and, truth to tell, I would make a very poor hand at it. I have never been able to face down our aunt, as you well know, whereas you have never had the least difficulty."

Lady Caroline did not know whether to laugh or to rage at him. It was not fair that he should force her into the decision to leave her childhood home so soon, while in the same breath request that she should perform his dirty work for him before she did go. She chose to laugh, feeling that it was better for her own self-respect. "Ned, you are a nodcock. I have always thought so and now I am more strengthened in my opinion than ever. Amaris would go quickly enough were you and Lady Eddington together to present the case to her, I am certain. Why, whatever could she say against it, pray? Berwicke Keep is your home, after all."

"But Aunt Amaris has been here very nearly as long as I can remember. She considers Berwicke more her home than anywhere else on earth. I cannot simply ask that she pack up her things, now, can I? Pray be reasonable, Caroline," Lord Eddington said.

Lady Caroline regarded her brother for a moment. She said quietly, "Berwicke Keep is more my home than it was ever Amaris', yet you have not had the least difficulty in indicating to me that you would prefer that I find another."

Lord Eddington flushed. He said uncomfortably, "Well, that is different. You are my sister, after all. I can talk to you with expectation of being heard out with some measure of quiet reason. Whereas with Aunt Amaris . . . well, you know what she is like."

"Yes, I know very well. I think I know better than you what Amaris is like. I know, also, that I am wearied to death of dealing with her on my own account and yours, and I really have no taste for becoming your second in this latest matter. Perhaps it is time that you were allowed to discover for yourself exactly how it is that you should deal with her, Ned," Lady Caroline said. She rose from her seat at the desk.

"You are angry!" Lord Eddington exclaimed, discovering it with surprise.

Lady Caroline rounded on him. There was no mistaking the temper in her flashing eyes or the high color in her cheeks, and he shrank back in his chair. "No, am I? Well, perhaps you should give a little thought as to why, Ned. And now, if you will excuse me, I shall go up to my room. I have the headache and I think that I shall lie down for a while before dinner." She whisked herself out of the library, leaving Lord Eddington to stare after her in the liveliest dismay.

Lady Caroline did, indeed, go upstairs to her room. She sent away her maid, saying again that she had the headache and wished to lie down quietly for a few moments. It was an unusual excuse for her, and well she knew it before she was ever treated to the maid's dubious expression, but she did not care. She was in full retreat for the second time in her life. She wanted to be alone in order to catch up her rampant emotions. Otherwise she suspected that she might fly apart in such a manner that it would embarrass both herself and whoever was witness to her unaccustomed fury.

For fury it was. She was unexpectedly consumed by it. She had endured a particularly grim week with Mrs. Burlington's strictures and malicious unpleasantries, only to have it all capped with Lord Eddington's startling though characteristically timid insinuation that she leave Berwicke Keep. What was most infuriating about the entire business, of course, was that she had been forewarned by her aunt.

Lady Caroline had thought it possible that Mrs. Burlington had exaggerated in her insistence that Lady Eddington would not wish to compete with a sister-in-law's presence, but she had succeeded in suspending judgment upon the matter until she had time to see how the wind might blow. She had never expected to be hit so swiftly by the possibility. She had been caught completely off-guard by Lord Eddington's confidences, and as a consequence had been hit harder than perhaps she should have been.

Lady Caroline had ample space for reflection before it became time to change and go downstairs for dinner. She made up her mind that no good purpose would be served if she were not to accept her brother's awkward hints as realistically as she was capable. Indeed, she was too used to her brother's sensitive nature not to realize that for her to treat him with the distant civility that her anger urged upon her would only bewilder and hurt him. Therefore she intended to make an effort to greet Lord Eddington in her usual convivial manner.

13

After the disastrous outcome of the interview earlier that day between himself and Lady Caroline, Lord Eddington was anxious at first of his reception at his sister's hands. However, when she met him in the drawing room before dinner was announced, she spoke to him in her usual fond fashion.

He was greatly relieved and thereafter put out of his mind the previous unpleasantness. He made himself agreeable to his sister and to his wife, and if his efforts fell somewhat flat with Mrs. Burlington, no fault could be laid to his lordship's door.

In truth, Mrs. Burlington was vaguely disgruntled. She had been surprised by the countess's faintly aloof air toward her, for she had been anticipating being at once able to establish herself somewhat in the guise of a mentor and confidante. She could not imagine what was wrong with the girl, for she had had that most respectful letter from Lady Eddington written not more than a month before. She could not complain that Lady Eddington was no longer respectful toward her, but there seemed to be an air of standoffishness that Mrs. Burlington did not recall had been in the girl's manner before the marriage.

Mrs. Burlington decided that perhaps Lady Eddington was simply overwhelmed by her new status. Once the young countess had settled a little more into her role, with gentle guidance from herself, naturally, Mrs. Burlington felt that she need have no doubt of her own indispensability.

The talk over the dinner table was desultory and ranged

from estate business and neighborhood gossip to travel anecdotes from Lord and Lady Eddington. The conversation changed tone, however, when Lord Eddington made the surprising announcement that he and his lady planned to leave Berwicke Keep.

"What! But you cannot be serious, Lord Eddington. Why, you have but just arrived at Berwicke," Mrs. Burlington said. She was taken so by surprise that she spilled her wine on her dress and in utmost irritation dabbed at the stained silk.

The Earl of Berwicke instantly sensed his aunt's strong disapprobation and sought refuge in an even heartier tone than was his habit. "Oh, well, there is not much happening here in the country this time of the year, and Lady Eddington and I are not much for rusticating at any time. We prefer town amusements and making a splash among the *ton* and such." Not wishing to be forced into argument by Mrs. Burlington, Lord Eddington turned to his sister. "May I rely upon you for the estate awhile longer, Caroline? I should be ever so grateful to you, as would my dear lady."

Though Lady Caroline's surprise at the announcement was at least equal to Mrs. Burlington's, she managed it better. "Of course you may rely upon me, Ned. But I had quite thought you and Lady Eddington were fixed here at Berwicke for a time. At least, that was the impression I gathered from you earlier this afternoon."

The questioning note in her voice made Lord Eddington flush. He waved his hand, saying uncomfortably, "Oh . . . as to that! The thing of it is, Caroline, I had not given the matter proper thought. My lady's family is not yet aware that we have returned to England, and naturally she wishes to call upon her father and his wife. I should like to pay my respects as well, of course." He eyed his sister in a half-apologetic fashion.

"I understand, dear brother," Lady Caroline said with a small laugh. Indeed she did, she thought. She had been given a reprieve of sorts because yet again her feckless brother needed her to take over the responsibilities of the estate. For the first time, Lady Caroline began to look upon her departure from Berwicke as a move in her own better interests. She simply could not allow herself to evolve any further into her brother's permanent crutch. Something must be done, and perhaps her best course would be to discuss the earl's indifference with his lordship's man of business, who was, after all, employed to look after Lord Eddington's concerns.

"Well, it is more than I can understand!" Mrs. Burlington exclaimed. "I do not know how long you mean to continue shirking your responsibilities here at Berwicke, my lord, but I think I must tell you that in my opinion it is a grave mistake. It should not be made your sister's position, for nothing could be more unseemly. And dear Lady Eddington must be wondering at the manner that you have kept her capering hither and yon, as though she were a Gypsy rather than the proud mistress of a grand and old house. I wonder at it, indeed I do!"

Lady Caroline threw a glance at her brother. Lord Eddington appeared more and more uncomfortable under his aunt's scolding tone of censure. His normally jovial face had lengthened into deep, unhappy lines. She sighed, for though she had meant what she said to him about learning to deal with their aunt, she found that the old habits of childhood were too strong. She could not sit idly by while he was bullied by Mrs. Burlington. "I think that the earl could be allowed to voice his decision without being subjected to these embarrassing exclamations, Amaris," she said quietly.

"By Jove, so I should," Lord Eddington muttered. A dull flush of resentment shaded his cheekbones.

"Mrs. Burlington, I shall look forward to our return to Berwicke, if for no other reason than to speak at length with you," Lady Eddington said.

On the point of addressing her nephew again, Mrs. Burlington instead shrugged as though the matter was one of indifference, after all. Though ill temper still hardened her eyes, she smiled at the countess. She said in a surprisingly tolerant manner, "As I am certain that I shall do also, dear Lady Eddington. It is all the same to me, of course, but I had thought to point out what I thought to be your own interests in the matter."

Lady Eddington inclined her head. She said softly, "I shall not forget that, I do assure you."

Mrs. Burlington's severe expression relaxed completely into a satisfied smile. She threw a rapid glance at Lady Caroline to be certain that her niece had not missed the progress she had made toward becoming the countess's ally. "That is most gracious of you, my lady."

Lord Eddington let out his breath on a long sigh. He said feelingly, "I am glad that is settled."

"But when shall you be leaving?" Lady Caroline asked.

The Earl of Berwicke warily eyed his aunt, unwilling to be the cause of another outburst. It was Lady Eddington who replied. "My lord intends to start off early in the morning, being most anxious to make London as speedily as possible so that we shall not be required to spend the night at some remote inn."

"Too right. One can never be certain of the airing of the sheets at those places," Lord Eddington said, nodding.

Lady Caroline lifted her napkin briefly to her lips to hide her smile. She had never before known her brother to express concerns over an inn's housekeeping. It was but another example of the ascendancy of Lady Eddington's quiet and pervasive influence over him. She dropped the napkin back to its place. "Indeed, Ned! Then I shall bid you and Lady Eddington a good journey this evening, for though I am usually a prompt riser, I might yet miss your departure if it is to be so very early. Or worse still, come upon you and Lady Eddington just as you are stepping up into the carriage. I do so dislike hurried farewells, as you know."

"Oh, indeed! The Earl of Walmesley could well testify to that," Mrs. Burlington said.

Lady Caroline did not acknowledge her aunt's interjection and she hoped that her brother and sister-in-law had not heard it, or, if they had, that neither would understand the allusion. In an effort to cover the awkward moment, she smiled at Lady Eddington and inquired, "Shall I request the usual coffee to be served in the drawing room, my lady, or do you have a preference for something else?"

Instantly Lady Caroline knew that she had erred.

Lady Eddington's eyes flashed and her voice was considerably chillier than it had been before. "Thank you for your kind consideration, Lady Caroline. However, I think that I shall relay my preferences myself." She beckoned the footman in attendance and spoke to him quietly.

A short laugh sounded from across the table. Lady Caroline did not need to glance at her aunt's face to know that that lady was wearing a malicious expression. Indeed, she had put her foot well into it, and as clumsily as the most awkward of debutantes, Lady Caroline thought resignedly.

After Lady Caroline's unintentional blunder in taking to herself the precedence reserved for the mistress of the house, the remainder of the evening was decidedly less convivial than it might have been. Lady Caroline excused herself soon after the coffee was served, saying that she was unaccountably tired and so she would retire early.

Lord Eddington looked upon his sister's exit from the drawing room with alarm, not wanting to be left without what he perceived as Lady Caroline's protection from Mrs. Burlington's caustic tongue. He instantly took his sister's declaration as his own cue. He reached for his wife's hand and pressed her fingers. "The hour is not so far advanced, but I know that you also must be wanting to retire, my lady. And so should we both, for it shall be an early morning."

"Quite so, my lord," Lady Eddington said, agreeing at once. "I should like to see how the packing is progressing too."

Mrs. Burlington pursed her mouth as Lord Eddington politely bade her good night. "I am not as easily readied for my pillow. The nights have become very indifferent for me and so I shall sit up yet awhile. You shall undoubtedly be gone before I rise, I am certain, so I shall say good-bye tonight."

Lord and Lady Eddington acknowledged the farewell and exited the drawing room to make their way upstairs.

There was a knock at Lady Caroline's bedroom door. A soft voice said, "May I come in, Lady Caroline?"

Lady Caroline realized with incredulity that her sister-in-law stood outside in the hall. She hesitated, for it had been a long and most emotional day. She certainly did not feel equal to the task of entertaining anyone at that hour, and particularly her sister-in-law after so stupidly giving offense by taking on the office of hostess. But Lady Caroline also felt constrained, by the strict social code in which she had been reared, not to send Lady Eddington away.

She gestured dismissal to her maid, who quietly went away to her adjoining sleeping closet. "Enter," Lady Caroline said, turning toward the door.

Lady Caroline waited until Lady Eddington entered the

room and closed the door before she spoke. "Yes, my lady?"

Lady Eddington advanced across the carpet. Her angelic blue eyes were fixed unwaveringly on Lady Caroline's face. "Forgive me if I have chosen an odd time to hold conversation with you, Lady Caroline. But I felt it imperative that I speak privately with you before our departure in the morning. I wished to discuss the interview that Lord Eddington had with you earlier today. He was naturally most distressed that he gave offense to you."

"I see. Am I to take it, then, that you have designated yourself as my brother's deputy?" Lady Caroline asked quietly.

Lady Eddington regarded her for a short moment. "I think you know all too well that his lordship relies on others in that capacity, my lady. Just as you were his deputy in administering this estate while he was in London and abroad, so am I here now on his behalf. However, in this instance, I am acting as much for myself as I am for Lord Eddington."

Lady Caroline regarded the countess for a silent moment. Then she gestured to the wing chair in front of the fire. "Pray forgive my lapse of courtesy. Will you not be seated, Lady Eddington?"

Lady Eddington smiled and seated herself, even as Lady Caroline took the opposite chair. "I am glad that you have granted me this time, Lady Caroline. After I heard what had passed between Lord Eddington and yourself, I was not at all certain of my reception at your hands. You had every right to your anger. So would I have felt if someone, especially one whom I loved, had suggested that I leave my childhood home."

"It was put to me in an intolerable fashion, otherwise I do not think that I would have responded in such a way. That is not my usual style," Lady Caroline said shortly. She misliked to be reminded of her regrettable lapse of control by Lady Eddington, for though the lady was her sister-in-law, she was still very much a stranger.

"So I thought, which is why I have taken it upon myself to come to you," Lady Eddington said. She hesitated a moment, her speculative gaze upon Lady Caroline's careful expression. "It is not my direct wish that you remove from Berwicke Keep, Lady Caroline, and I do apologize for my own defensiveness this evening. However, I shall not disguise from you that I should prefer to be the only mistress in residence. That circumstance would be of such help to my being able to establish a proper relationship with the household staff."

"You are brutally honest, my lady," Lady Caroline said quietly. She managed to summon up a small smile.

"I did not believe that you would respect less," Lady Eddington said.

That elicited a reluctant laugh from Lady Caroline. She regarded her sister-in-law with a degree of warmth that had not been present a moment before. "Indeed, I would not. In return, I shall be equally frank. It would pain me to leave Berwicke behind, but I do not think it will crush me to do so. My childhood memories are here, and in recent years, too, I have called Berwicke home. However, I have thought very recently that I have stayed overlong. I did not see it in the beginning, as I accepted more and more of the responsibility for the estate, but I realize now that my brother has become too dependent on me." She paused a moment before she smiled at her companion. "There are other reasons why I stayed, of course, but time has a way of showing one that some reasons become outdated and should be discarded."

Lady Eddington regarded her for a long moment. "I shall not ask you now what you mean. I do not think we are such good friends that I may do so. However, it is my hope that I shall one day be able to call you 'sister' in all truth."

"As do I," Lady Caroline said. She hesitated, then said, "I wish to ask you a most telling question at this time, my lady. Do you indeed love my brother?"

A flash crossed Lady Eddington's eyes. "Do you doubt it, then, my lady?"

"Perhaps I wish only to hear it from your own lips." Lady Caroline held up her hand, palm out. "Pray do not take offense, Lady Eddington. It is only that your manner has surprised me. You see, I recall you during your visit here with your stepmother as a retiring young woman, seemingly uncertain and untried. You gave no indication then of the purpose that I see in you now." She did not say so, but she was also curious how Mrs. Burlington might fare once she herself was no longer at Berwicke Keep.

Lady Eddington smiled. "That puzzles you greatly, no doubt. It is easily explained, Lady Caroline. My stepmother was not one to encourage any expression of opinion but her own. I discovered that it was much easier to get what I wanted when I played the mouse that she wished me to be. Do you find that reprehensible?"

"I know only that I could not have done the same," Lady Caroline said, thinking of her own girlhood and her constant struggles to deter her aunt's encroachments. She thought now she could understand how Mrs. Burlington could have been led to believe that in Lady Eddington she had discovered a malleable and powerful ally.

Lady Caroline looked at her sister-in-law and said slowly, "My mother was generous and loving to a fault. She was made unhappy when others whom she loved took advantage of her good nature. Whenever it happened, she chose not to acknowledge it so that her unhappiness would not spoil the way that she looked upon the world. I was not made from the same mold, which is perhaps why my aunt and I clash so frequently. I prefer to face my world as I find it and deal with whatever circumstances are given me."

"Whereas Lord Eddington prefers to believe in all that is good and turns a blind eye to the imperfections," Lady Eddington said, nodding. "Yes, that explains much that I had wondered about. In answer to your question, Lady Caroline, I do love your brother. More than you could possibly guess, for I shall do everything possible to enable him to continue to believe in the good nature of the world. It is his weakness and his flaw, but I find it an endearing quality as well, and I will not willingly see it destroyed."

Unspoken and yet understood was Mrs. Burlington's name.

"You have greatly relieved my mind, Lady Eddington," Lady Caroline said. She smiled in earnest and stretched out her hand. "I could not have asked for a better wife for my brother."

Lady Eddington joined her hand to Lady Caroline's for a brief moment. "Thank you, Lady Caroline." She rose and walked to the door. Before she opened it, she said over her shoulder, "Lord Eddington has told me that you were greatly courted once. It is a pity that you did not find a suitor to your liking." One last swift glance from those deceptively mild blue eyes was bestowed upon Lady Caroline before the countess quietly left the bedroom.

14

Lord and Lady Eddington left Berwicke Keep shortly after dawn.

Lady Caroline, rising an hour or so later, was not altogether disappointed to have missed their departure. She was grateful to have some peaceful time to herself before her next discordant meeting, for she had not forgotten that she had granted an interview to Lord Hathaway for the same morning.

Lady Caroline sighed over the teacup she had lifted.

"My lady, do you wish anything else?"

Lady Caroline glanced down at the virtually untouched plate that she had pushed aside. She shook her head. "I have no appetite this morning, Simpson." Shortly thereafter she left the breakfast room.

Lord Hathaway presented himself promptly at eleven o'clock.

Lord Hathaway knew that Lady Caroline was not one to sleep until luncheon. He knew, of course, that Mrs. Burlington would not yet be downstairs, since that lady was of rather indolent habits in the morning, and so he expected to find Lady Caroline alone. He was not mistaken.

Lady Caroline received Lord Hathaway in the drawing room. She awaited him standing near the settee, appearing elegant in an ivory day dress trimmed in brown velvet ribbons. As she took note of Lord Hathaway's austere expression, she was glad that neither her aunt nor her brother would be privy to this meeting. In particular, she was glad that Lord Eddington had already left and therefore would not be informed of an interview that she suspected must be uncomfortable at best.

She held out her hand to his lordship in a civil fashion. "Lord Hathaway."

Lord Hathaway bowed over her fingers in an excruciatingly correct manner. He did not linger over the salute as had formerly been his wont, but released her hand at once. "My dear lady, you appear in looks this morning."

Lady Caroline thanked him quietly for the compliment. She gestured to the wing chair opposite her own. "Pray be seated, my lord. Would you care for refreshment?"

"No, nothing." Lord Hathaway settled heavily into the chair, being careful to spread his coattails before he sat down.

Lady Caroline nodded to Simpson that he could leave them alone. The butler did so with an unusual show of reluctance, but the door eventually closed and Lady Caroline and Lord Hathaway were left staring at one another.

Lord Hathaway cleared his throat. "I have come this morning to state my thoughts to you, my lady, upon the unfortunate incident that occurred in this very room a few days ago." He paused to wait for her encouragement, but Lady Caroline merely lifted a slender brow.

Lord Hathaway puffed out his cheeks in faint annoyance that his hostess apparently did not mean to make the thing any easier for him. "I shall come to the point, my lady. I have come to apologize for my behavior and to beg your forgiveness. I might have done so earlier, on that very day, but for the unexpected interruption that we suffered. Lord Trilby's surprising appearance, however, put all such noble thoughts to flight. I assure you, it was not my intention to put either of us in such an ignoble position."

Lady Caroline saw that Lord Hathaway was not suffering

embarrassment over making his apology to her, but rather his lordship was feeling the still-ripe indignation that he had been found in such awkward and questionable circumstances. Therefore her response was drier and far less conciliatory than she had originally intended. "Your lordship's apology is acceptable to me, for what it is worth. However, I do not believe that I shall be able to return to our old friendly ways, my lord. It was made painfully obvious to me, through the incident that you have referred to, that your lordship has not taken in a serious light anything I have tried to impress upon you these last months. I ask, therefore, that you do not consider yourself as my admirer in any regard, for I shall not receive you as such."

Lord Hathaway stared at her in a disbelieving way. He could scarce credit his ears. He had difficulty containing his feelings, and his voice reflected his internal struggle. "Am I to understand that you will no longer receive me, my lady?"

"Not at all. Of course you will be welcomed at Berwicke as a good friend and neighbor, as always. I think what I am trying to convey to you, my lord, is that I will not entertain any longer your determined suit," Lady Caroline said quietly.

She gestured gracefully, regretfully, with her hand. "I trust that I do not give you pain, my lord, but—"

"Pain!"

Lord Hathaway's heavy countenance flushed dull red. The tenor of his voice was colored with outrage. "My dear lady, you greatly overrate your power over my heart! I am not so much pained as I am incensed by your selfish arrogance. I have taken care to illustrate to you the advantages of a marriage between us. I have endured your coquettish reservations, believing they were but the product of an unordered mind and would with time dissipate. I have proved to you, albeit in circumstances that in retrospect proved highly embarrassing to myself, that I am capable of harnessing your deplorable waywardness. I do not believe that I deserve this flippant dismissal."

Lady Caroline was taken aback by his lordship's unexpected and full-blown wrath. It was borne in on her suddenly that Lord Hathaway was incensed because she apparently regarded him in a lesser light than he did himself. She had not intentionally set out to insult him, and so she tried to minimize the blow. "Your pardon, my lord! I had no notion that you felt so strongly. Believe me, I do not regard you with the least degree of flippancy."

Lord Hathaway was not to be mollified. His ego had been cut to the quick. He got up from the chair to take a hasty turn about the room.

Lady Caroline watched his perambulations with astonishment as she realized that his lordship was operating under the influence of more powerful emotions than she would have believed him capable of sustaining. Perhaps she had misjudged him to a slight degree.

"My lady, I must tell you! Yes, I feel that I now have no alternative but to be brutally frank with you." Lord Hathaway turned to face her, and for the first time in their acquaintance he seemed to regard her with dislike. "Lady Caroline, I am aware that you do not often go to London or entertain extensively. I have observed that you do not have a court of several gentlemen about you, despite your beauty and birth and portion. I had thought myself eminently positioned to win your hand, in part because there was no one else to rival me. In short, my lady, I represent your one and your best opportunity to escape the fate of spinsterhood."

Lady Caroline rose in her turn. The sympathy she had felt for his lordship evaporated. His discourse was beyond what she would tolerate. She said coolly, "I think that will do, my lord. My fate is my concern. What I make of it is also my concern."

"Ah, if I but had the handling of you, my lady—"

"But you do not, nor ever shall," Lady Caroline said. Now at last there was the glitter of temper in her eyes. She went to the bell rope and tugged it. "I shall bid you good day, my lord."

The door to the drawing room opened instantly and Simpson stood waiting, his expression inscrutable.

Lord Hathaway recognized that unless he wished to make a scene, he had no choice but to make his adieus. He bowed stiffly and stalked out of the room.

Lady Caroline did not watch him go, but walked to the window, which framed an autumn day that appeared as bleak as her feelings.

The butler closed the door softly, leaving her to her thoughts.

Lord Hathaway had scarcely departed the house when Lord Trilby rode up to the door. The earl cast a glance after the rolling carriage and his brows knit thoughtfully. He bounded up the front steps to use the brass knocker, and was swiftly admitted.

"Is Lady Caroline in, Simpson?" he asked, handing over his low beaver and crop.

"Indeed she is, my lord. You will find my lady in the drawing room," Simpson said. "I shall see that your horse is attended to, my lord."

Thanking the butler with a smile, Lord Trilby crossed the entry hall and opened the drawing-room door. He stepped over the threshold, announcing himself cheerfully. "Good morning, Lady Caroline. I hope I am not again *de trop?*"

Lady Caroline, who had been staring pensively out of the window with her back to the door, turned swiftly. "My lord!

Pray do not be idiotic. I am always happy to see you."

As Lord Trilby closed the door behind him, he took swift note of her heightened color and the glitter in her eyes. He knew the signs well enough, and despite his own preoccupations, he asked, "Now what has put you out, my dear?"

Lady Caroline managed a short laugh. "Am I so transparent?"

"Like glass, my dear Caro. I observed Lord Hathaway's carriage leaving the drive as I rode up. What has his lordship done to have merited such a blaze in your eyes?" he said, going over to her and lifting her hand. He smiled down at her questioningly.

Lady Caroline sighed. "It is my fault, I suppose. I have been very irritable these past several days. My patience has been rubbed thin, and what has just passed between myself and Lord Hathaway . . . well, I shan't bore you with it. You have not come to listen to my complaints after all." She smiled up at him and gestured to the settee. She very much wanted to confide in someone, but it would be humiliating in the extreme to disclose to the earl all that Lord Hathaway had said to her.

Lord Trilby saw that she preferred not to go into the cause of her unusual discomposure, but he accepted her less-than-revealing explanation. "The Worthy sets up my back, as well. I don't wonder at your annoyance." He waited until she sat down before he did likewise. He regarded her expression thoughtfully. "Hathaway is still hanging on your sleeve, complacently expecting you to accept him, is he?"

Lady Caroline cast the earl a startled look. It was on the point of her tongue to ask him how he had known, but she caught herself back in time and instead shook her head. She looked away, saying, "Really, my lord!"

"If I were you, I'd be rid of his lordship. That insufferable conceit he has of his own worthiness makes one want to grind one's teeth," Lord Trilby said.

Lady Caroline laughed at that, her eyes flashing toward his face. The tension in her eased, and her smile became one of real amusement. "Indeed, how true! However, you need not concern yourself over Lord Hathaway. I believe that I have at last convinced him of my own unworthiness to become his wife."

Lord Trilby slanted a brow at his hostess. "I am glad to hear you say so. I have privately thought that your kindness in that direction was wasted, for it would never have occurred to Lord Hathaway that it stemmed from patience and inherent cordiality rather than admiration."

"Whereas you would have instantly understood it for what it was," Lady Caroline said, teasing him a little.

"But I am, you see, too uncaring to press myself forward on anyone's account."

"Oh, quite true," Lady Caroline agreed affably. "That explains how you have gotten yourself tangled up in your own polite fabrications with the Grandduchess of Schaffenzeits."

Lord Trilby regarded her with appreciation in his eyes. "*Touché!* I yield the field, my lady."

"You have always been of faint heart, Miles," Lady Caroline said, shaking her head.

"On the contrary, I am merely able to recognize a lost cause quicker than most," Lord Trilby said.

"Oh, well, then! I suppose that I shall not hear another word concerning your preposterous proposition that I pose as your future bride," said Lady Caroline with a wicked smile.

"You are too knowing for your own good, my lady," Lord Trilby said, narrowing his gaze on her face. "You have suspected, and quite rightly, that I have come to badger you once again."

Lady Caroline lifted her brows. "I admit to some surprise, my lord. I had *not* thought it, actually." She regarded him, puzzled, for the shortest moment before enlightenment entered her fine eyes. "Oh, the Grandduchess of Schaffenzeits has arrived! And she is even more formidable than you had supposed, is that it?"

Lord Trilby had watched the change in her expression, and a half-smile now touched his lips. "You have a marvelous capacity for understatement, my lady."

Lady Caroline laughed. "No, do I?" she asked in appreciation. "It must be very bad for you, indeed!"

"Tell me in all truth, Caro, can you not give me some hope?"

Lady Caroline shook her head and was about to reply to him when the door opened and her aunt entered the drawing room.

Mrs. Burlington paused a moment, her expression reflecting her disapproval that she should find her niece in obvious tête-à-tête.

"Well, I am astonished, my dear niece. Certainly Lord Trilby is an old and valued friend, but I think that it would have been courteous to send me word that you were entertaining. I would have joined you directly, of course."

"Of course you would have, Amaris. Your correspondence is not of such dire importance this morning as it was a few days past on a similar occasion," Lady Caroline said quietly. She disliked her aunt's tone, insinuating, as it did, that her behavior was more that of a recalcitrant schoolgirl sneaking a few moments with a lover rather than that of a mature woman visiting with an old and dear friend.

It angered her that her aunt had maneuvered to leave her alone with Lord Hathaway for that disastrous interview, perhaps even guessing what tactics his lordship meant to employ, and so now, in her own way, she let Mrs. Burlington know it.

Mrs. Burlington took Lady Caroline's meaning well enough, as was evidenced by the sliding away of her gaze. She advanced into the room and seated herself in a wing chair. "Such a production over a simple error of judgment, my dear!" She laughed as she turned to the Earl of Walmesley. "You will scarcely credit it, my lord, but my niece was discomfited to have received Lord Hathaway alone—Lord Hathaway, who is to my experience the most courteous and worthy of young gentlemen."

"Perhaps Lady Caroline did not inform you of his lordship's peculiar form of courtesy, Mrs. Burlington, I was witness to it and I do not think any lady of breeding should be mauled in her own drawing room," Lord Trilby said coolly.

Mrs. Burlington's mouth dropped open. She turned her eyes to her niece. "Caroline! You never once hinted at such a thing, I am sure. Why, I have never been more astonished in my life. I would never have expected to hear of such want of conduct in you, certainly, and as for Lord Hathaway—"

"I think enough has been said, Amaris. The incident is done with, and I have dealt with Lord Hathaway as I judged best. His lordship will not again presume to take such liberties," Lady Caroline said shortly.

Mrs. Burlington's eyes narrowed. She said sharply, "I suppose I must take it from that that you have been woolly-headed enough to bar his lordship from the house. That is very ill-thought-of, my dear niece. Forgive me, my lord. I would not speak so plainly in company except that I quite consider your lordship almost one of the family. My lady Caroline, excepting these all-too-rare visits by our dear Lord Trilby, Lord Hathaway is practically your only gentleman caller. Whom shall you call upon for diversion when Lord

Trilby returns to town, I should like to know?"

Lady Caroline had had quite enough. For several days she had endured slight and temper and malice and insensitivity from her aunt, from her brother, and from Lord Hathaway. Her eyes glittered with her renewed high temper. "Allow me to make you the first to know the news, Amaris. I shall not need to call upon Lord Hathaway or anyone else for *diversion*, as you put it! Lord Trilby has made an offer, which I am prepared to accept."

15

Lady Caroline felt a savage satisfaction when she saw the incredulity on her aunt's face.

Mrs. Burlington's mouth opened and shut several times, but no sound issued forth.

Lord Trilby, betraying by only the flicker of a brow his own surprise, took Lady Caroline's hand and raised it to brush his lips lightly across her fingers. Lowering her hand, he yet retained his clasp on it. "I am amazed, indeed, by my good fortune."

His lazy smile flickered over his face as he caught Lady Caroline's gaze. "In faith, when I rode down to Berwicke this morning, I had few expectations of finding success in my mission."

Lady Caroline's fingers turned in his and nipped smartly at his palm. She flashed a bright smile for her aunt's benefit, but in the depths of her eyes there was gathering horror at what she had done. She spoke directly to Lord Trilby, hoping that he understood all that she wanted to convey. "I admit that I had reservations, and still do, but impetuosity has always been a disastrous fault of mine. I hope that I do not live to regret my sudden change of heart, my lord!"

Lord Trilby laughed softly. He pressed her fingers once more and let go of her hand. "I hope not, indeed. But if you should do so, you may jilt me. I promise you that I shall harbor no ill feeling toward you for it."

Lady Caroline laughed in her turn, suddenly made giddy by the reckless danger she courted with what she had done.

She knew that Lord Trilby understood why she had abruptly and publicly announced that she had engaged herself to him. It was a measure of their relationship that he should not hold it against her. Indeed, he had even magnanimously provided her with the excuse that she would later need to free herself of him after the blunder of springing their private agreement into the open, and to her aunt, of all people.

"Jilt you, indeed! Why, whatever should put such a preposterous notion into your head, my lord! No, indeed, my niece has a finer sense of what is owed her family honor than to subject herself to such scandal," Mrs. Burlington said.

"I am glad you think so, Mrs. Burlington," Lord Trilby said suavely. "I trust, then, that this announcement has your approval?"

"Certainly it does, my lord! Why, I have been telling Lady Caroline for years that she should shake the dust of Berwicke Keep from her heels and set up her own establishment. I never expected that *you* . . . Well, that is neither here nor there."

Mrs. Burlington turned to Lady Caroline and reached out to grasp one of the younger lady's hands between hers. An odd triumph lit her eyes as she said, "My dear niece, I could not be happier for you. We must send word of the glad tidings to Lord Eddington at once."

"Is Lord Eddington returned to England?" Lord Trilby asked sharply, glancing swiftly at Lady Caroline. But it was Mrs. Burlington who answered him.

"Indeed he is, my lord, and great will be his astonished pleasure to learn that his dear sister is to be wedded at last. His lordship could not stay away from Berwicke then, and you, dear Caroline, will be finally relieved of the burden of carrying the estate business and the ordering of the household."

Mrs. Burlington showed her teeth in what she considered a conciliatory smile as she turned her eyes on her niece. "I hold myself ready to take on the necessary responsibility for the household at once, of course, in order that you might be freed to formulate plans for the wedding."

Lady Caroline laughed, retrieving her hand from her aunt's damp clasp. She well knew what primary emotion swayed her aunt, and she had no intention to play to Mrs. Burlington's huge satisfaction that at last Berwicke Keep would be under her own management. "Oh, I do not think Lord Eddington will see it quite the same way. My brother will in all probability wish me to see to the books even as I am measured for my robe."

Even as she saw the slightest stiffening of Mrs. Burlington's expression, Lady Caroline sensed Lord Trilby's own reaction. His gaze had locked onto her face, at once startled and thoughtful. The slightest flush colored her cheekbones as she realized how easily had come the reference to a bridal gown. She glanced swiftly up at his lordship's face. "Of course, it will be some time before such details must be seen to."

"Quite so, as the public announcement will not be made for some months. In view of that, it would be best to relay nothing of the matter even to Lord Eddington at this time," Lord Trilby said.

Mrs. Burlington looked from one to the other of them, her brows rising in polite displeasure. "I do not understand. Surely if it is to be a June wedding, then the planning must be put in motion at once. A notice must be sent in to the *Gazette* with the next post. Naturally you will want to attend the Season with the engagement well established so that you will be able to receive the well wishes of all of your friends and acquaintances. You will also want to supervise the redecorating of the town house and perhaps even Walmesley as well, dear Caroline."

Lady Caroline cast another glance up at the earl's face. Though his expression was polite, she knew him too well to believe that he listened to the enumeration of these pleasures gladly. But how to put off her aunt in a plausible fashion was quite beyond her own skills, she thought. "Perhaps it would be best if you should explain the thing, my lord."

Lord Trilby's stern expression relaxed into a half-smile as he glanced down into her anxious eyes. "I wonder how it is I anticipated that?" he asked softly.

"I really could not say," Lady Caroline said on a low laugh, her sense of the ridiculous affected.

Lord Trilby shrugged as he turned again to Mrs. Burlington, whose expression was beginning to reflect suspicion and impatience. "I have a particular reason for not wishing the understanding between myself and Lady Caroline to be commonly known, Mrs. Burlington," he said slowly, feeling his way. "I had the recent honor of receiving for a prolonged visit an elderly relation of mine whose notions of family descent are exceptionally demanding, and in particular the question of my own future heirs."

He ignored a peculiar choking sound from Lady Caroline, but he thought he could cheerfully have throttled her for her ill-timed irreverence. He scarcely controlled the quiver of his lips. "I have deemed it the wiser course to introduce Lady Caroline as my intended in a private way, so that her grace has time to adjust to the notion and grant her approval of the match."

"Her grace?" Mrs. Burlington searched her mind for some exalted connection of the Earl of Walmesley's that she had unaccountably missed in her avid reading of *Burke's Peerage*. "I do not seem to recall—"

130

"The Grandduchess of Schaffenzeits," Lady Caroline supplied.

Mrs. Burlington's eyes widened. "Oh, indeed! I had quite forgotten the continental connection. Why, this is exciting news indeed, my lord! You say that her grace is visiting you at this moment?"

"At Walmesley, yes," Lord Trilby said.

The earl exchanged a glance with Lady Caroline, which Mrs. Burlington instantly understood. She stared accusingly at her niece. "My lady, this obviously is not news to yourself. I wish to know what possible reason you have had in hiding the Grandduchess of Schaffenzeits' presence in the neighborhood from everyone? It is the height of rude manners for us not to have paid a courtesy call on her grace directly upon her arrival, as anyone could tell you."

"That was my doing, Mrs. Burlington. The journey from St. Petersburg is a lengthy and difficult one for any personage, and doubly so for a lady of such venerable age. I thought to shield her grace from any further fatigue," Lord Trilby said, dissembling swiftly.

"Oh, quite so! Of course, I understand perfectly. You must let us know when her grace is sufficiently recovered to receive callers, my lord, for I assure you that I, for one, will not be behind in paying my respects," Mrs. Burlington said.

"I did not really think that you would be, Amaris," Lady Caroline said.

Mrs. Burlington stared at her niece, suspecting the implication. With a glance at the earl, she decided that it would be politic to let pass Lady Caroline's disrespect. "Indeed, and as you well know, I pride myself on my correct manners. My lord, pray convey my regards to the Grandduchess of Schaffenzeits and assure her that I shall call on her in the next few days."

The Earl of Walmesley bowed. "Of course, Mrs. Burlington. Now, if it should not greatly outrage your sense of propriety, I would like to speak privately with Lady Caroline for a few moments."

It was on the point of Mrs. Burlington's tongue to utter an objection, but after taking note of the earl's expression, she summoned up a tight smile. "I shall just go inquire what is planned for luncheon. You will stay, will you not, my lord?"

"No, I think not today. My great-aunt will doubtless wonder where I have got off to, so I will not tarry long," Lord Trilby said.

Mrs. Burlington went to the door. "Very well, my lord. I shall bid you good day, then. Lady Caroline, I shall be in my sitting room if you should need me."

The earl bowed to Mrs. Burlington and she left the room, closing the door with obvious reluctance behind her.

Lady Caroline turned from the earl, clasping her hands before her with belated agitation. "It is a pretty mess I have created."

"Not at all. I am eminently content, my dear lady. After all, I have gained precisely what I hoped to from my audience with you. Though, in all honesty, I did not expect your surrender to come about through a flash of pique."

Lady Caroline turned around at that, a rueful laugh leaving her lips. "I do apologize, Miles. It was truly very bad of me."

"Yes, it was," he agreed. "My innate confidence in my powers of persuasion has been thoroughly trounced. I am a woeful creature indeed."

"On the contrary. Even provoked as I was, I would never have succumbed to the trap if it had not been presented to me before in such a reasonable fashion."

"Trap, Caroline?" he asked softly. "I was not aware that

an engagement to me was to be considered in the nature of a trap."

The blood rushed to her face. "I am sorry, my lord. I put it very badly."

The earl took her hand and smiled down at her. "I understand perfectly, my lady, believe me. I knew that I could rely upon you not to allow me to get into this thing over my head."

"I think that I have already failed you in that, my lord," Lady Caroline said on a sigh. She was thinking of her own very good reasons not to enter into the false engagement, and now they had all been knocked into a cocked hat.

"No, I forbid you to have regrets so soon, Caro," Lord Trilby slanted a quizzical glance at her. "Surely I am not so poor a suitor as that?"

Lady Caroline felt a shortening of breath. It was ridiculous what he could do to her with just a look. She attempted to make light of her feelings. "Oh, no, you could never be that, Miles. I do rate you a trifle higher than poor Lord Hathaway."

Lord Trilby laughed. He raised her fingers to his lips for the lightest of salutes, then released her hand. "Thank you for that much at least, my lady!"

Then his expression sobered a little. "I would appreciate it very much if you would come back to Walmesley with me this morning."

"Oh, dear. So soon?" Lady Caroline asked, dismayed. A rueful light entered her eyes as she watched the slow lazy smile enliven his face. "In for a penny, in for a pound. I cannot very well back down now, can I?"

"No, you most certainly cannot," Lord Trilby said firmly.

"Wretch! Very well, I shall make myself presentable to meet this most intimidating relation of yours. I shall rejoin you in the downstairs hall in a few moments, my lord."

Lord Trilby bowed her out of the drawing room. Lady

Caroline paused in the entry hall only long enough to request of a footman that her carriage be ready for her use in a quarter-hour.

Lady Caroline was aware that Lord Trilby stood watching while she climbed the stairs. She was glad when she turned the corner of the staircase and thus became hidden from his lordship's sight.

There was a strange churning in the pit of her stomach that she knew had nothing to do with indigestion. She also knew that if she stopped to think about it she would likely feel even worse, so instead of allowing herself a few moments of reflection when she reached her bedroom, as she had intended, she called immediately for her maid to help her change.

However, it was not so easy to put aside the whirling thoughts and speculations that rose to her mind. She knew the course that she had embarked upon courted disaster. She dreaded what must come, yet there was also an almost uncontrollable urge in her to give in to giddy laughter.

"What we need here is a liberal dose of courage and steady nerves," she told herself.

"What was that, my lady?"

Lady Caroline realized that she had spoken aloud and that her maid was regarding her with a puzzled expression. "Never mind, Spencer. Let me have the green carriage dress, if you please. Oh, and I shall want you to accompany me to Walmesley."

The maid had busied herself with locating the required carriage dress and the other things that her mistress would require for a drive on a cool autumn day, but at her mistress's words she paused. "Walmesley, my lady?"

Lady Caroline looked at her maid's reflection in the cheval glass, continuing to unbutton her cuffs. "Yes, Spencer." She offered no explanation and simply waited for whatever comment her henchwoman chose to make.

"Will Mrs. Burlington be joining you, my lady?"

A brief smile touched Lady Caroline's face. "No, my aunt will remain at Berwicke."

"Very good, my lady."

Spencer kept to herself the conviction that something of moment was to be marked by this unprecedented expedition. To her memory, Lady Caroline had never made a formal call at Walmesley, always preferring to ride over with only her groom in attendance on the infrequent occasion that the Earl of Walmesley had been in residence.

16

Lady Caroline returned downstairs attired in a hunter-green velvet carriage dress and matching bonnet. A silk-and-wool Norwich shawl was draped over her elbows and she was pulling on her gloves. Her reticule dangled from one slender wrist.

Not for the first time Lord Trilby observed her lovely face and figure with appreciation and enjoyed the innate grace of her movements. She presented a glowing picture of all that he found most attractive in a woman, and he felt the warmth that she invariably inspired in him. But as always, his pleasure in her appearance was tempered by an instinctive withdrawal and the hardening of his inner defenses.

He had never stopped to ponder why Lady Caroline Eddington had always affected him so oddly. It was enough to realize that she did so and hold a part of himself forever aloof from her charm.

He went to her as she descended the last step. He spared only a glance for the cloaked maid who followed in Lady Caroline's wake, but he approved of her foresight. Lady Caroline had supplied herself with the requisite companion that must accompany a well-bred lady when she paid a morning call. The Grandduchess of Schaffenzeits would naturally expect an unattached lady to conform to the conventions.

"You are in very fine looks, my lady," Lord Trilby said.

Lady Caroline cocked her head. She murmured quietly, for his ears only, "Indeed, and what else should I be when steeling myself to meet my fate?"

The earl laughed. His eyes were warm with rueful appreciation. "Quite. But I believe it is both our fates that you hold in your hand. I hope you are a good actress, my lady."

"So do I," Lady Caroline said with feeling.

Lord Trilby laughed again and drew her fingers through his elbow. "Come, it is time we were off. I shall have you back in time for dinner, I promise you."

Lady Caroline left quiet word with one of the footmen to let Mrs. Burlington know that she would not be in to luncheon, and accompanied the earl out the front door to where her carriage was waiting.

The maid, knowing what was required of her, lifted her skirts in one hand and climbed up into the coach to take the seat with its back to the horses.

Lord Trilby handed Lady Caroline up the iron step and saw that she was comfortably seated. Then he stepped back, closed the carriage door, and latched it.

Lady Caroline instantly put down the window. "My lord, you are not riding, surely?"

He looked up at her, his face taken by a sudden grin. "The grandduchess is a very high stickler. Unmarried ladies do not share their carriages with equally unattached gentlemen," he said with a shrug. He thought he heard an unladylike groan, quickly stifled as the window was raised, and he laughed.

Lord Trilby took the reins of his stallion from the groom who held them and stepped up into the saddle. He signaled the coach driver to whip up, and nudged his mount to follow the carriage.

The drive to Walmesley was generally one which Lady Caroline enjoyed. The countryside was rolling and hedged with low stands of trees. Though the previous rain had left its mark on the late-autumn countryside, the view was still one to excite admiration. However, this particular morning Lady Caroline was too preoccupied to enjoy the view moving past the carriage window.

She had had time to review her position, and her thoughts were not happy. She regretted already the hasty temper that had led to the impetuous declaration to Mrs. Burlington that she had accepted an offer from the Earl of Walmesley. With those ill-fated words she had entered into a subterfuge that she knew could only lead to harm and possibly scandal for herself and for the Earl of Walmesley.

Certainly nothing good could come of the farce that she was now embarked upon. Even if she and Lord Trilby were able to delude the Grandduchess of Schaffenzeits, and even if an open scandal could be avoided despite Mrs. Burlington's knowledge of the bogus engagement, there was still the matter of her own heart.

For a very long time she had managed to preserve her dignity by pretending to feel only a warm friendship toward Lord Trilby. She had succeeded so well that at times she had even persuaded herself that that was indeed the sum of her relationship with the earl.

But this morning she had agreed to participate in a pretense that would make her the object of a romantic courtship by Lord Trilby. With that one idiotic stroke she had stripped herself of her own carefully constructed defenses.

Lady Caroline berated herself for her own unthinking betrayal. Of what use was her shield of pride and self-control if it was to be laid aside in so reckless a fashion? she wondered.

Lady Caroline feared that it would take a more gifted actress than she could ever aspire to be to pretend that her very real feelings were only so much smoke to be blown in the eyes of a third party. She would betray herself again, this time to the Earl of Walmesley, with what must inevitably be disastrous consequences.

My girl, you are riding for a fall, she thought grimly.

Lady Caroline gave a small hollow laugh. The sporting phrase was absurd in its understatement.

"My lady?"

Lady Caroline glanced across the width of the carriage to meet her maid's inquiring expression. "It is nothing, Spencer, only an . . . amusing thought." She smiled, somewhat crookedly. Not wishing to encourage further conversation, she rested her head back against the leather squab and closed her eyes.

Perhaps it was just as well that his lordship had not chosen to tie his horse to the back of the carriage and take a seat within, she thought. Lord Trilby's presence would have required her to indulge in polite pleasantries for the maid's benefit, and she did not think that she could have borne it. For now, at least, she could remain true to herself and spend a few quiet moments in gathering her courage for the coming ordeal.

Lady Caroline had no illusions about her introduction to the Grandduchess of Schaffenzeits. Lord Trilby had told her enough about his great-aunt for her to have gathered that the grand lady was a formidable personality, being autocratic and haughty in the extreme. The grandduchess was obviously used to gaining her own way in every instance. Undoubtedly she would naturally be entrenched in the belief that her own opinion must weigh extraordinarily heavily with lesser mortals.

Lady Caroline was not without experience in dealing with such individuals, having come into contact during the course of her London career with a few society ladies who had held similar high opinions of themselves. Her own aunt could be added to that company, and until quite recently she had done fairly well in maintaining an even relationship with that lady. It was to be hoped that her regrettable lapses would not work to her disadvantage with the Grandduchess of Schaffenzeits.

The granduchess was of very different importance than those others of her past, however, even more so than Mrs. Burlington, because the outcome of the next hour or two would determine Lord Trilby's own relationship with the *grande dame.* Lady Caroline's nerves were not soothed by the knowledge that it would be her own efforts that would heavily influence the outcome.

Lady Caroline's countenance mirrored outer calm, but her mind worked as she thought about and discarded half a dozen approaches that might earn for herself the granduchess's approval. She had plunged recklessly into the fray and she was determined to do her best for the Earl of Walmesley's cause, but that did not mean she wished to prolong the business. The sooner the desired result had been gained, the sooner it would be that she could put off this uneasy role.

The remainder of the drive to Walmesley was accomplished in rather a shorter time than Lady Caroline could have wished.

Lord Trilby dismounted. He gave the reins of his mount into the care of the groom who had been on the lookout for his return and walked around the coach in time to give his hand to Lady Caroline as she decended to the ground.

He saw that her face was pale, and as he drew her hand through his elbow, he asked softly. "Have you second thoughts, Caro? For I shall not force you to go on, you know."

She threw a swift glance up to meet the concern in his eyes. It served to brace her faltering resolve, and she managed to summon a smile to her lips. "I do not easily cry craven, my lord!"

He pressed her fingers. "Thank you. I could not ask for a greater show of friendship than that."

Lady Caroline laughed, a little bleakly, and allowed him to usher her into the house. Her maid followed discreetly behind.

In the entryway they were met by the footman, and Lord Trilby surrendered his crop and riding gloves and hat. While she waited, Lady Caroline looked about her. She had always felt completely at home at Walmesley, but on this particular occasion her pleasure in her surroundings was marred by the purpose of her visit.

Lord Trilby inquired quietly as to the grandduchess's whereabouts. He turned to Lady Caroline. "Her grace awaits my return in the drawing room. Shall we join her, my lady?"

"Of course. I have a lively wish to meet her grace," Lady Caroline said, dreading the interview but also anxious simply to have it done with. She signaled to her maid, and that dame understood that she was dismissed until further notice.

"I am happy to hear you say so, my lady," Lord Trilby could plainly discern the shadow of anxiety that darkened Lady Caroline's eyes and he appreciated anew the generosity and determination that were an essential part of her character. He had felt from the first that he could rely upon her in his extremity, and she had proved him correct.

Lady Caroline lifted her head proudly and entered the drawing room on Lord Trilby's arm.

An elderly woman looked up at their entrance. Mingled astonishment and outrage crossed her face before her countenance hardened into autocratic hauteur.

The Grandduchess of Schaffenzeits, for it could have been no other, thought Lady Caroline, watched with stony eyes as she and Lord Trilby approached. Lady Caroline realized in that frozen moment that this autocrat would not and could not be wheedled and charmed by deferring and conciliatory words. The grandduchess would dismiss such attempts as beneath contempt. That would be the end of the little masquerade, and she would have failed Lord Trilby in the shambles of it.

Feeling that she had very little to lose, Lady Caroline decided upon a most reckless and daring approach.

"Madam, I have brought you a surprise," Lord Trilby said. He smiled down at Lady Caroline in reassurance. "Grandduchess Wilhelmina Hildebrande, allow me to present to you Lady Caroline Eddington, my intended. Lady Caroline, my great-aunt, the Grandduchess of Schaffenzeits."

The Grandduchess of Schaffenzeits registered a deliberate flicker of surprise in her expression. Then she slowly inclined her head. "Lady Caroline."

Lady Caroline curtsied, advanced to extend her hand. Her heart was hammering in her breast, yet there was nothing of her inner agitation in her friendly gaze or pleasant smile. "I am happy to meet you, madam. Lord Trilby has often mentioned you, and with the greatest fondness, I might add."

The grandduchess accepted the familiarity of the handshake even as she threw a sharp glance in the Earl of Walmesley's direction. "Indeed? I find this most difficult to believe, my lady. My grandnephew does not easily accept suggestion or advice from those who might be expected to hold his best interests close at heart." Her tone was forbidding, even cold.

Lord Trilby felt himself tensing. He feared the worst for Lady Caroline, and for himself. Yet there was nothing that he could do to circumvent the disaster.

Lady Caroline gave an easy laugh. She cast a glance at the

earl's inscrutable countenance. "I have often observed that to be true of his lordship, madam. But I believe it is often so with most gentlemen, and most particularly with those whom one has known for the greatest length of time."

The Grandduchess Wilhelmina Hildebrande regarded Lady Caroline with an unreadable expression. She indicated that her visitor should be seated on the settee beside her. "So. I assume from what you say that your acquaintance with Lord Trilby is of lengthy duration."

Lady Caroline sat down and began to remove her gloves, signifying that she intended a lengthy stay. She pretended not to notice the grandduchess's jaundiced observation of this signal.

Observing his great-aunt's increasingly frosty stare, Lord Trilby stood in admiration of Lady Caroline's cool audacity. "Lady Caroline and I are old friends," he said.

The grandduchess spared the earl a contemptuous glance before her gaze refastened on Lady Caroline's face.

"Oh, yes, indeed. Lord Trilby and I have known one another for years. In point of fact, our families visited often when we were both young children," Lady Caroline said, smoothing her gloves on her silken velvet skirt.

"It is astonishing to me then that we have not previously met, my lady, for I came to England many times when his lordship was but a boy," said the Grandduchess Wilhelmina Hildebrande. She showed her teeth in a predatory smile. "Nor do I recall that Lord Trilby has ever mentioned your existence in more recent times in his letters to me."

Lord Trilby had an almost overwhelming urge to loosen his neckcloth, which suddenly felt tighter than it should. The feeling startled him, for it recalled quite vividly his salad days when he had made his first bows to society.

"It is not surprising at all, actually," Lady Caroline said

coolly. "My family divided their time between London and the country, whereas it is my understanding that you never cared overmuch for London and so rarely visited anywhere else but here at Walmesley even during the height of the Season."

Lady Caroline smiled slightly. "As for Lord Trilby's omitting my name in his correspondence, I am not at all surprised. After all, it could quite conceivably have been because he feared that your grace might leap to the conclusion that I was of romantic interest to him."

Lord Trilby, who had been leaning with one shoulder against the mantel in a counterfeit attitude of relaxed interest, abruptly straightened. "Caro!"

The Grandduchess of Schaffenzeits shot a fleeting and very keen glance at the earl. "Indeed, my lady. I am most profoundly intrigued why that should be," she murmured.

17

Lord Trilby reschooled his features. Pretending a nonchalance that he was far from feeling, he said in a voice of teasing reproof, which nevertheless managed to convey his feelings to the lady he addressed, "I do not tittle-tattle about *any* of my friends, Lady Caroline, as you should have guessed, knowing my negligent character so well as you do."

"True, my lord." Lady Caroline bestowed a warm smile upon the earl. "You do cultivate a reputation for indifference, and certainly to discuss your friends to any extent would betray an intensity of feeling which must be avoided at all costs by one so set upon giving an impression of carelessness."

The earl was left speechless by Lady Caroline's thorough and uncomplimentary reading of his character.

Lady Caroline turned back to the Grandduchess of Schaffenzeits, who had listened with every evidence of growing interest. Lady Caroline shook her head in a tolerant fashion, smiling as she did so. "My lord is not nearly as cold-blooded as he wishes all of us to believe, as I am certain you are already well aware, madam. But of course, you must already have suspected why it is that he has never mentioned me! While it is true that I am a great friend, I am also a female, which is undoubtedly a shocking combination for one with my lord's studied attitude of carelessness."

The Grandduchess Wilhelmina Hildebrande shot another glance at her grandnephew, catching an impression of outrage, swiftly hooded. "Indeed, so I find it in truth, and in particular when I recall that his lordship claimed ignorance of

145

the existence of any lady worthy of pursuit. I believe that you indicated the scarcity of such in the breadth and width of all of England, did you not, my lord? I am disappointed in you, sir, for I had believed our relationship to be such that you would have felt able to confide even your most negligible thoughts to me."

There was a short silence while the earl weighed his options. He could express his outrage over Lady Caroline's slanderous maligning of his character by delivering a stiff set-down, or he could swallow his indignation and play the role that she had outlined for him. He decided to take the jump. With a sigh he said, "I am beginning to wonder just what I have done to myself in bringing you here today, Lady Caroline. In the space of fifteen minutes you have managed to shred my reputation, wound my sensibilities, and set me up for a raking-down by my illustrious and high-minded great-aunt, who, as I recall, is particularly fond of ringing a peal over the head of anyone who is so misguided as to think himself qualified to govern his own life."

The Grandduchess of Schaffenzeits unbent enough to give a cackling laugh. She did not comment upon the earl's accurate observation and instead confined herself to a pronouncement of judgment. "I find Lady Caroline to be charming." She turned to the younger woman with a thin smile on her face. "You will stay to luncheon if you please, my lady. I would very much enjoy talking more with you." It was not a civil request, but rather a dictum couched in polite language.

Lady Caroline let out a careful breath. She met Lord Trilby's eyes, the quizzical expression of which was tempered by a reflection of her own sense of relief. The first hurdle had been successfully met. "Thank you, your grace. I would be delighted," she said quietly.

As Lord Trilby seated himself in a wing chair, he remarked, "I suspect that between the pair of you, I am to be further pilloried. I shall resign myself to the inevitable, therefore, and put my energies into proving my reputation for indifference."

It had not taken him above a heartbeat to realize the object behind Lady Caroline's surprisingly aggressive style in this first meeting with the grandduchess. Once more he was impressed with her quick understanding of a difficult situation.

When he had presented her to his great-aunt, he had seen instantly that the Grandduchess of Schaffenzeits fully intended to reject all civil overtures. Lady Caroline had dispensed with the merely polite, and boldly carried the field to the grandduchess. The Grandduchess of Schaffenzeits respected strength more than anything else, and she had therefore chosen to allow Lady Caroline the benefit of the doubt.

Assessing the result, Lord Trilby could only admire Lady Caroline's strategy. She had at one stroke acknowledged a long acquaintance between them and established herself as one too secure in her own position to fear anything that the Grandduchess of Schaffenzeits might muster forth.

It had but remained for him to adjust his own manner to reflect Lady Caroline's, and the thing had been done. Before many more hours the Grandduchess of Schaffenzeits would be entirely convinced of the authenticity of the supposed match between Lady Caroline and himself.

The Earl of Walmesley anticipated the remainder of Lady Caroline's visit with equanimity. He was already considering whether future performances would be necessary. But then his peace of mine was once more cut up.

The grandduchess said softly, "Lady Caroline, I observe that you do not wear an engagement ring upon your finger."

Lady Caroline's eyes flew to the earl's face. His lordship

appeared as startled and consternated as she felt. She had not a single thought to offer. Lord Trilby stared down at her, appearing equally at a standstill. She felt herself ready to sink. In the next few moments would come unendurable humiliation, for what could she possibly say that would sound halfway reasonable for such an obvious oversight.

Damn Miles and his easy assurances, she thought, more distressed by her own culpability than by the lack of foresight shown by the earl.

"Well, my lady?"

The grandduchess's voice was inexorable.

Lady Caroline turned her head slowly until she met the elderly woman's cold stare. It would be far better to own up to the deception at once, she thought, than to squirm and writhe in the tightening net of yet more lies while the Grandduchess of Schaffenzeits probed mercilessly for the truth.

Lady Caroline opened her reluctant lips. Already she imagined she could feel the scorching heat of the grandduchess's scorn. "I am sorry, madam. I wish with all my heart that—"

Lord Trilby's hard voice cut across hers. "You do not have to say a word, Caroline. I am perfectly capable of speaking in my own defense."

While Lady Caroline practically gaped at him, he got up from the wing chair and sauntered over to the mantel. With his studied movement, the Grandduchess of Schaffenzeits transferred her sharp attention from Lady Caroline to the earl. Suddenly Lady Caroline realized that that had been his lordship's intent, and she was grateful to him for it.

"I am waiting, my lord." There was no compromise in the grim voice or in the arctic hauteur of the grandduchess's eyes.

Lord Trilby smiled slightly. The expression in his eyes was guarded. "I have no doubt at all of that, madam. It is a feeble excuse at best, as you will naturally point out to me. I originally thought it best not to reveal my engagement to Lady Caroline to you, for reasons well known to us both and which are best left unsaid if we are to maintain civility."

The Grandduchess Wilhelmina Hildebrande gestured her acknowledgment. However, her smile remained cold. "Yes, it is true that we have not yet come to agreement upon the oft-discussed subject of your impending marriage."

Lord Trilby made a mocking bow. "When you announced plans for your visit, and the object of it, I had no alternative but to inform you that I had formed an understanding with a young lady. But still I concealed Lady Caroline's identity from you, for I suspected that given the opportunity, you would make your presence felt in her ladyship's life."

The grandduchess covered with a cough the home force of the earl's observation.

Lord Trilby smiled briefly. "You did not accept the news as I had anticipated, madam. I thought that you would be overjoyed that I had at last begun to fulfill your long-held ambition for me. However, from your letter it was quite painfully obvious that you did not believe that such an understanding existed."

"No, nor do I believe in it now," the grandduchess said forcibly. "Lady Caroline is a charming lady and has put herself forth in a very creditable fashion. One who was less observant, perhaps, might have succumbed to the pretty tale. However, I am not yet in my dotage, Miles. I have the wit to understand the meaning of a finger naked of the requisite proof."

The Grandduchess Wilhelmina Hildebrande held up a weary hand. "And pray do not insult my intelligence further by insisting that the pretty bauble is at the jeweler's to be cleaned or to have its loosened stones reset. I should not believe it, you see."

The Earl of Walmesley allowed the faintest of smiles to touch his lips. "Indeed, I had no such intention. I meant to tell you quite truthfully that I have not given a ring to Lady Caroline at all."

Surprise flashed across the grandduchess's face. She glanced curiously at Lady Caroline, who had averted her face. What could be seen of her cheek had flushed rose. It would have been apparent even to the least discerning eye that Lady Caroline was suffering acute embarrassment.

"I do not understand this in the least," the Grandduchess Wilhelmina Hildebrande said disapprovingly. She did not like obscurities. She was invariably made cross by the few things that escaped her swift comprehension, and this instance was proving no exception. "You tell me that you have an understanding with Lady Caroline. Her ladyship confirms this, yet she had no ring. Why is this, Miles? You have not told me why, sirrah. I shall know the reason upon the instant, my lord!"

"I have not your approval, your grace," Lord Trilby said simply.

There was a short silence while the grandduchess digested this most astonishing of statements.

The Grandduchess Wilhelmina Hildebrande contemplated the pleasurable feeling that the earl's declaration had given rise to in her heart, but reluctantly she set it aside as being false. In sudden fury she stared at her grandnephew for his temerity in playing to her vulnerabilities. "Pah! I do not believe it for a moment, my lord, do you hear? I have observed you for all of your life. Your stubborn nature is well known to me. You have rarely sought my opinions. *Never* have you sought my approval! No, I do not believe it!"

"But I value your approval, madam."

Lady Caroline's voice was soft, and yet immediately riveted the grandduchess's attention. "I know how very fond his lordship is of you, and I suspect that you hold him in high esteem, as well. It would not rest well with my conscience if my understanding with his lordship were to drive a harmful wedge between you."

That much at least was true, Lady Caroline thought, attempting to assuage her conscience.

The Grandduchess Wilhelmina Hildebrande stared coldly at Lady Caroline. Her ladyship had dared to interrupt the scolding that she had intended to unleash on the earl. The impertinence was utterly remarkable. But it seemed that Lady Caroline felt no shame, for she met the grandduchess's fierce eyes with a calm expression. The grandduchess snapped, "You have refused to accept a ring from my grandnephew?"

Lady Caroline glanced apologetically at the earl, who was regarding her with a rising brow. "Not in so many words, madam. But our understanding is at the moment a relatively private matter, and as you have yourself observed, an engagement ring would most definitely call attention to it."

The Grandduchess Wilhelmina Hildebrande appeared to stiffen even further. "A private matter, my lady? Am I to understand, then, that you deem my grandnephew not worthy of you?"

"Not at all!" Lady Caroline exclaimed, truly disconcerted. "It is just that Lord Trilby has never . . . that is, he does not pretend to . . ." She saw with each disjointed utterance, the Grandduchess of Schaffenzeits was growing steadily grimmer and colder of expression.

With a wild look she appealed to her companion in deceit.

The Earl of Walmesley felt it incumbent upon him to step

into the breach. "I am such a never-may-care, you see, madam," Lord Trilby said apologetically.

The Grandduchess Wilhelmina Hildebrande shot a sulfurous glance at him. "As I am all too aware," she agreed cuttingly. "Many times have I observed that selfsame thing about you, Miles, which has in turn led me to lament the lack of vigor and fortitude it bespeaks. Any relationship, whether personal or political, requires those singular traits of strength if one is to weld the connection successfully."

"I am all too aware that I am something of a disappointment to you, madam," Lord Trilby said stiffly.

"Pah! You know nothing about it, my lord! Nothing at all! Would I demand to see your progeny about you if I held you in contempt?"

The grandduchess appeared to be genuinely distressed. His affront forgotten, Lord Trilby stepped forward hastily to catch up her withered hand. "Your grace, it was not my intent to overset you."

The Grandduchess Wilhelmina Hildebrande gave a wavering cackle of laughter. She snapped her fan against his sleeve, indicating that she wished to be freed, and his lordship obliged with a rueful look. "You never intend to do so, Miles, but you have still managed it on several occasions. Now, you must tell me this. Is anyone outside this room aware of the understanding between Lady Caroline and yourself?"

Lord Trilby glanced at Lady Caroline. A faint smile suddenly tugged at his lips at her look of guilty consternation. "Lady Caroline has dutifully informed her aunt, Mrs. Burlington."

Lady Caroline bent her head, biting her lip in order to keep from smiling. It was infamous of the earl to refer to her lamentable indiscretion so blandly, as though it had not been the beginning of this outrageous situation that she found herself caught up in.

The grandduchess flashed a sharp look between the pair. The earl's reply had astonished her and given rise to a germ of belief in their story. "Indeed! I am very much surprised to hear this, my lady."

"It was an unfortunate indiscretion on my part, your grace," Lady Caroline said. She threw a reproving glance at the Earl of Walmesley when he laughed. "My aunt very much wishes to see me wedded and in my own establishment, and I fear that I have raised hopes that may yet prove unfounded."

The Grandduchess Wilhelmina Hildebrande regarded Lady Caroline for a long moment. Finally she asked, "Then I am to assume that this understanding between you and my nephew depends entirely upon my approval of the match?"

"Yes," Lady Caroline agreed. Almost instantly she realized her error, but it was too late.

18

Lord Trilby closed his eyes for a pained second.

The grandduchess's expression became all amiability and her previous harshness was gone as though it had never been. "My dear Lady Caroline, this has been a most enlightening conversation. I am so very glad that we three have had this amazing little talk. You are staying to luncheon, of course."

"I had already asked Lady Caroline to join us," Lord Trilby said.

"I shall naturally be happy to do so," Lady Caroline said, inclining her head.

The Grandduchess Wilhelmina Hildebrande bestowed a smile of immense affability upon Lady Caroline. "I will introduce you to my protégée, my lady. Fräulein Gutenberg is most fascinated by England and all things English. I know that she will be delighted to make your acquaintance, especially in light of your long friendship with Lord Trilby, with whom she is also quite fascinated. She has many questions about English gentlemen, you see, and I feel certain you are in a position to educate her."

Lady Caroline allowed her brows to lift in politest disbelief. "I am honored by your confidence in me, madam."

The Grandduchess Wilhelmina Hildebrande showed her teeth in her original predatory smile. Her eyes were bright as she glanced at her companions' faces. "Pray do not fear that I shall give the game away, my dears. It would be in thoroughly bad taste for me to be so insensitive as to disregard your wishes and publicize your private understanding, so naturally I shall not say a word about it to Fräulein Gutenberg. We shall simply allow her to remain in the dark for a time."

Lord Trilby looked startled and he would have said something if the grandduchess had not ruthlessly pressed on. "Yes, I think that would be the wisest course, for if I should not give my approval to the match that you have made for yourself, Miles, you will still require a suitable bride. And it would be cruel indeed to make it so obvious to Fräulein Gutenberg that she was second choice. I am certain that you must agree, my lord."

"I doubt whether my opinion makes much difference in the matter," Lord Trilby said, rather grimly. He was neatly trapped by his own and by Lady Caroline's half-truths. Though he had succeeded in establishing Lady Caroline as his intended, as he had hoped, it still would not free him of Fräulein Gutenberg's speculative scrutiny. The irony did not escape him.

"None whatsoever, my lord." The grandduchess's smile widened while she watched the inscrutable mask drop into place over the Earl of Walmesley's countenance.

She transferred her attention to Lady Caroline. "I am actually rather glad that you have so precipitately told your aunt about the tentative engagement, my lady."

Lady Caroline warily regarded the grandduchess. "Indeed, madam?"

"Oh, indeed. I look forward with great eagerness to meeting a member of your family. We shall have Mrs. Burlington over for a small intimate dinner party. Miles, you shall arrange it, of course."

Lord Trilby's mouth twisted in a faint smile. "Of course," he agreed.

The door opened and there was the swish of skirts.

"Ah, here is Marie! My dear Fräulein, come meet Lady Caroline Eddington."

Lady Caroline looked around, curious to have her first glimpse of the lady that had been chosen for Lord Trilby. She felt her smile freeze. She did not know what she had expected, but certainly nothing Lord Trilby had said had prepared her for the young lady who crossed the room with such ineffable grace.

Fräulein Gutenberg was easily one of the most beautiful women she had ever seen. Lady Caroline could not take her eyes off the young woman, while confusion and outrage vied inside her.

Lord Trilby had scarcely referred to Fräulein Gutenberg except in a dismissive fashion, and his reticence had given her the vague impression of a rather dowdily turned-out and plain young lady. Lady Caroline had been prepared to greet the Fräulein with a friendly manner best calculated to put at ease a timid girl who was perhaps feeling overpowered by the grandduchess's stronger personality. She was totally unprepared for the self-possessed creature who claimed her place beside the grandduchess and who offered Lord Trilby a smile of possessive recognition.

"Marie, Lady Caroline is a neighbor to Walmesley and an old friend of my nephew's. She will be staying for luncheon. Lady Caroline, my young protégée, Fräulein Marie Gutenberg." The Grandduchess Wilhelmina Hildebrande had not missed the complete shock that had appeared on Lady Caroline's face upon Fräulein Gutenberg's entrance. It was quite obvious that the earl had not thought to apprise her ladyship of certain qualities possessed by the Fräulein. It would be most interesting to observe how Lady Caroline handled herself in the face of a stunning beauty.

"I am pleased to make your acquaintance, Fräulein

Gutenberg," Lady Caroline said.

The young woman's eyes briefly met Lady Caroline's gaze. Her expression registered acceptance and a disconcerting instant of assessment. Then with scarcely concealed indifference she said, "As I am to meet you, Lady Caroline." She turned her shoulder and smiled at the Earl of Walmesley. "Tell me, my lord, do you spend much of your time in London? I should like to hear of the amusements one might be expected to find there."

Lady Caroline swallowed wordless indignation. She had not been so lightly dismissed since her salad days, when she had crossed paths with a couple of society dames who had made a regular habit of snubbing self-conscious misses just out of the schoolroom for the sole object of puffing out their own consequence. Fortunately, she had already been secure in her own esteem after years of acting as mistress of her father's household and so she had been nearly impervious to such pointless cruelties. She had looked upon such instances as part of one's rite of passage into society, to be endured but never to be taken to heart.

However, this had been very personal indeed. Fräulein Gutenberg's deliberate snub had made it abundantly clear that Lady Caroline was to be dismissed as being of negligible importance.

Lady Caroline's fine eyes flew storm signals. Her feathery brows lifted in perfect emphasis of the delivery of an affable set-down. "The Season can be quite exciting to one unused to such an abundance of amusements. I am certain if Lord Trilby and I put our heads together we shall come up with the names of a few young gentlemen who can be depended upon to entertain a newly liberated schoolroom miss."

Fräulein Gutenberg's eyes narrowed, but she said civilly, "You are too kind, my lady. However, it would not be necessary, for I have been out in society for several Seasons."

"Have you, indeed," Lady Caroline murmured with the faintest touch of amused disbelief. She had the satisfaction of seeing annoyance flit over the Fräulein's lovely face. *That should teach you to mind your manners, my girl.*

Lord Trilby hid a smile. His choice of ally was proving herself more than adequate to the task. He had not witnessed any emotion of strength on the Fräulein's face before, even when he had been at pains to present himself at his coolest, and it was pleasant indeed to discover that the Fräulein was not quite the unshakable ice maiden he had begun to think her. "I do not believe that my great-aunt has formed any plans to attend a Season in London."

"What a pity, for we do have a great many genial acquaintances who would undoubtedly make the Season a memorable one for her grace and for Fräulein Gutenberg," Lady Caroline said regretfully.

The Grandduchess of Schaffenzeits decided it had come time to put an end to these pleasantries. Her protégée was beginning to appear quite unhappy by the turn of the conversation, which reaction but served to point up even more sharply that Lady Caroline was taking the honors in the genteel confrontation. "Miles, I discover that I grow irritated with this eternal waiting. Why have we not been notified to come to table? Pray relay my request that luncheon is to be served at once."

The earl got up to pull the bell rope hanging to one side of the fireplace, glancing at the ormolu clock on the mantel as he did so. "It but lacks a few minutes to the hour in any event, madam. I am certain that we will be notified at any moment."

The servant who answered the bell's summons assured the earl that the company could repair to the dining room directly.

"Your staff is learning what is expected of them, my lord! That is excellent, indeed. Lady Caroline, you would be amazed at the number of households that are let go to rack and ruin for want of a little direction or firm prodding," the Grandduchess Wilhelmina Hildebrande said.

"I am sure that is very true, your grace."

The grandduchess rose from her chair. "Miles, you shall escort me into the dining room."

The Earl of Walmesley offered his arm to the grandduchess and formally escorted her grace from the drawing room, leaving Lady Caroline and Fräulein Gutenberg to trail behind.

In the dining room the Grandduchess of Schaffenzeits was seated at the table on one side of the earl and Lady Caroline upon the other. Fräulein Gutenberg, as the most junior in precedence, was seated on the grandduchess's far side. Lady Caroline suspected that the arrangement did not particularly please the Fräulein, but she failed to detect any hint of ill-usage in the young woman's countenance.

As the first course was served, the grandduchess addressed some remark to the Fräulein, and Lady Caroline seized what might possibly be her only opportunity to speak privately with Lord Trilby during luncheon. Lowering her voice so that it could not be heard over the noise of the dishes and cutlery, Lady Caroline said reproachfully, "I wish you had forewarned me, Miles. I was never so bowled out in my life as when I saw the Fräulein."

Lord Trilby glanced thoughtfully at the Fräulein. "A veritable mantrap if ever there was one," he commented.

Lady Caroline also looked in the Fräulein's direction, a bit wistfully. "She is very beautiful. Do you . . . do you not *wish* to marry her, Miles?"

"I do not intend to leg-shackle myself for the remainder of

my life to that rabbity chit," Lord Trilby said.

Lady Caroline turned astonished eyes on him. "*Rabbity,* my lord? However can you say so?"

"I have it on excellent authority that Fräulein Gutenberg's ancestry is such that it is virtually guaranteed that she will breed like a rabbit," Lord Trilby said, his face perfectly straight.

"Miles! That is positively atrocious!" Lady Caroline exclaimed, her voice wobbling.

"Upon my honor, it is true," Lord Trilby said with a laugh.

Lady Caroline chortled at the absurdity.

Their shared amusement drew the attention of the grandduchess and Fräulein Gutenberg. The Grandduchess of Schaffenzeits smiled in a benign fashion, but the faintest of creases appeared between the Fräulein's perfectly formed brows. Her dark eyes rested on Lady Caroline with sharper interest than previously.

Luncheon was dispensed with quickly. Lady Caroline felt that it was time to take her leave, and said so. The Grandduchess of Schaffenzeits expressed regret but did not attempt to detain her. Fräulein Gutenberg merely inclined her head as though it was a matter of little moment. However, when Lord Trilby said that he would walk out with Lady Caroline, her eyes followed them with a sudden narrowed expression.

Lady Caroline's maid was collected and the servant woman got into the coach. At the carriage door Lady Caroline turned to hold out her hand to the earl. "Thank you for a most interesting visit, my lord. I do not think I have ever spent a more anxious morning," she said dryly.

Lord Trilby laughed. He pressed her fingers in gratitude before letting go of her hand. "It is I who should thank you, my lady. I do not know how I could have managed otherwise."

"No, nor do I," Lady Caroline said frankly.

The earl acknowledged her hit with a grin. "I shall call on you again quite soon, if for no other purpose than to personally deliver an invitation for that cursed dinner party."

"That will be an interesting evening indeed," Lady Caroline said, lifting her skirts and stepping up into the carriage. Behind her, Lord Trilby shut the door. She leaned forward to wave to him from the window as the carriage jolted forward.

A half-hour later, when Lady Caroline had returned to Berwicke, she was met with the intelligence that Mrs. Burlington awaited her in the drawing room.

"Please inform my aunt I shall be with her directly after I put off my bonnet and gloves," Lady Caroline said calmly. It did not at all surprise her that her aunt wanted speech with her. She had anticipated that her absence at luncheon would be sufficient reason for Mrs. Burlington to take one of her pets. Without pausing any longer, she swept up the stairs.

When Lady Caroline returned downstairs, having put on her ivory day dress, she found that she had not been mistaken in Mrs. Burlington's temper.

Upon Lady Caroline's entrance into the drawing room, Mrs. Burlington snapped, "Well, the prodigal niece doth return." She tossed aside the *Lady's Magazine* that she had been discontentedly perusing and stared with an unfriendly gaze at her niece.

Lady Caroline calmly seated herself in her customary place and took up her embroidery. "How kind of you to notice, Amaris," she murmured.

"What have you to say for yourself, my lady? I assure you, I have never been more insulted in my life than to discover from the servants that you had traipsed off in the Earl of

Walmesley's company. It was very ill-thought of, too. One does not luncheon alone with unattached gentlemen, Lady Caroline!"

Lady Caroline knew quite well that her aunt's seething distemper had little do with her having been with the Earl of Walmesley, but everything to do with not being invited along to be presented to the Grandduchess of Schaffenzeits. "As you might have guessed, Amaris, I took luncheon with the earl and the Grandduchess of Schaffenzeits. Her grace's protégée, Fräulein Gutenberg, was also present, so I do not think there was any impropriety attached to my visit to Walmesley." For good measure she added, "I took Spencer with me so that everything was perfectly respectable."

At once she knew that she had made a mistake.

Ruddy color flushed Mrs. Burlington's face. "I see. I am to be slighted in favor of your maid! Fine civilities indeed, my lady! And when, pray, am *I* to have the honor of an invite to Walmesley?"

Lady Caroline gave the faintest of smiles, not at all discomposed by her aunt's high dramatics. She knew exactly how to take the wind out of her aunt's sails. "The earl is to get up a small dinner party, quite soon I believe, at the Grandduchess of Schaffenzeits' request. Her grace expressed a wish to meet you, Aunt."

Mrs. Burlington's wrath was whisked neatly aside. She stared openmouthed at Lady Caroline, as though suspecting her niece of making game of her. Then a gratified expression settled over her features. "Well! That is very much more the thing. I am sure I never expected such kind condescension from the grandduchess. Her grace obviously knows what is due to one's family."

"Yes, indeed." Lady Caroline did not look up from her embroidery. On the return drive from Walmesley she had pondered how best to persuade Mrs. Burlington that it would not be in the best interests of herself and the Earl of Walmesley to trumpet abroad word of the understanding between them, and now her aunt had given her precisely the opening that she required. "Her grace wishes to assure herself that the family Lord Trilby has chosen to ally himself with is worthy of her approval."

As she had expected, Mrs. Burlington took instant umbrage. "The effrontry of such an aspersion! Why, the Eddingtons are one of the most ancient landed families in England, while your mother and I are descended from a truly noble line!" She abruptly realized the full ramifications of Lady Caroline's casual statement. "Do you mean to say that the grandduchess may refuse to countenance a connection between Lord Trilby and yourself? What has she to say to it, pray? It is not as though Lord Trilby is dependent upon her for an inheritance!"

"I do not anticipate any such thing, Amaris, but still, it is a possibility. The Grandduchess of Schaffenzeits is a very proud woman, and from what Lord Trilby has revealed to me, nothing sets up her back more than to discover that one has presumed to make a decision without first consulting her opinion. Lord Trilby is quite fond of the grandduchess, and he wishes to preserve his peace with her, so naturally he has respectfully and quite privately presented me to her," Lady Caroline said.

She was amazed at her own capacity for half-truths. She had never considered herself to be a devious person, but apparently she did have some talents in that direction. It was a most sobering reflection.

Mrs. Burlington pursed her mouth. "I suppose that the grandduchess reserves to herself the announcement of the engagement?"

"As to that, I do not know. However, certainly it would never do for the topic to be brought to her grace's attention before she has given it her benediction." Lady Caroline said.

Mrs. Burlington nodded sharply. "I understand perfectly. You may rely upon me, niece. Not a word regarding this topic shall pass my lips until the grandduchess herself raises the matter. This fortuitous engagement shall not be jeopardized by me, you may be certain of that!"

Mrs. Burlington wore a determined expression that Lady Caroline knew of old. Her aunt had looked just so during the whole of her first Season. Mrs. Burlington had not stinted in her efforts to see Lady Caroline launched well, and it had been a bitter disappointment when her niece had refused the offers she had received. Now a new challenge had arisen, which, from every appearance, Mrs. Burlington was fully prepared to meet. The Grandduchess of Schaffenzeits would be assiduously courted, but there would be no arch asides about weddings.

"I do appreciate your consideration, Amaris," Lady Caroline said. For once, she and her aunt were in perfect accord. Lady Caroline contemplated the curious phenomenon as she continued to stitch her embroidery. It could not last, of course.

19

Several days passed without word or visit from the Earl of Walmesley.

Lady Caroline thought it could scarcely be hoped that the grandduchess had been persuaded so easily by the performance that she and Lord Trilby had given to abandon her determination to see him wedded to Fräulein Gutenberg. It could not be denied, however, that as the days faded one into another with nothing more remarkable to mark them than grayer weather, Lady Caroline was encouraged to think that there would not be an invitation to dinner at Walmesley at all. She began to recover her former sanguinity and was quite able to put out of her mind any thought of a communication from Walmesley.

Mrs. Burlington was not so content. One morning when she had risen earlier than her wont for the sole purpose of checking the post, she exclaimed, "Whatever is keeping Lord Trilby, I should like to know? Surely the grandduchess is sufficiently recovered that she may begin to receive morning calls, at the least! It is the height of rude manners for me to delay in making my respects to the Grandduchess of Schaffenzeits."

Lady Caroline put forth her best argument to persuade her aunt to wait awhile longer. "We do not know what is transpiring, Amaris. Lord Trilby has his reasons, I am sure. The grandduchess may be behaving in a most difficult manner at present."

She spoke more truly than she knew.

Lord Trilby had put off the matter of the dinner party with a handful of valid reasons, delivered one after the other in the most logical fashion. Though the Grandduchess of Schaffenzeits received each excuse politely, she was not a stupid woman. She recognized a delaying tactic when she was faced with it, and when the earl's fertile explanations began to bore her, she decided it was time to force his lordship's hand.

The matter was done in the simplest way imaginable, through the simple expedient of a morning call paid to Berwicke Keep.

Minutes after Lady Caroline counseled patience to her aunt, she was shocked by the announcement that the Grandduchess of Schaffenzeits had come to call.

Simpson stood aside to bow in the august visitor.

The Grandduchess Wilhelmina Hildebrande swept past the butler, saying, "Good morning, Lady Caroline. I had hoped to catch you at home on such a dreary, damp morning."

Lady Caroline recovered quickly from the shock of seeing the Grandduchess of Schaffenzeits in her own drawing room. She went forward to meet the elderly woman, her hand extended. "Your grace! This is a pleasant surprise, indeed. Oh, allow me to present my aunt, Mrs. Burlington. Amaris, the Grandduchess of Schaffenzeits."

The two ladies exchanged pleasantries while they took one another's measure. The grandduchess smiled slightly at the aunt's extremely civil manner, sensing behind it a will nearly as steely as her own.

Lady Caroline requested the butler to bring some light refreshments. "A ratafia and some biscuits, I think."

"Very good, my lady."

Inviting their unexpected guest to take a seat, Lady Caroline said, "I do not see Fräulein Gutenberg with you. I hope she is well?"

"Oh, Fräulein Gutenberg is never so inconsiderate as to take ill. She begged me make her excuses to you, and sends her greetings," the Grandduchess Wilhelmina Hildebrande said.

Lady Caroline smiled. She was quite certain that the Fräulein had done no such thing, but she accepted the civility with a proper word or two. The refreshments were brought in and she offered the grandduchess a glass of ratafia and her choice of the sweet biscuits. The Grandduchess of Schaffenzeits condescended to take the ratafia, remarking that she preferred a fine cordial over wine.

Mrs. Burlington also accepted some of the sweet cordial, ignoring the surprised lift of Lady Caroline's brows. Under other circumstances she would have rejected the ratafia with abhorrence, but at the moment it seemed politic to display pleasure in its oversweet quality.

The ladies talked of several things of polite interest, such as the weather and the likelihood of snow appearing in a few days' time, before at last the Grandduchess of Schaffenzeits judged the time had come to broach the point of her visit, and she launched the topic that Mrs. Burlington, for one, had been waiting to hear in discussion. "Of late, my grandnephew has unaccountably become too caught up in estate business to arrange the promised dinner party. You will be pleased to know, Lady Caroline, that I have taken matters into my own hands and given the necessary orders."

Mrs. Burlington sighed softly in satisfaction. She settled back in her chair and sipped genteelly at her ratafia.

"How very nice, to be sure. I shall certainly look forward to it," Lady Caroline said, forcing enthusiasm into her voice. She had so very nearly convinced herself that she would not again have to playact in concert with the Earl of Walmesley that now she felt only the liveliest dismay.

"It is to be on the fourth," the grandduchess said. She smiled at Mrs. Burlington, who had not quite disguised her distaste for the ratafia and thus in the grandduchess's estimation had marked herself as a foolish woman. "I am much looking forward to your attendance as well, ma'am. Your presence will certainly be a welcome addition to our little company."

"I am positive that both my niece and I could not think of anything finer than an evening at Walmesley, your grace. We have been rather dull of late, I fear, what with the lack of company at this time of year," Mrs. Burlington said.

The butler entered to quietly inform Lady Caroline of another caller. He bent near her ear to give the visitor's name in a low voice. Lady Caroline looked around in consternation. It was on the tip of her tongue to deny admittance. But Lord Hathaway had followed straight after the butler. He had long since stopped standing on ceremony when he called at Berwicke, and such was his own heightened sense of self-worth that it never occurred to him that his call could be construed as awkward.

Lord Hathaway made his bows to Lady Caroline and to Mrs. Burlington, expressing gravely his hopes of the ladies' continued good health in the increasingly chill and damp weather. Then he begged to be presented to their companion.

Lady Caroline resignedly made the proper introduction.

Lord Hathaway's heavy brows shot up at learning the elderly lady's identity and at once his manner was all deference. He bowed low over the grandduchess's hand. "I am pleasantly overwhelmed to make your acquaintance, your grace. Truly, this is an unlooked-for honor."

Lady Caroline was amused by his lordship's fawning behavior. However, when she glanced at the grandduchess's frosted eyes, she realized that that *grande dame* was not at all taken with Lord Hathaway's heavy-handed compliments and ponderous manners. The grandduchess became increasingly haughty and condescending in her conduct, which served to impress Lord Hathaway further. However, Lady Caroline could easily tell that a crushing snub was in all probability but a breath away.

"Do you reside in the neighborhood, Lord Hathaway?" the Grandduchess Wilhelmina Hildebrande asked. Her bored expression openly conveyed her desire to send his lordship on his way, but Lord Hathaway was impervious to even such open hints.

"Indeed I do. I possess a very fine estate which is but a short carriage distance from Berwicke. I fancy that though my manor is not so steeped in history as Berwicke Keep, it compares very well. Very well indeed," Lord Hathaway said. "I have commissioned several modern improvements that must quite make up for any deficiencies of that sort. I shall be most honored if I may show you all about my small kingdom one day, your grace. You will be fascinated by the acres of new rooms that I have had erected, I expect."

The Grandduchess of Schaffenzeits did not appear to think that that was a recommendation to her. As little as she herself liked Lord Hathaway's style of gallantry, Lady Caroline liked even less for anyone to receive the sort of raking setdown that she could see building in the grandduchess's eyes, and to spare Lord Hathaway the humiliation, she interjected, "Lord Hathaway is known as a very worthy gentleman and an excellent neighbor, and certainly he has proved to be just that to us here at Berwicke."

"Yes, true, niece. His lordship has been quite accustomed to sitting in our pockets, as the saying goes," Mrs. Burlington said. She thought that a clever little hint to the grandduchess would not be amiss, and therefore she cast an amused glance in Lady Caroline's direction. "I do not know that it is so much my company that Lord Hathaway is most desirous of obtaining, however. Oh, no, indeed! I am sure his lordship will agree with me when I say that he has been a friendly admirer of Lady Caroline's for several months."

Lord Hathaway nodded, though his own glance in Lady Caroline's direction could have been said to lack that particular satisfaction that it once had held. "I have always stood in admiration of her ladyship's many excellent qualities," he said ponderously.

"Amaris, such things can be of little interest to her grace," Lady Caroline was embarrassed that it had been made so blatantly clear that Lord Hathaway considered himself to be her suitor. She did not know what her aunt could be thinking about to make such a pointed reference. Mrs. Burlington was not usually so free in exalted company.

The Grandduchess Wilhelmina Hildebrande put up her thin brows. "On the contrary, I find everything about this charming place to be of some interest. For instance, I should like to hear more of the improvements that you have made at your estate, Lord Hathaway. Unfortunately, good manners will not allow me to outstay my welcome today. However, in light of the friendly—one might almost say intimate— standing that you are on with the ladies of Berwicke, I would be most pleased if you would condescend to join us at a small dinner that I am giving at Walmesley. Then you may tell me more about your holdings."

"I would be extremely honored to do so, your grace," Lord Hathaway said, gratified. He thought it most satisfactory that one of such high distinction should have immediately recognized his worthiness of character. He blew out his cheeks in a pleased way.

Lady Caroline was appalled. She could not imagine a worse calamity than to have her former suitor present at a dinner that in some respects must be treated as an engagement party.

"I shall now take my leave of you all. I have thoroughly enjoyed the kind hospitality, and most particularly the present company. Lady Caroline, Mrs. Burlington, good day. Lord Hathaway."

As Lady Caroline took the grandduchess's extended hand, her gaze met the lazy amusement in the elderly lady's eyes. Lady Caroline realized that the grandduchess knew exactly what Lord Hathaway was to her and it had been for that precise reason that she had issued him an invitation to Walmesley. With a great deal of indignation Lady Caroline thought she had rarely been privileged to meet a more devious or more dangerous old woman than the Grandduchess of Schaffenzeits.

"I am anticipating the evening of the fourth," she said defiantly.

"Are you, my dear? I would not wish my guests to be disappointed. I do hope that your anticipation is justified and that it will prove to be an entertaining evening." The Grandduchess Wilhelmina Hildebrande bestowed a last smile on the company and swept out of the drawing room.

Lady Caroline shook her head as she turned to her aunt and Lord Hathaway and spoke some of her thoughts aloud. "I do not think I have ever been in the presence of a shrewder or more determined lady."

"What an odd thing to say, Lady Caroline. I am sure that there was nothing in the grandduchess's manner to make one think her grace of a devious nature or possessing of a pushing manner. Quite the contrary, I thought. Her grace was most properly aware of her position, of course, but exceptionally affable for all that. I was personally most gratified by her interest," Lord Hathaway said.

Mrs. Burlington cast an indulgent glance at his lordship. "Be that as it may, my dear Lord Hathaway, Lady Caroline is undoubtedly correct. The Grandduchess of Schaffenzeits is of a very quick understanding indeed."

Lady Caroline looked at her aunt, realization coming to her, and she sighed. "Oh, Amaris. It was not at all the wisest thing to do. It serves only to complicate matters."

"That is just as well, my lady, as you shall admit, once this matter is straightened tidily away," Mrs. Burlington said. "You must leave it in my hands, for I daresay I am something of a match for our grandduchess."

Lady Caroline was alarmed by this declaration. "Truly, Amaris, there is no need to exert yourself."

Mrs. Burlington merely smiled. With a touch of her characteristic malice she murmured. "Oh, but I think that I would be completely derelict in my duty if I did not do so, my lady."

Lord Hathaway looked from one lady to the other, completely bewildered. There were undercurrents that he did not understand, and he was not certain that he wished to, for there was that in Lady Caroline's eyes that reminded him most strongly of her temper on that day upon which he had explained himself to her so forthrightly. He was not normally a timid man, but on this occasion he thought it would be the prudent course to bow himself out, which he did so in short order.

20

On the afternoon of the fourth, tiny snowflakes commenced to drift gently down in the first snowfall of the season. The snow did not stick long, the ground being still too warm for it to do so, and melted to muddy slush.

Lord Trilby, notified by his butler of unexpected arrivals, emerged from his study into the entry hall. He paused before bringing himself to the notice of his friends. The gentlemen brushed powdery snow off their shoulders and tapped their hats against their arms to dislodge the flakes on the brims, laughing and commenting all the while.

The stir of dismay he had felt upon hearing of their arrival strengthened, for he could already tell, by a cursory overview and a short snatch of conversation he heard, that this was not to be a flying visit that they paid him.

He sauntered forward, his demeanor reflecting only faint amusement. "I suppose I must voice a certain pleasure at this unexpected visit, gentlemen."

The three gentlemen turned as one to regard him. Mr. Underwood stepped forward, his hand out in greeting. A large grin lit his face as he shook the earl's hand. "My lord! I fling myself upon your mercy. If you do not protect me from these brigands, I am sure I do not know what else may yet befall me this day," he said.

Lord Trilby looked him up and down, taking note for the first time of a coat streaked by wet and pantaloons and boots that had been muddied. "You look as though you have been tossed into a ditch, Carey."

Lord Heatherton, normally so mournful of countenance and manner, snorted laughter.

The viscount, who stood beside Lord Heatherton, gave a smile unusually free of bitterness. "Be careful how you answer, Underwood," he counseled.

"I suppose by that you mean that you will mill me down otherwise," Mr. Underwood said.

"That is a possibility," the viscount agreed.

By this time Lord Heatherton and the viscount had finished giving over their damp greatcoats and beavers to the attentive footmen and joined their host and Mr. Underwood.

"But what has brought you to this inglorious pass, sir?" Lord Trilby asked politely.

Mr. Underwood cast a severe glance in the direction of his traveling companions. "You may well ask, my lord! My grievances are several, but I shall tell you instantly that of all of them, *that* was the worst indignity. I was indeed tossed into a ditch, as you so inelegantly phrase it. Yes, you may laugh, Miles, but it was not at all amusing at the time, I assure you! Of all the clunch-headed, cow-handed—!"

"Cow-handed, Carey?" Viscount Weemswood inquired softly.

Lord Trilby saw that his friend was winding himself up to deliver a vilification of some proportion, unwise in the extreme when its object was the viscount, and he took Mr. Underwood's arm. "Come into the parlor, Carey. You will feel much more the thing with a warm fire at your back and a good brandy in your hand. Then you may rail to your heart's content at poor Heatherton and Weemswood, who I gather are in the nature of being the authors of your sense of ill-usage."

"Poor Heatherton and Weemswood! Well, I like that! When I have just been telling you that I have suffered unimaginable indignities at their hands," Mr. Underwood said. He shook his head and sighed as he accompanied his host into the parlor. "I fear that I am but a lone voice in a vast wilderness of indifference."

Lord Heatherton and the viscount entered the parlor in their turn.

Viscount Weemswood sauntered to a chair and dropped into it with his careless athletic grace. "Is that so surprising to you, Carey? It is, after all, Miles to whom you have made your complaint," he said, flashing his peculiar twisted smile. The characteristic coolness had returned to his eyes.

"Quite true," Mr. Underwood said, still enjoying his dramatic role. He accepted the filled wineglass that was offered to him by the earl with grateful thanks and put it to his chilled lips. He tasted the brandy, rolling and warming it on his tongue, and nodded his approval.

The viscount also accepted a portion of brandy, and Lord Trilby crooked a brow at Lord Heatherton. "What will you have, Nana?"

"Tea," Lord Heatherton said promptly. "I shall wait for a proper tea. I am famished." He had placed his back to the fireplace and lifted the tails of his coat so that the back of his trousers would warm the quicker. "Sinjin did not stop for luncheon, for fear that Carey would slip us at the posting house, you see, and so we have all had nothing but a bite of breakfast since this morning."

Lord Trilby's dark brows rose. He glanced at the viscount, whose expression was at its blandest. The earl sighed, knowing what was required of him. "Very well. I admit it, Sinjin. My curiosity grows by leaps and bounds and even threatens to consume me whole. Shall my reputation suffer greatly when it becomes known, do you think?"

Viscount Weemswood's teeth flashed in a reluctant grin.

"No, I believe that subtlest of disclaimers allows your reputation to remain fairly well intact, my lord."

"You relieve me profoundly, my lord. Now, Carey, you must tell me the whole, and pray do not think to spare my finer sensibilities, for I apprehend already that it is a lurid tale. So you may well draw it out to its fullest limits," Lord Trilby said, seating himself in a wing chair.

"Very well, my lord." Mr. Underwood joined Lord Heatherton at the mantel and leaned one shoulder against it. Relaxed and at his ease, he said, "The full and sum total of the matter is that I have been foully tricked, betrayed, abducted, and starved to within an inch of my life. Yes, and had my best overcoat ruined by that toss into the snow. As for my boots, they have been ruined by the enforced march endured at the hands of these merciless miscreants."

"Here, here! It wasn't as bad as all that," Lord Heatherton said, looking at Mr. Underwood with dawning indignation. "You quite liked the notion of posting down to Walmesley. You said that as you were at point-non-plus with those two ladybirds of yours, it was just the thing to give your spirits a fresh turn."

"Devil a bit!" Mr. Underwood protested.

Viscount Weemswood grinned up at his friend from the depths of his chair. "Indeed you did, Underwood! As I recall, your exact sentiments were that you heartily wished to be gone from town until the hue and cry had spent itself, even if it meant burying yourself in the country for a fortnight or more."

Lord Trilby slanted a glance at Mr. Underwood's direction. Mr. Underwood had the grace to look appropriately shamefaced. "I am positively overwhelmed that my roof engenders such handsome accolades, my friend. Er . . . two ladybirds, Carey? Is that not rather complicated?"

"The expense is nothing to sneeze at, I assure you. As for the other, it is not at all complicated, as long as one takes care that neither of the fair lovelies in question knows anything of the other," Mr. Underwood said.

At this, Lord Heatherton and the viscount began to laugh. Mr. Underwood sent his riotous companions what he fully intended to be a dignified look of reproach, but it was quite ruined by the twitch of his own lips.

"I think I begin to see the light," Lord Trilby said. "How did the ladies discover your perfidy, Carey?"

Lord Heatherton took out his kerchief to carefully dry his eyes, and it was he who answered. "Oh, it was the most monstrous piece of luck, my lord. Sinjin and I were tooling down the street, and there was Carey handing one lady in the door of a milliner's shop, when out pops the other from the same shop! She takes one look and lets out a hideous screech. Ours was not the only carriage that slowed, believe me. Then it was bellows to mend for poor Carey, what with the tremendous scoldings that were heaped upon his head by the two harpies and the hoots of the gathering curious besides."

"I assure you, it was a most deplorable scene, my lord," Viscount Weemswood said.

"I can only too well imagine," Lord Trilby said, laughing. "My poor Carey, however did you come to be so careless as to patronize the same shop for both?"

"How was I to guess that Nancy would take it into her pretty little head to exchange a hat this morning? Yes, and before noon, too! I have never known her to rouse herself before one o'clock in the afternoon," Mr. Underwood complained.

There was general laughter again.

"Certainly you have had a most trying day, Carey. But I still fail to see how any of this is connected to Nana or Sinjin," Lord Trilby said.

"Ah! Now we come to it, my lord. Sinjin fairly dragged me into his curricle whilst Nana tossed a few conciliatory coins to the two lovely rioters, and they bore me off to the Ale and Drum."

"A good thing, too. Those two furies appeared set to do violence to poor Carey in another moment," Lord Heatherton said thoughtfully.

"Such is the result of my enviable charm," Mr. Underwood said with a modest cough.

Viscount Weemswood tilted a mocking smile in his friend's direction. "It is hardly a source of envy to me, Underwood. You may keep your honeyed tongue and amiable countenance. For myself, I vastly prefer to conduct my little *affaires d'amour* in the privacy of my own quarters or at the lady's apartment."

"The open street does seem a mildly outlandish place to put an end to one's amours," Lord Trilby said.

"The circumstances left much to be desired," Mr. Underwood agreed feelingly. "I was never more taken aback in my life than when Nancy appeared outside the shop. It all left me a bit blue-deviled, as you may imagine. However, once I had left the Ale and Drum, where, I may add, I made my rash declaration that I wished to leave town, I was quickly made more cheerful by stumbling upon the fair Melinda. What a beauty she is—great sloe eyes and the most delectable mouth!"

Lord Trilby glanced at Lord Heatherton and the viscount for clarification. "The fair Melinda?"

"Nancy's sister," Viscount Weemswood supplied blandly. Lord Trilby's brows lifted incredulously. "The same Nancy who was expected to be still abed?"

"The very same," the viscount said, not bothering any longer to hide his sardonic amusement.

"Good God! Carey, I suspect you to be quite mad," Lord Trilby said.

"No, no! I am simply unable to refrain from passing by a pretty face," Mr. Underwood said, laughing.

Viscount Weemswood pointedly ignored Mr. Underwood's rejoinder. "So we believed also, my lord, when Carey met us for luncheon and declared his intention to meet the fair Melinda the same afternoon. Believing Carey incapable of preserving himself, Nana and I conspired to whisk him safe out of harm's way."

Lord Heatherton nodded, his eyes doleful. "Aye, we were honor-bound to do it. Mind, it was a near-run thing, for Carey would have it that he did not want to luncheon on the outskirts of town, but Sinjin persuaded him that it was the very place, and off we went."

"You see how I am treated, my lord," Mr. Underwood said simply. "I never received my luncheon."

Lord Trilby nodded, amusement prominent in his eyes. "Quite reprehensible, indeed. I am persuaded that you did not accept such barbarity in a tame fashion."

"Carey threatened to leap from the phaeton," Viscount Weemswood said. His teeth flashed in the swiftest of smiles. "I was obliged to spring my horses."

Lord Trilby laughed, understanding that Mr. Underwood had not dared to jump from the swift-moving carriage.

"He drove like a veritable devil, Miles. Nana and I were in fear for our lives more than once when we chanced upon other vehicles and Sinjin hardly paused, but swept past with but an inch to spare on either side."

Lord Heatherton rocked on his heels. "It was a most splendid example of driving."

Viscount Weemswood made a mocking bow in acknowledgment of the compliment.

"Quite! But fool that I was, I shouted that I did not think Sinjin could make that sharp turn at the crossroads. Sinjin simply gave that strange smile of his, dropped the reins, and let his cattle have their heads. The hair was raised up on my head, I can tell you," Mr. Underwood said.

He reflected a moment, then said fairly, "You would have done it, too, Sinjin, but for that coach coming unexpectedly round the corner. Lord, weren't those passengers rattled when we flew under the coach horses' noses!"

Viscount Weemswood laughed with Mr. Underwood, and even Lord Heatherton smiled reminiscently.

"I take it that is where you took the toss into the snow, Carey," Lord Trilby said.

"Oh, aye." Mr. Underwood waved dismissively, having let go of his staged indignation. "But that was of little moment. Would you believe it, my lord? The coachman bawled only an inquiry after Sinjin's horses, and when assured that none had suffered more than a sprained hock, he whipped up his jobbers and left us to make our way on foot to your door, leading the horses, of course. One of the back wheels of the phaeton was splintered, and we had to leave it."

"It was the rudest thing I have ever experienced," Lord Heatherton said with a heavy frown. "I am in half a mind to report the man for willful malice, for after all, it is not as though Sinjin had locked wheels or some such thing."

Mr. Underwood made a derisive sound at the very idea that the viscount would have been so careless. "Sinjin is the consummate whip even at his most disguised. Of course there was no question of clumsy driving."

"I am overcome by such fulsome praise," Viscount Weemswood murmured, his peculiar smile appearing.

"It is an edifying tale indeed," Lord Trilby said. "Of course you are all welcome to accept my humble hospitality until you feel the urge to return to town or at least until Sinjin's phaeton has been repaired, but I warn you that Walmesley is deadly dull at this time of year. I have even found the hunting to be somewhat indifferent."

"Then what is it that drew you so abruptly away from town, Miles?" Viscount Weemswood asked curiously.

Lord Trilby's reply was never uttered, for the door opened and a lady glided into the room. She checked at sight of the gentlemen, who all rose hastily to their feet at her entrance. With the exception of the earl, the gentlemen stared open-mouthed at the unexpected vision of beauty.

Fräulein Gutenberg glanced coolly at the three unknowns before her gaze fixed itself on the Earl of Walmesley's unreadable face. When she spoke, her throaty voice was very soft. "Pardon the intrusion, my lord. Madam thought she left her shawl on the settee."

There was a sharp crash. Startled, all turned to see the cause of the noise.

Mr. Underwood's wineglass had slipped from his suddenly nerveless fingers to shatter on the hearthstones. Heedless of the stares of his friends or, indeed, of anything but the lady standing near the door, he enunciated, "Good God!"

Viscount Weemswood shot a keen glance first at Mr. Underwood and then at the earl. Himself not entirely immune to the staggering effect of the lady's beauty, he could not but realize that others might be even less impervious. "I believe that my previous question has been answered," he murmured.

21

Lord Trilby was not able to stop the flicker of annoyance that crossed his face at the viscount's words. Recovering almost instantly, however, he went to the young lady and offered his hand to her in order to draw her forward into the room.

"Gentlemen, this is Fräulein Gutenberg. She has accompanied my great-aunt the Grandduchess of Schaffenzeits on her grace's latest visit to England. Fräulein, allow me to present to you Lord John St. John, Viscount Weemswood, Mr. Carey Underwood, and Lord Edward Heatherton."

Lord Heatherton and the viscount had recovered sufficiently to voice the usual pleasantries. Mr. Underwood, however, seemed incapable of speech and merely made a deep bow over the Fräulein's small slender hand.

After exchanging greetings with the earl's friends, Fräulein Gutenberg was faintly smiling when she returned her gaze to Lord Trilby. "I should return abovestairs now, my lord. Madam is waiting for me."

"Of course, Fräulein. We shall see you and the grandduchess at tea? Very good. Oh, thank you, Heatherton. You have found it. Here is the missing shawl, Fräulein," Lord Trilby said.

Fräulein Gutenberg accepted the garment from Lord Heatherton, who alone had had the presence of mind to glance about for it and had discovered it draped over one arm of the settee. With a graceful inclination of her head and a softly murmured excuse, Fräulein Gutenberg left the parlor.

"Carey appears to be in a state of suspension," Viscount

Weemswood observed dispassionately.

Their attention thus directed, the earl and Lord Heatherton looked over at Mr. Underwood. He was pale of face and his eyes held a dazed expression.

Lord Heatherton patted him kindly on the shoulder, much as one would do for an old dog caught up in the throes of a dream. "Wake up, Carey. She is gone now."

Mr. Underwood seemed to come to a partial return of his senses. He sank down into a convenient chair, but looked up agonizingly at Lord Heatherton. "Did you see her, Nana? Pray say that I did not conjure up that vision from the fumes of the earl's excellent brandy."

"Brandy which you have shamelessly squandered," Lord Trilby said. He pulled the bell rope in order to call a servant to clean up the shards of glass and to sponge the stains from the carpet where the wine had splashed. "And, yes, the Fräulein does exist, very much so."

There was a curious inflection to his voice that the viscount, at that moment the most perceptive of the earl's friends, found very odd.

Viscount Weemswood looked hard at the Earl of Walmesley, wondering what there could possibly be about the beautiful young Fräulein that had brought that peculiar edge to his lordship's statement.

Mr. Underwood put his head in his hands, groaning. "Then I am lost, utterly and completely lost."

"What of the fair Melinda?" Viscount Weemswood asked, shifting his attention from the puzzle suddenly presented him by the Earl of Walmesley with that single betraying comment.

"Who?" Mr. Underwood looked up, and his vague eyes focused briefly. "Oh, Melinda. She is eclipsed, my lord, by the brightness of my revelation."

Lord Heatherton shook his head mournfully. "I am persuaded his brain is addled. Perhaps he grazed his head in taking that tumble, Sinjin?"

"Not at all, Nana. Do you not recall? Carey confessed himself 'incapable of passing by a pretty face.' I do not think it an exaggeration to say that the Fräulein is no mere pretty face, but a diamond of the first water. It does not surprise me in the least, given our friend's admitted weakness, that he has once more become the victim of *coup de foudre*," Viscount Weemswood said.

His gaze rested thoughtfully on the Earl of Walmesley's face, but if he had thought to discover anything of interest from his lordship's expression, he was disappointed.

Lord Trilby appeared undisturbed, exhibiting neither undue interest nor boredom in the conversation while he directed the footman who had come in response to the bell's summons to clean up the remains of Mr. Underwood's drink.

"A dashed pretty girl," Lord Heatherton allowed, nodding. The gross understatement provoked laughter from Lord Trilby and the viscount, but elicited only another dull groan from Mr. Underwood.

Somewhat bewildered, Lord Heatherton looked at each of his friends. "Well, is she not? I may be a slow-top with the ladies, but even I could see that."

"Indeed, Fräulein Gutenberg is quite pretty, Nana. But I pray you to be circumspect with your admiration, my friends. The Grandduchess of Schaffenzeits will look with disfavor on anything which might, however faintly, be construed to be a liberty taken with her lovely protégée," Lord Trilby said.

"The grandduchess is your great-aunt, I believe you said? Is that perhaps the same formidable dame whom I had the doubtful pleasure of meeting some years ago whilst rusticating once at Walmesley during our Cambridge years?" Viscount Weemswood asked.

Lord Trilby grinned and said cheerfully, "The very same, Sinjin."

"Then I will go upstairs on the instant to smooth my appearance." Viscount Weemswood said reflectively, "I still recall that her grace caught me with dirt clinging to my boots, and after a resounding scold dismissed me as no better than an untutored stable lad."

Lord Trilby laughed outright.

Lord Heatherton exclaimed in amazement at this story. "You, Sinjin? Why, you are a veritable Corinthian! Everyone has always said so!"

"You must perceive, then, that the Grandduchess of Schaffenzeits was a considerable influence upon me in my impressionable youth," the viscount said.

Mr. Underwood had been taking a gathering interest in the conversation. Now he leapt to his feet, saying in determination, "Miles, I must make myself presentable if I am to get the grandduchess to smile on me with favor."

"Surely it is the Fräulein's favor that you desire?" Viscount Weemswood murmured.

Mr. Underwood turned on the viscount and regarded him with pardonable resentment. "Damn you thrice over, Sinjin! I am streaked all over with mud and I have not my man with me, no, nor even a change of neckcloth!"

"Rest easy, my anxious friend. Nana made arrangements for our valets to follow us shortly, even sending round a note to your man. You may yet appear to tea in perfect sartorial splendor," Viscount Weemswood said.

Mr. Underwood's countenance cleared as though by magic. "Did you indeed, Nana? You are the best of fellows!"

"Oh, well, as to that I don't know," Lord Heatherton said with an embarrassed cough. "I do know that one must have one's man, however, if one means to go into the country, and so I told Sinjin."

"Nana insisted that we could not in honor abduct you without first making certain of your creature comforts," Viscount Weemswood said.

"And thus I was made to endure a tumble into a ditch and a hike of three miles. I truly appreciate the effort, Nana!"

"Think nothing of it, for I am sure I do not," Lord Heatherton said in his open way. He smiled in a good-natured fashion when the others laughed at him.

"It is already approaching the hour. I shall go up at once and do what I can to refurbish my appearance," Mr. Underwood said. "You will send my man to me the moment he arrives, will you not, Miles?"

At the reminder of the time, the gentlemen had all risen.

Lord Trilby smiled as he accompanied Mr. Underwood to the door. "Certainly I shall do so. In the meantime, I shall send my own valet round to your room to sponge and press your coat."

Mr. Underwood gratefully accepted this offer. "I stand in your eternal debt, Miles."

"All obstacles must fall away in face of the inexorable pursuit of love," Lord Trilby said dryly.

Mr. Underwood laughed. His good humor completely restored, he said, "I shall be making a longer visit with you than I intended, my lord. I find I've a taste for a deadly dull rustication."

Then, along with the viscount and Lord Heatherton, he followed a footman who was to show them to their rooms.

Lord Trilby stood in the entry hall below, watching the three gentlemen ascend the stairs. A frown came to his face, as though he were contemplating a peculiarly difficult puzzle.

He knew that he could not cancel the dinner party at that

late hour, especially not when the Grandduchess of Schaffenzeits had virtually arranged it herself. She had given it out that she was particularly interested in making the acquaintance of Lady Caroline's aunt.

Lord Trilby had his own suspicions regarding the truth of that. In any event, her grace would never accept another trumped-up excuse without asking penetrating questions for which he had no answers.

Lord Trilby grimaced slightly. He had no alternative but to allow the dinner party to take place with the addition of three extra gentlemen at table. Three gentlemen, moreover, who were well enough acquainted with the state of the friendship between himself and Lady Caroline that they would be most surprised at any mention of an engagement.

He felt that he could trust his great-aunt to keep her word to maintain her discretion, but Mrs. Burlington was another matter altogether. That lady had always been beforehand in putting forward her opinions, and she had a magnificent disregard for anyone else's sensibilities.

Mrs. Burlington also had a thirst for claiming illustrious acquaintances. Lord Trilby could well imagine the pleasure Mrs. Burlington would take in establishing herself in the eyes of a trio of London gentlemen as the future-in-law to the Grandduchess of Schaffenzeits. He could also imagine the lengths to which he himself would be driven to stop Mrs. Burlington from informing the whole party of the same interesting item.

"What a damnable farce it will be," he muttered.

What had previously seemed so simple was fast assuming unmanageable proportions. The deception casually entered into for the Grandduchess of Schaffenzeits' benefit was becoming more complicated than he could ever have conceived.

If he had been wiser, he would have listened more closely to his secretary's cautionings.

The earl's thoughts came full circle and he wondered again how he was to keep his friends ignorant of his supposed engagement to Lady Caroline.

It was impossible, of course. Mrs. Burlington was bound to make some sort of reference to it that he would not be able to smooth over in time. Though Lord Heatherton might not catch it up on the instant, Lord Trilby had no such doubts about either Viscount Weemswood or Mr. Underwood. Those gentlemen would certainly wonder to hear such a fantastic claim, and he would not be able to refute it without creating just the sort of scene that he most desired to avoid with the grandduchess.

In addition, it had never been Lord Trilby's intention to expose Lady Caroline to public speculation. It was not only this dinner party that would be involved, but the servants, in position to overhear the rumpus, would carry the tale throughout the neighborhood. Lady Caroline's reputation would be wholly ruined and his own besmirched.

It went hard against the grain to even contemplate Lady Caroline placed in such an ignoble position. He felt that he could not leave something of such importance to the whims of chance and a simple hope for the best.

After a moment's more reflection, Lord Trilby came to the unwelcome conclusion that he had no alternative but to take his friends at least partially into his confidence. He was certain that he could trust to their own innate discretion and good manners to spare Lady Caroline undue embarrassment. In addition, the gentlemen would carry no word of the unusual matter outside Walmesley, and in time it would be quite forgotten.

The difficult decision was made. Still to be sorted out was

how he could best carry it out and, more to the point, what he would tell Lady Caroline concerning the matter. Somehow, Lord Trilby had the feeling that her ladyship would not be at all accepting of his decision.

Lord Trilby turned and made his way back to his study, his boots rapping sharply against the tiles.

22

An hour later the gentlemen reassembled downstairs.

The Earl of Walmesley's valet had waited on each of the gentlemen from London, expertly brushing coats and overseeing the cleaning of boots. The valet's time had been most commandeered by Mr. Underwood, who understandably had withstood more damage to his attire than his companions owing to his unfortunate experience earlier that day.

Though there was nothing of the dandy about him, Mr. Underwood was nevertheless always careful of his appearance. In this instance, however, he took more care than was his usual wont. His hair was brushed neatly back and his pantaloons were smoothed creaseless into freshly polished boots. He fretted over what appeared to his eyes the crumpled state of his cravat, but he knew that there was nothing much that could be done with it. He restored the neckcloth as best as he was able, cursing the viscount again, and submitted to being aided back into his newly pressed coat by the earl's valet.

A last inspection in the glass, a brushing away of an invisible mote of lint from his sleeve, and Mr. Underwood was at last satisfied with the effects of his limited toilet.

He was the last gentleman to emerge from his bedroom and therefore he had the exclusive gratification of meeting the ladies on the stairs.

Mr. Underwood civilly brought himself to the Grandduchess of Schaffenzeits' notice, remarking that he had had the honor of meeting Fräulein Gutenberg earlier when she had come down to the parlor in pursuit of the missing shawl. He managed to confine himself to a polite nod in the younger lady's direction, even though it cost him dear not to express himself with more warmth. However he might have wished to do so, though, he could not disguise the light of admiration in his eyes.

"Indeed!" The Grandduchess Wilhelmina Hildebrande glanced thoughtfully from Mr. Underwood's kindling glance to the Fräulein's quiet smile. Fräulein Gutenberg's dark eyes revealed only mild pleasure. "I have not had the opportunity to hear of your earlier meeting with Mr. Underwood, Marie."

"I did not wish to disturb your rest unnecessarily, madam," Fräulein Gutenberg said with perfect calm.

Mr. Underwood had always been swift with the feminine nuances, and he realized that the grandduchess was not best pleased to learn in such a roundabout fashion of the Fräulein's small social adventure. He said quickly, "Then your grace was not aware that I and the others had arrived. Forgive me, madam. I would not have presumed to bring myself so familiarly to your notice if I had known. Despite the informality of our meeting, I hope that you will allow me to escort you downstairs."

The Grandduchess Wilhelmina Hildebrande accepted the support of Mr. Underwood's arm. As the trio started down the stairs, she said, "I confess to mild surprise to learn of the arrival of you and your companions. I was not aware that the earl planned to entertain us with company."

"Oh, we can hardly be called invited guests," Mr. Underwood said with a chuckle. "My friends and I simply took a notion to drop in at Walmesley for a short visit. We suffered an unfortunate carriage accident, requiring a new wheel, so I suppose we shall be fixed here for several days while we await repairs."

The grandduchess slanted a skeptical glance toward Mr. Underwood, but remarked only, "Walmesley is often very quiet at this time of the year, as I recall. It is why I vastly prefer it over London. However, I daresay that we will all become acquainted over tea and be quite comfortable."

Mr. Underwood, ever inclined to be the optimist, decided to overlook the grandduchess's tepid courtesy and instead chose to consider the fortuitous meeting as an auspicious beginning. As a consequence, Mr. Underwood was well-pleased with himself as he ushered the ladies into the drawing room.

Lord Trilby made the introductions all around. The grandduchess chose to ensconce herself on a wide settee, with Fräulein Gutenberg beside her. The gentlemen distributed themselves in a loose ring about the ladies as the servants brought in the tea.

The grandduchess requested that Fräulein Gutenberg pour the tea. Her grace accepted the first cup with a gracious nod and addressed herself to the gentlemen, drawing them out to talk about themselves.

While her mentor chatted in a seemingly idle manner, Fräulein Gutenberg quietly inquired each gentleman's preferences, serving herself last. Though she did not appear to be listening closely, she nevertheless carefully collected those bits of information that the gentlemen let drop about themselves, their circumstances, and their way of life. The Fräulein had learned much from the Grandduchess of Schaffenzeits about the importance of discovering as much as possible about those about her.

Lord Heatherton, who had spurned inferior refreshment in anticipation of the tea, was at once intent on consuming an enormous amount to make up for the missed luncheon. His lordship, ever polite, carried his share of the conversation when he was addressed, but it was apparent to all that nothing interested him so much at the moment as the sandwiches, sweet biscuits, cake, and tea.

Viscount Weemswood recalled to the grandduchess their original meeting and he endured with surprisingly good grace the lady's short humorous recounting of his past indiscretion. In the midst of his friends' laughter he observed, "I was a mere bantling in those days."

The Grandduchess of Schaffenzeits inspected the viscount's thin intelligent face and his handsomely turned-out form again with more interest than before. She gave a sharp nod and in her guttural accents said, "You have done yourself credit, my lord. The awkward scruff-mannered cub that I remember is no more. I suspect, however, that there is yet something left of that undisciplined character lurking beneath the present polished exterior."

Viscount Weemswood cracked a laugh. His cold eyes gleamed. "I fear that is true, your grace."

Mr. Underwood seized the opportunity afforded by the viscount's conversation with the Grandduchess of Schaffenzeits to lean close to Fräulein Gutenberg's shoulder and engage her attention for a few moments.

He became quickly aware that the grandduchess was not so deep in her own conversation that she did not manage to overhear what was said between himself and the Fräulein. Mr. Underwood therefore prudently began to address himself to the grandduchess as well.

Lord Trilby overwatched it all with an expression of faint amusement, contributing to the conversation only as it behooved him.

At one point, when both the viscount and Mr. Underwood urged Fräulein Gutenberg to rise from her place and go over to play the pianoforte for the company, he encountered a glance from the Grandduchess of Schaffenzeits that was unmistakable.

Lord Trilby obeyed the unspoken summons, and when he sat down beside his great-aunt, he was surprised to be greeted with a look of eloquent amusement.

"My dear Miles, you have surprised me yet again. I did not know you were so capable. I shall take care not to underestimate you in future," the grandduchess said.

Lord Trilby slanted a brow at her. "Oh? Pray enlighten me, ma'am, for I cry ignorance."

The grandduchess smiled fondly at the earl. "Very well, my lord, I shall stroke your sense of satisfaction. I am never behind in giving credit where it is due. You managed to produce a most charming young lady as your intended when I felt certain that none existed. That in itself was a marvelous feat. However, it pales in comparison to this. It was a masterful stroke indeed to invite your friends to Walmesley. I compliment you, Miles, for it is not often that I am faced with the completely unanticipated."

Lord Trilby was taken aback. He took care to maintain his mild expression, however. "I am not certain I know what you mean, your grace. I was thoroughly taken by surprise by the arrival of my friends. They have always been assured of a welcome at Walmesley, of course. I am sorry if you do not care for the company."

The Grandduchess Wilhelmina Hildebrande expressed her disbelief with an unladylike snort. "Come, Miles, let us have done with this feinting. I have listened politely to the sad story of an incapacitated phaeton and I have agreed that it was a great inconvenience, as was obviously expected of me. That was the role assigned to me, after all, was it not? However, I would think it beneath me not to acknowledge my respect on a most successful foray. Yes, indeed, I suspect that your ploy to provide my dear ambitious Fräulein with a surfeit of eligible *partis* to choose from may prove unexpectedly vexatious for my own plans." She directed a nod at the small knot of gallants gathered about Fräulein Gutenberg.

Quite astonished, Lord Trilby followed his great-aunt's glance. His friends were obviously paying court to Fräulein Gutenberg. Even Lord Heatherton, having sated himself, had become willing to pay pretty compliments to the beauty. As for Fräulein Gutenberg, she fairly radiated satisfaction as her eyes dwelt on each of the gentlemen's faces in turn.

The earl's face lit up with a slow delighted smile. He glanced again at the Grandduchess of Schaffenzeits and discovered that that dame was regarding him with a sharp speculation that instantly made him wary. It would not do to let the grandduchess guess that the astonishing result he witnessed had indeed come about merely by chance. Surely it was far better to leave her on her guard, Lord Trilby thought. Perhaps then she might think twice before trying to engineer another assault upon his defenses.

With the aplomb for which he was well-known, Lord Trilby made a courtly bow from the waist. "Very well, madam. I accept your congratulations, for I don't doubt that you will speedily conspire to counter whatever happy effects this situation has gained for me."

The grandduchess cackled. Her world-weary eyes were bright with affection as she looked on him. "Indeed, you may consider it as a foregone conclusion that I shall do so. However, I think I shall be content, for now, to allow you mastery of the field. Savor your small triumph, my lord, for I warn you it may well be your last."

"It is early days yet, madam," Lord Trilby said cheerfully. Soon afterward, the Grandduchess of Schaffenzeits indicated that she wished to retire to her afternoon rest. Since she required the Fräulein to attend her, this effectively broke up the pleasant gathering.

Mr. Underwood looked closely for some sign that Fräulein Gutenberg was reluctant to leave in company with her exacting mentor, but she offered only the most correct civilities, scattered impartially amongst the gentlemen, before she exited.

The viscount requested wine from one of the footmen who entered to clear away the remnants of the tea. When the wine was brought, all of the gentlemen accepted a glass and talked idly of what had been transpiring in London during the earl's absence.

After the servants had withdrawn, Mr. Underwood said, "I am now deuced glad that you fellows carried me off. Otherwise I might never have had the felicity of meeting Fräulein Gutenberg." He raised his glass. "A toast, gentlemen. A toast to the lady who has at last succeeded in stealing my heart."

"Carey, you are not contemplating anything foolish, I trust?" Lord Heatherton asked with an anxious air.

"Of course not," Mr. Underwood said, but with such a faraway look in his eyes as he stared into the fire that Lord Heatherton was not at all reassured.

"Fear not, Nana. He will have no chance to fix his interest with the beauteous Fräulein," Viscount Weemswood said.

Mr. Underwood looked around, shooting the viscount a concentrated look of suspicion. "Whatever do you mean?"

The viscount contemplated the wine in his glass, swirling it gently and admiring the rich color. "Why, surely it is plain, Carey. The Fräulein is meant for our host."

On the words he lifted his gaze to look at the Earl of Walmesley.

"Damn your eyes, Sinjin. They are too perceptive by

half," Lord Trilby said mildly.

Mr. Underwood, who had quickly switched his attention to the earl, was now staring narrowly at his lordship. "It is true, then my lord?"

Lord Trilby made an irritated motion with his hand. "It is the grandduchess's intention, yes. It is not mine, however."

He frowned, misliking the turn that the conversation had taken but recognizing as well that it was inevitable. Obviously the time had come to take his friends into his confidence, yet he found himself most reluctant to do so. It was against his innate pride even to acknowledge the ridiculous situation, let alone authenticate its gravity by referring to it.

"The Grandduchess of Schaffenzeits is one of the most willful and autocratic ladies I have ever had occasion to meet," Viscount Weemswood observed softly.

The Earl of Walmesley shot another glance at the viscount. A reluctant smile began to tug at his lips. "I suppose that next you will offer your opinion that I am rather too fond of my great-aunt for my own good."

Viscount Weemswood gave a negligent shrug of his shoulders, forbearing to reply.

"I am too fond of her grace," Lord Trilby acknowledged. "Otherwise, I would cheerfully have told her to go to the devil long since. As it stands, I cannot wound the grand old lady so cruelly, and so, as a result of my lamentable sentimentality, I find myself in something of a predicament." Lord Trilby frowned slightly as he stared into his wineglass.

"Whatever the trouble, Miles, rest assured that you may call upon any one of us," Mr. Underwood said.

The earl raised his eyes. Rueful amusement leapt into their depths. "Actually, I believe that all of you have already done me a service. According to my great-aunt, it seems that your untimely arrival has worked to my advantage, in that the Fräulein's thoughts have been given a new turn."

"I do not quite follow you, my lord," Lord Heatherton said.

"I do, however. What you have said interests me most profoundly, Miles," Mr. Underwood said on a laugh. His brown eyes danced. "You may count on my enthusiastic co-operation, my lord. In point of fact, I shall do my damnedest to cut you out."

"I thought I might count on you at least, Carey," Lord Trilby said dryly.

"Oh, of course, I see it at last. Well, I am not quite the favorite with the ladies that Carey is, or that Sinjin can make of himself when he puts a bit of effort into behaving with common civility, but I shall do my part in making myself agreeable," Lord Heatherton said stoutly.

"I do not know why I accept such undeserved insults from my friends. I am sure I am no more rude than the next fellow," Viscount Weemswood said. The flicker of a smile crossed his face at the derisive sound made by Mr. Underwood and seconded by Lord Heatherton's discreet cough.

He addressed the earl. "I had no notion that a visit to Walmesley at this time of year would prove so entertaining. My commitments in London are not of such moment that I cannot remain a fortnight or longer."

"I am deeply appreciative of your support, gentlemen," Lord Trilby said. "I know I need not point out that I rely upon your complete discretion. My reputation would suffer a harsh blow if it were known that I would go to such lengths to spare an elderly lady a shocking set-down."

"Of course you may rely upon us, my lord. I am certain there is not one in this room who would allow a word in your disfavor," Lord Heatherton said.

There was a murmur of agreement from the other two gentlemen.

"I am glad to hear it, for I have a confession to make which will most certainly astound you all and possibly cause you to reexamine your declaration of loyalty."

23

The Earl of Walmesley saw that he had gained their undivided attention. He could not but smile at the profound somberness that had promptly fallen over Lord Heatherton's features. His lordship always anticipated the worst, but perhaps in this instance his apprehension would prove to be justified.

Lord Trilby's eyes traveled to his other companions. Mr. Underwood regarded him with the alert look of a loyal retainer, while the viscount had of a sudden gone quite still and only by the wariness in his cold eyes betrayed that his interest had been engaged to an extraordinary degree.

Lord Trilby set his wineglass down on the table, the click of its base sounding a contrast to the waiting silence.

"As all of you are now aware, my great-aunt has made shift to provide me with a suitable candidate for roping me into marriage, in the delectable person of Fräulein Gutenberg," he said.

At their nods, he continued in a colorless voice, "I have countered her grace's inspiration by enlisting the help of a certain lady who has agreed, most reluctantly I may add, to stand as my intended until the grandduchess chooses to leave England behind."

"Good God!"

Viscount Weemswood abruptly straightened in his chair. His eyes, igniting in twin points of angry disbelief, narrowed on the earl. His long fingers clenched suddenly on the chair arms. "You must be mad, my lord!"

Mr. Underwood confined himself to a low thoughtful whistle.

It was left to Lord Heatherton to ask the obvious question. He cleared his throat in a diffident fashion and sought a delicacy of phrasing, deciding finally that there was none. "My lord, this lady . . . is she perhaps known to any of us?"

Lord Trilby glanced at the savage expression on the viscount's face. He held himself very still, knowing full well that gentleman's capacity for fury, yet not fearing it. The friendship between them had survived a tumultuous history, one which had irrevocably linked them. "Yes, I fear that the lady in question is quite familiar to each of you. It is Lady Caroline Eddington."

"You should be thrashed within an inch of your life for dragging that lady into your filthy mire, my lord," Viscount Weemswood ground out, looking very much as though he were just the individual to mete out such harsh punishment.

"You are undoubtedly correct," Lord Trilby said in a quiet voice. He and the viscount clashed stares for a long tense moment.

Realizing that a crisis was in the making, Mr. Underwood snapped sharply, "Sinjin, leave off! Cool heads are required, do you not see?"

Still the viscount regarded the Earl of Walmesley with hard glittering eyes, then slowly nodded. But he threw out a last barb. "I have always thought you too careless of your friendship with Lady Caroline. Someone should have married her years ago and with a cuff to the head sent you to perdition. She is too fine a lady to be taken for granted by a gentleman of your deliberately careless stamp."

The Earl of Walmesley's face reflected his surprise at the unexpected direction of attack. The viscount's charge was unpleasant to hear, astonishingly so, and in response he felt a surge of ferocious anger. "Have you yourself in mind to do the thing, Weemswood? For I shall tell you to your face that I would not willingly stand by whilst one of your rack-and-ruin character made free with Lady Caroline's affections."

The viscount threw himself out of his chair to his feet, a curse snarling from between his lips.

"Enough, I say!" Mr. Underwood exclaimed, leaping forward to put himself between the two antagonists. He said urgently, "Miles, you know how Sinjin is when he takes one of his freakish starts! Come to your senses, man! What will it profit either of you to come to blows?"

Lord Trilby spared a glance for Mr. Underwood, and that gentleman's appalled expression served to clear the angry mists from his head. He discovered that his fists were clenched. Slowly he loosened his fingers. "You are right, Carey. There is nothing to gain. Sinjin, I owe you an apology. As my friend, you have every right to question my ethics in this matter. So should I have done, in your shoes."

"It is forgotten, my lord," Viscount Weemswood spoke somewhat stiffly. His anger was not so easily let go of, but apparently his response reassured Mr. Underwood, for that gentleman sighed and his defensive stance relaxed.

Lord Heatherton regarded the earl in open reproach. "I cannot fathom how you could have asked it of Lady Caroline, my lord. Dash it, she is a gentlewoman to her fingertips. No, and another thing! It further mystifies me why she ever agreed to take part in such a havey-cavey business."

The viscount briefly caught the Earl of Walmesley's inscrutable eyes, and his lips twisted in a mirthless smile. He had his own thoughts on that score, but such speculations were not to be bandied about even in this company. Viscount Weemswood spoke quietly but with an underlying violence. "No one was to know of it, Nana. One does not parade one's attachments, for fear of disillusion, does one, my lord?"

"It was to be a completely private matter between myself and Lady Caroline," Lord Trilby said, with equal quiet. He again met the viscount's eyes, and for a long moment their glances visibly clashed.

"Then why have you made us party to this conspiracy, Miles? Lady Caroline's good name should not be risked even among us who may be considered her friends. We have naught but the utmost regard for Lady Caroline, yet this sordid tangle cannot but raise unseemly curiosity in our breasts," Mr. Underwood said.

He was very disturbed by what he considered a flagrant disregard for the lady's reputation and her sensibilities. For himself, he thought it was certain that he could never again meet Lady Caroline without wondering what had ever possessed her to agree to participate in such a mad scheme. His curiosity would almost certainly color his acquaintance with her and perhaps even cause him to treat her to a wounding reserve.

"Lady Caroline comes to dinner tonight, Carey. She will be accompanied by her maternal aunt, Mrs. Burlington. I do not believe that either of you or Nana has previously had the pleasure of making Mrs. Burlington's acquaintance. She is a somewhat difficult woman, being both malicious and free-handed with her opinions," Lord Trilby said.

Once again Viscount Weemswood was a step ahead of the other gentlemen in the quickness of his understanding. He unleashed a disgusted expletive and threw himself back into the wing chair in a careless fashion.

Mr. Underwood's mouth fell open in astonishment. "You don't mean to say that the talkative aunt is in on it too?"

"Quite the opposite, Carey. Mrs. Burlington labors under the mistaken impression that the engagement is genuine. My fear was that if Mrs. Burlington chanced to mention an engagement to you, without some forewarning you gentlemen would express such astonishment that must instantly shed suspicion on my and Lady Caroline's farrago," Lord Trilby said.

Viscount Weemswood let out a crack of laughter. "Whose farrago, my lord?"

Lord Trilby stared at the viscount without a trace of expression. "If you will have it so, mine is the sole responsibility."

"What if this pretty scheme of yours goes awry, my lord?" Viscount Weemswood asked softly. "What matters then your declaration of responsibility? Somehow I do not think that will be of much comfort to Lady Caroline. It will be far too late."

"Damn you, Sinjin!" Lord Trilby's voice was thin. His eyes blazed with rare fury at the viscount, who but smiled in the face of the earl's wholly unwarranted reaction.

"I cannot believe in any of it!" Mr. Underwood exclaimed.

"This is not at all the thing, my lord."

Lord Heatherton's voice was heavy with disapproval. "I am sorry to say that I have grossly misjudged your character, and so has society in general. Lord, if I were to breathe but half of what I have heard today to m'mother, she would instantly bar the house to you. Yes, and begin to receive Sinjin and Carey with open arms as the more respectable."

There was an instant of astonishment before Lord Heatherton's companions roared with laughter. His lordship's long expression loosened into a smile. "Well, so she would," he said, which brought further guffaws and a dissipation of the former tension.

Lord Trilby bowed to Lord Heatherton. "Thank you, Nana. You have delivered to me a singular set-down, one which I most richly deserve and that I embrace with alacrity. I had feared myself to have become too respectable. It relieves me to learn that I would share, along with Sinjin and Carey, your esteemed mother's stern disapprobation."

"Well, you don't, for m'mother doesn't know about this business. No, nor will she. Wouldn't do at all, for m'mother knows everyone in London," Lord Heatherton said.

"We shall all take strictest care that Lady Caroline's part in this regrettable charade is never known," Mr. Underwood said.

A faint smile began to form in his eyes as he reviewed in his mind the personages who would be in attendance that evening. "My word, Miles, you could not have contrived a more uncomfortable party if you had tried."

"I fear that I must agree with that sentiment. I can only hope it is gotten over quickly, and with my great-aunt none the wiser."

"I'll lay a monkey that within the fortnight the Grandduchess of Schaffenzeits will be in possession of all the particulars of your deception, my lord," Viscount Weemswood said.

Lord Trilby met his friend's eyes and he laughed. The fact that Viscount Weemswood had reverted to form told him all that he needed to know. Of the three gentlemen, he had been most uncertain of the viscount's support. For the first time in over an hour he relaxed. "Done, sir! That is one wager that on my honor I cannot refuse."

"Done!" Mr. Underwood exclaimed. "I'll put my faith in the earl, and more to the point, in Lady Caroline's quick wits."

Mr. Underwood looked over at Lord Heatherton, whose brows had drawn together in a prodigious frown. "What of you, Nana? Will you back our host as well?"

Lord Heatherton shook his head even as he glanced apologetically at the Earl of Walmesley. "No, I shan't. Elderly ladies are deuced shrewd at ferreting out just what one most particularly wishes to keep close between one's teeth. One need only consider m'mother to see that." None of Mr. Underwood's many persuasions could sway him from his position.

Lord Trilby suggested a round of cards, and the hours were whiled away pleasantly enough in good-natured raillery and respectable stakes. The card game came to an end when the gentlemen were notified of the arrival of their valets.

The gentlemen went their separate ways to dress for dinner. Not one did not wonder what the evening might hold.

24

The snow continued to fall and the temperature to drop. It was thought by those interested in such matters that by late evening a thin cover of winter white might form over the countryside. Lady Caroline, looking out her window at dusk, thought the pristine snow would make the drive between Berwicke and Walmesley breathtakingly lovely in the moonlight.

As she was helped to dress by her maid, Lady Caroline thought she should have been dreading the dinner party at Walmesley more than she was. Strangely enough, as the time to depart approached closer, she began to actually look forward to the appointed hour.

Despite her nervousness at the thought of performing once more for the Grandduchess of Schaffenzeits' benefit, despite her anxiety over what Mrs. Burlington might feel herself compelled to do, despite her dismay that Lord Hathaway would make up one of the company, Lady Caroline was feeling remarkably cheerful.

The game had become peculiarly intoxicating, she thought. She was to play a gentleman's intended to fool one person while at the same time pretend to the gentleman that she was not in love with him. It was a thorny role indeed.

At last she added the last touch to her appearance, placing about her neck a diamond-and-emerald necklace. The maid did the clasp and Lady Caroline's hands slid lightly over the jewels in their settings.

For a long moment Lady Caroline looked at her reflection

in the cheval glass. Her fine eyes glowed with satisfaction and excitement, rivaling the sparkle of the emerald ear studs and the jewels about her throat.

"I have seldom seen you appear so lovely, my lady," her maid said.

Lady Caroline smiled. "Thank you, Spencer."

That was it, of course. That was the reason she was actually anticipating the evening. She had dressed for Lord Trilby and she knew herself to be at her most beautiful.

Her gleaming chestnut hair was arranged in a flattering knot of curls, soft tendrils escaping to wisp about her brow. She wore an emerald-green satin gown overlaid with silver lace tissue, and it showed her figure to excellent advantage, molding to breast and thigh as she moved. The color emphasized the rise of her creamy throat and shoulders and an elegant show of rounded bosom.

Fräulein Gutenberg would not be the only swan this night.

Spencer handed a velvet cloak to her mistress, which Lady Caroline laid over her arm.

With a departing word to the maid, Lady Caroline gathered up her muff and reticule and went downstairs. She had taken longer with her toilet than was her habit and she fully expected that her aunt would greet her with unbridled impatience.

Lady Caroline swept across the threshold of the drawing room, saying cheerfully, "Here I am at last, Amaris. Now we may be off."

Mrs. Burlington turned, exclaiming, "My dear Lady Caroline, I was just telling . . . Oh, but you do not know. Only look who is here!"

But Lady Caroline had already seen those standing across the room. "Ned! Lady Eddington!" She left the doorway and went quickly to meet her brother, who stepped forward to greet her. As he caught her hands, she demanded, "Whatever are you doing at Berwicke?"

Lord Eddington laughed at her. "A fine welcome, I must say!" He raised his sister's hands higher so that he could better admire her attire. "You look as fine as sixpence, Caroline."

Lady Caroline laughed, disengaging herself so that she could offer a hand to her sister-in-law. "Lady Eddington. I cannot tell you what a welcome surprise this is." She glanced inquiringly at her brother, then again at Lady Eddington. "But I thought you meant to stay in London for the remainder of the Little Season."

Lady Eddington flushed slightly. "Our visit was cut short. It proved not to be as convival as I had hoped it would be."

Lord Eddington lifted his wife's small hand and pressed it comfortingly. "Never mind, love. You must not think about it any longer." He addressed his sister and Mrs. Burlington. "There's no need to wrap it up in clean linen for you two, I know. The truth of the matter is that the pair of them acted in a deuced scaly fashion toward my lady and I would not tolerate it. Neither of you would believe what that cold fish-eyed harpy had the audacity to say to her. I was never more inflamed in my life. My lady's father and I had words, and in the end . . . well, here we are."

"Oh, no, how dreadful for you both! But you are home now and may be comfortable again," Mrs. Burlington said. She was immensely pleased by the turn of events. It was a pity, of course, that Lady Eddington had quarreled with her family, but perhaps it was all for the best. Lord and Lady Eddington would not be going up to London as often as they might have done otherwise.

Lady Caroline smiled with ready sympathy at her sister-in-law. "One's family can be such a trial to one at times. Pray do try to disregard the unpleasantness, for I am certain that your visits will not always be so difficult."

"Thank you, Lady Caroline." There was a shadow in Lady Eddington's expression, but she recognized her sister-in-law's attempt at kindness for what it was, and her lips curved faintly.

"We were not blue-deviled the whole time. We spent a jolly afternoon at the Tower Zoo. There was Astley's Circus too, and the theater," Lord Eddington said, anxious to bring the happy light back to his bride's eyes.

Lady Eddington awarded his lordship with a widening smile. "Quite true, my lord! We could pass hours enumerating the little pleasures that we enjoyed."

"We shall have all of tomorrow to visit at our leisure, my lady, but now you and Lord Eddington must hurry and change out of those travel clothes, for we are due at Walmesley for dinner," Mrs. Burlington said.

"What, is Trilby down from town as well? Well, this is something grand. We shall pay our respects hot-foot," Lord Eddington said.

"Oh, no! You must not!"

Three pairs of startled eyes found Lady Caroline.

She was embarrassed by her own unthinking discourtesy. Despite her heightened color, she managed to produce a creditable smile. "Lord and Lady Eddington have but just arrived after a long tiring journey, Amaris. I am persuaded that mingling in company this evening is the last thing that they would wish."

"Now, there you are out, Caroline," Lord Eddington said frankly. "I am of no mind to kick my heels here and sup on slivers of yesterday's ham when I could be at Walmesley enjoying a bang-up dinner and cheerful society. It would be just the thing to chase away the pall that has hung over us since leaving London. Do you not agree, my dear love?"

"Oh, yes, indeed! I do adore to be in company," Lady Eddington said, perceptibly brightening at the thought.

"There! Didn't I tell you?" Lord Eddington said with satisfaction.

"Really, my lady! It is almost as though you do not *wish* his lordship and dear Lady Eddington to accompany us," Mrs. Burlington said, her eyes narrowing in speculation.

Lady Caroline felt the situation slipping inexorably away from her, but she made a gallant attempt to salvage it. "The grandduchess is such a high stickler, Amaris, as you well know. I cannot help but wonder whether she would—"

"What grandduchess?" Lord Eddington interrupted. "Oh, I say! Never tell me that old dragon of an aunt of Trilby's is in England again. I never met her myself, of course, but what one has heard over the years positively curls one's toes. Why, I would have thought she had perished ages ago!"

"Great-aunt, and her grace is still exceedingly lively," Lady Caroline corrected, distracted. She could not think what to say to persuade her brother and sister-in-law to remain at Berwicke, but it was of paramount importance that they do so, for their presence at Walmesley could hardly be thought of as a welcome fortuity.

The problem was that dear Ned knew her and her mannerisms too well. It could complicate matters immensely if her brother were to come to suspect that something was afoot between herself and the earl. Lord Eddington's character did not lead him to indulge in deep reflection. He was more likely to blurt out whatever was on his mind at the most inopportune moment.

"Pray recall, dear niece, that when Lord Hathaway was presented to the Grandduchess of Schaffenzeits, she very graciously extended an invitation to his lordship on the basis of his acquaintance with us. In that light, I do not think there can be the least objection to the inclusion of family members to our party," Mrs. Burlington said.

Lady Caroline was forced to concede the logic of her aunt's argument. "Very well, then. We shall all go, if that is truly your wish, Lady Eddington."

Assured that it was indeed Lady Eddington's fondest desire, Lady Caroline sighed defeat. She cast a glance at the mantel clock. "Dinner is for ten o'clock, Ned."

Thus adjured, Lord Eddington reassured his sister that he and his lady would scramble into their evening clothes without delay.

As Lady Eddington accompanied him out of the drawing room, she protested laughingly, "Surely we shall not *scramble*, my lord!"

"Not precisely that, no. Lord, just wouldn't we look a pair of quizzes with our buttons askew and our shoes mismatched."

The young couple laughed together as they mounted the stairs. Standing below in the entry hall, Lady Caroline envied their lightheartedness.

Lord Eddington threw back over his shoulder that they should all go together in the large coach. "For I do not mean to ride squeezed up against the window in the smaller carriage, Caroline," he warned.

"I shall see to it, Ned," Lady Caroline said, and gave the necessary instructions for the smaller carriage to be returned to the stables and exchange for the larger equipage. Staying the servant from his errand for a moment, she said that she also wished a missive to be carried to Walmesley, and requested that pen and paper and an inkwell be brought to her.

The servant returned to the drawing room with the required articles. Lady Caroline placed them on the occasional table, dipped the pen, and began scratching swiftly over the sheet.

For her aunt's benefit, Lady Caroline explained, "I shall dash off a note to notify Lord Trilby that there will be two more than anticipated at his table. I am sure that his cook will be grateful for at least that much notice."

Mrs. Burlington nodded in rare approval of her niece's way of taking the initiative. "What a good thought, for if the grandduchess does chance to cut up stiff over our enlarged party, his lordship will be obliged to point out the courtesy of your note."

Lady Caroline cast an unreadable glance at her aunt. Quickly she finished the note, sanded and folded it, and gave it to the servant. "Yes, indeed. We must not forget the grandduchess even for a moment."

However, it was not the Grandduchess of Schaffenzeits, nor the earl's cook, of whom she was thinking. She thought Lord Trilby might appreciate an advance warning that her brother and sister-in-law would be in attendance. Not that it changed matters in the least, she thought, but now she would not be alone in feeling herself to be caught on tenterhooks.

All of her former anticipation of the evening was quite dashed.

The Earl of Walmesley's expression whenever he should first set eyes on her was not likely to be filled with admiration for her lovely gown. Instead, his lordship was likely to lift his brows with just that show of assumed surprise that was so very maddening.

"Lady Caroline, are you quite all right? You are wearing the most prodigious frown! Quite unbecoming, I must say!"

Lady Caroline sighed. "Amaris, would you think it wonderful if I were to say I am developing the headache?"

"Not at all, dear niece. I am quite used to your wayward

idiosyncrasies by now, I assure you," Mrs. Burlington said waspishly. "However, I do think you might exert a little effort for your brother's and Lady Eddington's sake. They are quite looking forward to this little outing, and to discover that you meant to be so disobliging as to cry off, for I assume that is what you are hinting at, would quite ruin their harmless pleasure."

Lady Caroline sighed again. In a resigned voice she said, "Yes, quite true. That would be most unfortunate."

25

The butler came to the door, requesting a word with his lord-ship.

Lord Trilby left the other gentlemen and walked into the entry hall, where he was informed that an urgent note had come from Berwicke Keep. Lord Trilby thanked the man, taking the note and unfolding it.

Quickly scanning the contents of the note, Lord Trilby creased his brows in a deep frown. Lady Caroline Ed-dington would be accompanied that evening not only by her aunt, Mrs. Burlington, but also by Lord and Lady Ed-dington.

The earl swore.

"Miles, whatever has caused you to resort to such shocking utterances?"

Lord Trilby looked up quickly to see that his great-aunt, accompanied by Fräulein Gutenberg, had come down the stairs. He smiled for their benefit. As he went over to meet them he casually slipped the note into his coat pocket.

Lord Trilby took the gloved hand that the Grandduchess of Schaffenzeits had extended and carried it to his lips with a flourish.

He released her hand and, eyeing her elaborate coif ad-miringly, said, "My dear ma'am, that is a most becoming turban. I do not believe I have ever before seen—let me see—four plumes of such extravagance on any one head-dress."

"It is five plumes, and you cannot shift my attention quite

215

so easily as that, my lord! Now, what has served to annoy you?"

Lord Trilby allowed a faint smile to play about his lips. "You are too discerning, madam. But I fear that you will say I am guilty of overreaction. I have received word that Lady Caroline will also be accompanied by her brother, Lord Eddington, and his lady."

The Grandduchess Wilhelmina Hildebrande put up thin brows in interrogation. "What of that, pray? Are Lord and Lady Eddington not quite the thing, then?"

Lord Trilby smiled again. "Hardly that, madam. I was merely annoyed to learn so late in the evening of their attendance. We may have to wait dinner, you see, and I know that there is little else that irritates your grace more."

"I shall not regard it in the least, I assure you. I have a great wish to meet all of Lady Caroline's family, as you must have guessed." The grandduchess slid a sly glance in Fräulein Gutenberg's direction. "Lady Caroline is a charming lady. She will undoubtedly make some gentleman a most worthy wife."

Lord Trilby saw the start of surprise given by the Fräulein, as well as the momentary tightening of the lady's soft mouth. He could almost find it in himself to feel sympathy for her, when Fräulein Gutenberg lifted her eyes. The cool self-assurance of her gaze was enough to remind him that the Fräulein had definite intentions in regard to himself.

Not for the first time Lord Trilby considered it a great pity that the Fräulein did not know of Lady Caroline's role.

Lord Trilby nodded politely to Fräulein Gutenberg before he offered his arm to the grandduchess. "Allow me to escort you in, madam." He said teasingly, "The rest are already assembled, so you shall be able to make a grand entrance."

The Grandduchess Wilhelmina Hildebrande nodded, appreciating his wit. "Good. It is what I most like. Marie, pray do not just stand there! His lordship has two arms and so is perfectly capable of escorting two ladies. There, that is better." She cackled, quite pleased with herself. "Your friends will envy you, Miles. On the one arm you have power and wisdom; on the other you have beauty and pleasure. You are a fortunate man indeed."

"As you say, madam," Lord Trilby said. He was annoyed that his great-aunt had maneuvered him so adroitly in bestowing a courtesy on Fräulein Gutenberg that must at once be commented upon, yet he was amused as well. The grandduchess was always alert to any advantage that could be had for the taking, and he had literally handed this one to her.

He was not mistaken about the impact that the sight of himself with the ladies would make upon their entrance into the drawing room. Mr. Underwood shook his head. Viscount Weemswood gave that peculiar twisted smile and made a low comment to Lord Heatherton. Lord Heatherton appeared momentarily startled. Then he sent the viscount a glance of reproach, which that gentleman impatiently shrugged aside.

Lord Heatherton was the first to step forward and make his bow to the ladies. Mr. Underwood, never to be outdone, was swift to follow. Viscount Weemswood was content to wait until the grandduchess and Fräulein Gutenberg were seated before he came forward to convey his own pleasure that the ladies had joined them.

Conversation was so general and light of topic that Lord Trilby was persuaded he was the only member of the company who was tense. He kept one ear attuned for some hint of the rest of the party even while he smiled and conversed.

At last his vigilance was rewarded.

The sounds of arrival heralded the party from Berwicke Keep. Lord Trilby excused himself to those already gathered and stepped just outside the drawing room in order to greet his other guests. "Good evening, Mrs. Burlington, Lady Caroline. Lord, Ned, it has been this age since I have seen you. I was astonished when I heard that you and your bride had returned to England."

Lord Eddington shook the earl's hand. "Foreign parts are all very well, but after a while one begins to pine for dear old England," he said, grinning. He proudly drew forward his wife and introduced her.

Lord Trilby bowed over the countess's hand, genuinely curious about her. It would be interesting to discover what sort of lady had accepted Lord Eddington, whom he knew to be a gentleman sometimes too amiable of character for his own benefit. "Lady Eddington, your servant. I am most happy to make your acquaintance."

"And I yours, my lord." Lady Eddington gave her sweet smile.

Lord Trilby urged the arrivals to finish putting off their wraps and to come into the drawing room, where the other guests were assembled. As he ushered them past him into the drawing room, further greetings and introductions were begun among old and new acquaintances. Lady Caroline, who had lingered behind, joined the earl in the doorway.

Under cover of the flurry of greetings, Lady Caroline whispered urgently, "I am so very sorry, Miles. I did not know what to do. Amaris would have it that Ned and Lady Eddington should accompany us. There was nothing I could possibly have said that would not have sounded suspiciously feeble."

They had deliberately paused a moment before actually entering the drawing room. "I, too, have bad news to relate," Lord Trilby said grimly. "Weemswood, Underwood, and Heatherton have all graced Walmesley with their presence.

They arrived this afternoon and mean to stay at least a fort-night."

"Oh, no!" Consternation deepened the color of her eyes. She quickly glanced around to look into the drawing room as though to confirm it for herself.

"Oh, yes. Caro, I think I must warn you—"

But what Lord Trilby would have said, Lady Caroline was not to hear, for at that moment the Grandduchess of Schaffenzeits came to them. "Whatever are you doing still lurking in the entryway with Lady Caroline, my lord? Come, I insist that you join the rest of the company."

She put her arm through Lady Caroline's and neatly sepa-rated her from the earl. "My dear, Miles has told me that you are well-acquainted with the other gentlemen, so I know that you will not take it amiss that I should ask you to take Marie under your wing and not allow her to be teased too unmerci-fully. Poor girl, she is quite bewildered to be surrounded by so many smart London gentlemen."

As she was borne off, Lady Caroline cast a helpless glance back at Lord Trilby. The earl shook his head and lifted his shoulders in the smallest of shrugs, as though to express his own powerlessness over the proceedings.

As it chanced, Fräulein Gutenberg did not appear at all at sea. She was smiling at something Viscount Weemswood had said, and her quiet amusement simply appeared to deepen when the Grandduchess of Schaffenzeits brought Lady Caro-line up to her and reiterated the opinion that Lady Caroline could be of some use to her.

"Of course, madam. I will be glad to share my present ad-mirers with Lady Caroline, if that is what my lady desires," the Fräulein said.

Lady Caroline chose to ignore the faint derision in her voice. She exchanged nods with the viscount, saying lightly,

"I should not wish to arouse your ill-favor, Fräulein. I am content enough merely to greet my acquaintances." She shook hands with Viscount Weemswood. "How are you, Sinjin?"

The viscount shrugged in a negligent fashion. "I am as always, my lady."

"Oh, dear, as bad as that?" Lady Caroline asked, deadpan. Her small joke was received with chuckles by the gentlemen gathered about.

The Fräulein rose and lightly touched the viscount's sleeve. "My lord, I am desirous of a small glass of wine. Will you escort me, please?"

Viscount Weemswood smiled, his sardonic eyes reflecting his amusement at the subtle vying between the ladies. He glanced at Lady Caroline as he said, "Of course, Fräulein. It will be my pleasure." Murmuring polite excuses, he and Fräulein Gutenberg strolled off in the direction of the decanters on the occasional table.

"Well, I like that! Sinjin knows I have been trying this past quarter-hour to induce Fräulein Gutenberg to go in to dinner with me, and off he goes with her without a single by-your-leave," Mr. Underwood said. There was an underlying note of seriousness in his flippant tone that was underscored by the way his eyes followed the handsome couple.

"Have you been bitten again, then, Carey?" Lady Caroline asked with a sympathetic smile. She held out her hand. "Other than that, how are you keeping yourself, sir?" To her surprise, rather than shaking her hand in his usual friendly manner, Mr. Underwood made a formal bow to her. Awkwardly her hand dropped to her side.

"I am very well, thank you, my lady," he said.

Lady Caroline's bewildered gaze crossed to Lord Heatherton. His lordship cleared his throat. "You mustn't mind Carey, my lady. It is the worst case yet, you see. He is all about in the head over the Fräulein." His lordship was uncharacteristically fiddling with the fob that hung from a black ribbon around his neck. Lady Caroline's gaze dropped momentarily to the nervous movement, then rose again to meet Lord Heatherton's anxious expression.

"Oh, then, everything is made perfectly clear," she said lightly, disguising the hurt she felt.

Mr. Underwood smiled fleetingly. He would not quite meet Lady Caroline's eyes as he excused himself, saying that he was desirous of becoming better acquainted with Lady Eddington.

Mrs. Burlington appeared abruptly at Lady Caroline's side. She demanded in a low sharp voice, "Why did you not tell me about Fräulein Gutenberg?"

"I did do so, Amaris."

"You never told me that . . ." Mrs. Burlington relowered her voice. "You must beware, niece. The Fräulein watches the earl with a peculiarly predatory gaze."

Lord Hathaway came up. He greeted Mrs. Burlington and exchanged bows with Lord Heatherton before he turned to Lady Caroline. "Lady Caroline, I hope to be allowed to escort you in to dinner."

"Oh! But . . ." Lady Caroline had little desire to be partnered by Lord Hathaway, and glanced around to catch Lord Heatherton's eye. But that gentleman was bowing to Mrs. Burlington as he gravely requested the honor of taking her in to dinner.

The rest of the company was already forming up couples, Lady Caroline realized. Her brother had bravely solicited the Grandduchess of Schaffenzeits' hand, which had earned for him that lady's most gracious nod. Lady Eddington had risen to place her fingers on the Earl of Walmesley's elbow, and

Fräulein Gutenberg had bestowed her favor upon Viscount Weemswood. Mr. Underwood had been neatly cut out, and he was obviously of no mind to come to Lady Caroline's rescue.

Lady Caroline turned back to Lord Hathaway, her smile keeping well hidden the hurt she felt at the inexplicable desertion of her friends. "I shall be delighted, Lord Hathaway."

For Lady Caroline, the evening was suddenly interminable. Wrapped in her own thoughts, she paid but half an ear to Lord Hathaway's monotonous conversation. She did not realize that he was attempting to justify himself to her yet again, but merely felt his unending monologue to be much in the same class as the irritation of a persistent fly.

Momentarily emerging from her thoughts, she said impatiently, "Yes, yes, my lord."

She would have been appalled if she had been told that she had agreed to reconsider him as her most devoted admirer.

Lord Hathaway felt that Lady Caroline's response lacked some measure of enthusiasm, but after a moment's reflection he was persuaded to the notion that more could not be expected of a lady of proud and whimsical character. Thereafter he was content enough to abandon polite conversation and fully enjoy the several excellent dishes served up by the Walmesley cook.

As for Lady Caroline, she had little appetite and merely picked at her plate. Her mind was wholly absorbed by the horrid and growing suspicion that something had gone very wrong with the Earl of Walmesley's little plot.

She had greeted the gentlemen who were known to her with the familiarity of an old acquaintance. Viscount Weemswood was as he had always been, but she had been surprised and made uneasy by the odd reserve she felt in Mr. Underwood's and Lord Heatherton's manner toward her.

Lady Caroline could not shake the dread feeling that worse was yet to come of the evening.

26

Dinner was concluded and coffee was being served in the drawing room when Lady Caroline succeeded in buttonholing Lord Heatherton. "Nana, I wish to know what is wrong. Why have I become of a sudden such a pariah?"

Lord Heatherton gave a warning shake of his head. He glanced meaningfully around the crowded room as he said, "Miles wouldn't like it if I were to say anything, my lady, especially in light of the wager. No, nor would I, if it comes to that. I have too much respect for you to do so, Lady Caroline." He bowed and hastily retreated, feeling that even by association he might say more than he thought.

Lady Caroline allowed Lord Heatherton to go. She felt quite ill.

A wager!

Slowly her eyes roved the room, her glance touching on the grandduchess, Mrs. Burlington, Lord Heatherton, Mr. Underwood and Viscount Weemswood. However it had happened, they had all in one fashion or another been made privy to the false engagement.

That alone was scarcely to be borne, but to discover that some sort of wager rested upon it was not to be endured.

Lady Caroline's stricken eyes fastened at last on the Earl of Walmesley. His head was tilted attentively as he conversed with Lord and Lady Eddington, and he appeared oblivious of all but enjoyment of the gathering.

Her fingers clenched of their own volition.

Without giving a thought to how it might be construed, Lady Caroline swept down on the trio and requested a private word with the earl.

Lord Eddington looked at his sister in troubled astonishment. Her eyes were dark with emotion, while her breast rose and fell in witness to some distress. "Caroline?"

She spared her brother a scarce glance. "It is quite all right, Ned. I merely have a matter that I wish to discuss privately with Lord Trilby."

Lord Trilby regarded Lady Caroline with equal surprise. "Of course, my lady." He excused himself to Lord and Lady Eddington and drew Lady Caroline with him.

Lord Eddington frowned after them. Lady Eddington, always quick to discern his lordship's moods, shook her head at him. "You must not perturb yourself, my lord. I am quite certain that whatever has transpired will quickly be found to be of little moment." He glanced down, his expression at once lightening, and agreed.

Lord Trilby showed Lady Caroline into a small sitting room near the drawing room. He closed the door quietly and crossed over to her as she turned to face him.

"My dear Caro, you are trembling. What has happened?" he asked, beginning to feel alarm.

The earl attempted to catch her hands.

She warded him off, stepping back a pace. "Do not 'dear Caro' me! I am so furious and humiliated that I can scarcely speak! How could you, Miles? How *could* you tell your friends, and mine, about this stupid masquerade? And then, having done so, you thought so little of me that you wa-wagered on the outcome!"

"How the devil did you hear of that?" Lord Trilby saw from the flash of her eyes that that was not the most salutary opening and he said hastily, "Never mind that now. Caro, you must believe me. I had no choice but to confide in the others. The wager simply cropped up. Believe me, it has nothing to do with you."

"Nothing to do . . . ! Forgive me, my lord, but I cannot conceive how it might be otherwise."

Lord Trilby shook his head. "Caroline, please listen for one moment. The wager was put to me that within a fortnight my great-aunt would discover that our understanding was a hoax. Of course I disagreed. Can you not see? It in no wise reflects upon you."

Her eyes glittering, Lady Caroline snapped her fingers at him. "*That* for your protestation, my lord!" She gave a furious laugh. "Lord, what an utter fool I have allowed you to make of us. A wager! When I imagine what Carey and Sinjin and, yes, even dear sweet Nana, must think of me, I am quite sunk with mortification."

Lord Trilby held fast to his composure. "You must see that I had to take them into my confidence, Caro. It was imperative that they be forewarned. I could not chance an inadvertent word from Mrs. Burlington."

"Why did you not consult with me, my lord? *I* had persuaded my aunt to say nothing!"

Her outraged words left silence in their wake.

Lord Trilby and Lady Caroline stared at one another.

Suddenly the earl laughed. "Oh, Caro! The shifts to which we have been put."

Lady Caroline's eyes still glittered, but now with tears. "I do not think it in the least amusing." She turned away hurriedly.

Lord Trilby sobered instantly, at once regretting his ill-timed sense of irony. "No. No, of course it is not." He gently placed his hands on the outside of her shoulders and was not surprised when he felt her stiffen. "My apologies, Caroline. I should never have asked it of you."

His voice was curiously tender.

He knew her so very well, and yet in some ways not at all. Since they had embarked upon this mad plot, he had several times thought he caught sight of a certain expression in her eyes. When he had glanced at her more fully, the expression had vanished or, if it had even existed, seemed to have been but a trick of the light.

Through her fury and her misery, Lady Caroline felt her traitorous heart bump uncomfortably against her ribs. She said with feeling, "Damn your eyes, Miles."

He tightened his fingers briefly, then forced his hands to drop away. It was perhaps one of the most difficult things he had ever required of himself. "I should return to the drawing room before anyone begins to wonder at our continued absence."

He hesitated. "Will you be quite all right alone, my lady?"

A hollow laugh came from her. She did not turn around to look at him. Her voice carried an uncharacteristic bitter note. "Of course I shall. How could it be otherwise?"

It was an odd thing for her to say. There was something just beneath the surface of her words that he intuitively sensed.

Again Lord Trilby hesitated.

As he looked down on her bowed head, he felt the most extraordinary compulsion to gather her up into his arms and kiss her thoroughly.

Suppressing the impulse ruthlessly, afraid that if he remained he would do something that he would later regret, he turned quickly and exited the sitting room.

With a sigh, Caroline sank down into a chair.

She was staring meditatively into the fire when the door to the sitting room opened. She turned her head quickly, thinking that the earl had returned. She was dismayed when she met Fräulein Gutenberg's contemplative gaze.

"Fräulein! You startled me. I am sorry, were you seeking a bit of privacy? I . . . I was on the point of leaving." Lady Caroline had risen to her feet as she spoke, and now she moved toward the door.

"No. Stay a moment, Lady Caroline. I came in to speak with you," Fräulein Gutenberg said. She closed the door. Walking gracefully to a chair and sinking into it, she gestured for Lady Caroline to resume her own seat.

Lady Caroline remained standing, regarding the Fräulein with puzzled surprise. "I do not understand."

"Please, Lady Caroline. Pray be seated."

Reluctantly Lady Caroline did as she was bidden. She was curious despite her wariness. Fräulein Gutenberg had deigned to take only as much notice of her as she had been compelled to by circumstances, yet now the Fräulein had actually sought her out. "Very well, Fräulein. What is it you wish to say to me?"

Fräulein Gutenberg glanced at the flames, and back at Lady Caroline. "You do not care overmuch for me, my lady, nor I for you. So it always is when two beautiful women become rivals over the gentlemen." She paused a heartbeat. "I shall marry one of your Englishmen, my lady. I shall marry Lord Trilby if I so desire. That is what I wish to say to you, my lady."

"You saw that I left the drawing room in the earl's company and you followed us. Your jealousy ill becomes you, Fräulein," Lady Caroline said evenly. She started to rise from the chair.

"The understanding that lies between you and his lordship is not of importance to me, Lady Caroline."

Lady Caroline stared in consternation at the Fräulein's

calm expression. Slowly she sank back onto the chair. "How knew you of that, Fräulein?" A flush rose to her face. "Perhaps from the grandduchess?"

Fräulein Gutenberg gave a low amused laugh. "Madam confides in me only what she wishes me to know, my lady. I do not think that particular piece of information was meant for my ears. No, your good aunt was very kind and quite sympathetic of my position." She laughed again. "Mrs. Burlington does not wish me to harbor false hopes over Lord Trilby."

"Amaris," Lady Caroline breathed, recalling how her aunt had warned her earlier against the Fräulein. She had not paid particular attention, and now wished bitterly that she had.

The corners of Fräulein Gutenberg's mouth lifted in another lovely smile. "Pray do not think too harshly of Mrs. Burlington, Lady Caroline. She, at least, has your interests at heart. I have only myself to rely upon."

Lady Caroline's anger was checked by the curious inflection in the Fräulein's voice. "But you have a formidable sponsor in the Grandduchess of Schaffenzeits, surely?"

The Fräulein lifted slim shoulders. "For the moment, perhaps, it suits her grace to take an interest in me. The grandduchess's sponsorship is very like a child's sand castle. It appears strong and solid, but the wind and the waves always make quick work of it in the end. No, I am not so foolish as to play my future blindly into the grandduchess's hands. I shall marry one of your Englishmen instead."

"But do you not care, then, whom you wed?" Lady Caroline asked, fascinated despite herself.

Again came the lift of the Fräulein's shoulders. "One man is much like any other. Two arms, two legs. Any significant difference is determined by the depth of his pocketbook."

"My word, I have never heard such a cold-blooded thing,"

Lady Caroline said, repelled. "Have you never taken into account love or even simple liking? I cannot imagine the sort of match you contemplate, Fräulein."

"Can you not? Then I shall tell you how to imagine it, my lady. Imagine that you are the fifth of twelve daughters. Imagine that you have observed how each of your elder sisters has chosen her husband, not by birth alone, nor by wealth, nor again by this love you speak of. Instead, each has chosen out of necessity to contract a marriage that will weld strong political ties for her family."

Fräulein Gutenberg gestured with her slender hand. "It is an illustrious family, to be sure, but one impoverished and in exile, its survival dependent upon the whims of those in power. Now the family is politically secure, but still the remaining daughters are urged to barter themselves, and in return they will receive the discontent that became their sisters' lot."

After a moment Lady Caroline gestured eloquently. "I am sorry, Fräulein. I did not realize."

"Do not pity me, Lady Caroline, for I am the fortunate one. The Grandduchess of Schaffenzeits has made possible my escape. I shall not return to be displayed like a freshly trimmed joint of beef to the innumerable petty princes of St. Petersburg. I shall marry an Englishman, one wealthy enough to provide me with all that I could ever desire."

At last there was a passionate note in Fräulein Gutenberg's voice, and in the firelight her eyes flashed with the radiance of jewels. Lady Caroline regarded her in amazement.

The Fräulein abruptly became aware of her wide-eyed scrutiny, for she caught herself up, and the mask of calm indifference once more shadowed her beautiful face.

"I shall marry an Englishman, Lady Caroline, and it may

well be that my choice shall fall upon Lord Trilby."

Without another word, Fräulein Gutenberg rose from her chair, walked to the door, and let herself out.

Lady Caroline stared after the young woman, feeling more pity than she would ever have believed possible for the woman who had declared that she intended to marry the Earl of Walmesley.

When the horrid evening had at last come to an end and Lady Caroline was able to take her leave with the rest of her party, she discovered that the phantom headache that she had suggested to her aunt had become a pounding reality. Her discomfort was not eased in the least by the sharp and garrulous discourse that Mrs. Burlington sustained the whole of the drive back to Berwicke Keep. Upon entering the house, Lady Caroline excused herself immediately, pleading the headache and fatigue, and retired to her bed.

27

Lady Caroline woke late the next morning, heavy-eyed and with a sore throat. She rose listlessly and suffered her maid to attend her before she went downstairs to the breakfast room.

Mrs. Burlington, breakfasting in company with Lord and Lady Eddington, said, "Well! It appears that you do not always rise with the cock's-crow, Lady Caroline. But far be it from me to point out the disregard you have shown toward his lordship and Lady Eddington on their first morning home," Mrs. Burlington said waspishly.

Lady Caroline sighed wearily. "I can only assume that you suffered an indifferent night, Amaris. It is the only fitting explanation I can imagine for your spleen." She ignored her aunt's angry intake of breath. "Good morning, Ned, Lady Eddington. I trust that you at least spent a restful night."

Lord Eddington glanced up briefly from his plate to nod at his sister. "A vastly better night than you did, from all signs. You look ghastly, Caroline."

Lady Caroline gave the ghost of a laugh. "Why, thank you! I did not expect such gallantry so early in the day, I must say. Yes, Simpson. Tea will be all, thank you."

Lord Eddington looked up, startled. "What is toward, Caroline? Why, I cannot recall the last time you turned down breakfast. Surely you must wish to have a few of these excellent kidneys and biscuits, or perhaps some toast and marmalade. Here, I shall spread it for you myself."

Lady Caroline suppressed a slight shudder. "No, nothing else, truly."

"Perhaps our dear Lady Caroline has resolved to cultivate a daintier appetite," Mrs. Burlington said acidly.

Lady Eddington had quietly observed the interchange, and now she reached over to place a hand on her sister-in-law's wrist. "My dear Lady Caroline, I hesitate to intrude on your privacy, but you do not appear at all well. Are you certain that you would not prefer taking your tea in your room and resting for a short time? I am sure that none of us would think the less of your courtesy." Her glance flickered in Mrs. Burlington's direction, and that lady, on the point of making another acid observation, felt unusually constrained to hold her tongue.

To her surprise, Lady Caroline felt relief at the gentle suggestion. It was true that she did not feel the least like being in company. The headache had persisted to nag her even after she had awoken, and she felt inordinately tired and melancholy.

She contributed it to the fretful sleep that she had endured, interrupted, as it was, several times as she tossed on her pillow, quite unable to still her unhappy reflections. She could not imagine how she would ever be able to greet her friends again without wondering what thoughts might be going through their heads about her scandalous behavior.

"Perhaps I should do exactly that, Lady Eddington. I am feeling rather pulled this morning," Lady Caroline said.

"Then you must not give us another thought. We shall do very well without you, you know. I have it in mind to trespass upon Mrs. Burlington's good nature and request her to show me about Berwicke this morning," Lady Eddington said.

"Of course, Lady Eddington! I would be most pleased to do so," Mrs. Burlington exclaimed, delighted.

Lord Eddington appeared startled at the proposed itinerary. He cleared his throat diffidently. "If you should not mind it, my love, I think that I shall spend a little time with my bailiff. My sister has urged me to acquaint myself with the workings of the estate, and I may as well make a start of it, do you not think?"

While Lady Caroline stared, astonished, at her brother, Lady Eddington bestowed a warm smile on his lordship. "I know you will do just as you ought, my lord."

Lord Eddington straightened his shoulders, basking in his wife's approval. "Well, I do think it just the thing to while away a few hours."

As it turned out, Lady Caroline's slight indisposition developed into a light bout of influenza that kept her abed for several days. She therefore missed the morning calls paid by Lord Trilby and the granduchess. Lord Hathaway came faithfully each day to ask after her, and when Lady Caroline heard it, she could not but be grateful that she had a valid excuse not to be compelled to endure his company.

The second day after Lady Caroline returned downstairs, Fräulein Gutenberg came to tea at Berwicke. She made the granduchess's excuses, saying that her grace had declined Lady Eddington's kind invitation because she had taken a chill and did not wish to expose herself to the cold.

"I know I must not expect any of the gentlemen, for Lord Eddington informed me this morning that he had been invited to go hunting at Walmesley," Lady Eddington said on a laugh.

"Viscount Weemswood may yet surprise us with his presence, my lady, for I understood that he meant to consult with a wheelwright about the repairs of his phaeton instead. Surely that will not take the remainder of the afternoon," Fräulein Gutenberg said.

"I would not be too certain," Lady Caroline said humorously. "The viscount is a perfectionist when it comes to his sporting vehicles. He will not be easily satisfied."

"Then it will be a cozy tea indeed, with just the four of us," Lady Eddington said.

Tea was poured and the biscuits had been passed around before Fräulein Gutenberg referred again to the gentlemen. "I find the manners of the English a little different from what I was used to in St. Petersburg, and in particular those of English gentlemen," she said.

"Oh? In what way, Fräulein?" Lady Caroline asked.

Fräulein Gutenberg shrugged slightly. "The Russian princes are very boastful. They will tell you about everything they own, their accomplishments, their physical prowess."

"Yes, I suppose our English gentlemen are more reticent. However, I do think that you shall hear a great deal of boasting of physical prowess this evening when the results of the day's hunting are served up for dinner," Lady Caroline said.

"My lord Eddington will certainly entertain me with a minutely detailed description of his outing today," Lady Eddington agreed.

"I suspect that gentlemen are much alike everywhere, dear Fräulein. They like to tell us what they wish us to hear, which may or may not be the whole truth, and leave it to us to make what we will of it all," Mrs. Burlington said. She threw a malicious glance at her niece. "That is why young ladies should allow themselves to be guided by the counsel of those wiser and perhaps better informed than themselves, for that is how the best possible matches are contracted."

"True enough, Amaris, but I believe the young lady in question should have some opinion in the matter," Lady Caroline said amiably, not to be drawn into a discussion of her personal history. "Would you not agree, Lady Eddington?"

"Oh, yes. But it is not always possible, as it is dependent upon one's circumstances. I was very fortunate. I developed a decided partiality for Lord Eddington quite apart from the advantages of his lordship's birth or material possessions," Lady Eddington said. "There were other suitors, of course, but none I liked quite so well or who proved quite so eligible in my father's eyes."

"That is what has me in a puzzle, Lady Eddington. How does one discern the wheat from the chaff, for very nearly any gentleman may represent himself well," Fräulein Gutenberg said. "For instance, if I had not met the Earl of Walmesley or his friends under the Grandduchess of Schaffenzeits' patronage, I should not have been so completely certain of their characters." She raised her shoulders in an eloquent shrug.

"Oh, *well!* Even when one meets a gentleman under the auspices of a trusted acquaintance, one cannot always be certain of that gentleman's personal circumstances," Mrs. Burlington said. "Of course, I do not speak specifically of the earl's friends, you must understand, but even they have their crosses. Viscount Weemswood is the perfect example. He was heir apparent to a dukedom and quite squandered on his expectations, from what I have heard. Now the old duke is remarried and his younger wife is in expectation of producing a new heir. Quite shocking, of course."

"Amaris, I daresay that the viscount would not care to have his private affairs quite so well-aired," Lady Caroline said quietly, though with pointed authority.

Mrs. Burlington was offended at the rebuke, but she attempted to cover it with a titter. "Lord, my dear, I do not forget that you count the viscount one of your bosom bows, just as you do Mr. Underwood and Lord Heatherton.

Though how one may be friends with a libertine is beyond me, I am sure!"

"Lord Heatherton is a libertine?" Fräulein Gutenberg asked with such palpable amazement that the other ladies laughed.

"Oh, no, *not* Lord Heatherton," Lady Eddington tactfully left unvoiced the obvious conclusion to be drawn about Mr. Underwood. "I have the acquaintance of his lordship's mother, who is a very good friend of my stepmother's. I doubt very much that Lord Heatherton would dare go counter to anything *she* may frown upon."

"Lord Heatherton is a dear, but perhaps he does stand a trifle too in awe of his mother," Lady Caroline conceded.

"A regular cat's-paw!" Mrs. Burlington exclaimed scornfully. "I doubt that his lordship will ever pluck up the necessary courage to take proper control of his own interests. Not but what that gorgon is quite enough to cow the stoutest of hearts!"

"Why, Amaris, one would suppose that you do not yourself care overmuch for the lady," Lady Caroline said, putting up her brows.

"I had the misfortune to share the same coming-out Season with that female. I have always suspected that once she latched on to the earlier Lord Heatherton she positively bullied him to the altar," Mrs. Burlington said.

Lady Eddington glanced at her guest's polite expression. "I fear none of this can be of much interest to Fräulein Gutenberg. Nothing is more boring than to be obliged to listen courteously to old gossip, isn't that so? Do let us talk of something else. Perhaps we may put our heads together and agree on a date for another dinner party, this time to be hosted by Berwicke. I did so enjoy the last."

Lady Caroline, taking note of the almost indiscernible

flicker of disappointment in Fräulein Gutenberg's eyes, was certain that the lady had been far more interested than Lady Eddington had assumed. However, she herself was more than willing to follow the countess's lead, for she had not felt comfortable while Mrs. Burlington gossiped so disparagingly of the gentlemen.

Soon afterward, Fräulein Gutenberg rose to take her leave. She remarked that it had been a most entertaining tea and she promised to carry word back to Walmesley of the informal soiree that was to be held at Berwicke Keep.

Lady Caroline chose to ride over to Walmesley the following day.

When she arrived she was astonished to see a familiar high-bred team being backed into the traces of a sporting phaeton. She deduced instantly that the phaeton was being readied for travel. Accepting the assistance of a groom to descend from her mount, she tossed the man the reins and entered Walmesley's open door.

She discovered Lord Heatherton in the entry hall, engaged in pulling on his gloves. "Nana, never tell me that you are leaving!"

Lord Heatherton greeted her with one of his usual open smiles. "Lady Caroline! I had hoped to see you before we left. I was meaning to have Sinjin drive over to Berwicke before we returned to town, for I wished to convey my apologies. I have been fretting this age that I offended you over that little matter we talked of the other evening."

Lady Caroline laughed and shook her head. She felt a rush of glad relief. Tucking her gloved hand into his elbow, she said, "I do not regard it in the least, I assure you. Now, you must tell me why you and my two other friends have decided to abandon the neighborhood so suddenly, for I must have a plausible excuse to convey to Lady Eddington."

"The soiree, of course!" Lord Heatherton frowned, as though weighing something in his mind. "Come into the drawing room a moment, my lady. I think it best if we are not overheard."

Lady Caroline accompanied his lordship, wondering and curious. When Lord Heatherton closed the door, she said lightly, "Now I am certain that you have a secret to tell, my lord."

"As it chances, I have. But it is not altogether mine, so you must not tout it about," Lord Heatherton said.

Lady Caroline instantly sobered. "Why, Nana, what is it about?"

"The thing of it is, you shall have to contrive an excuse for us to Lady Eddington, for the truth would never do," Lord Heatherton said. "We are returning to town because Carey has suffered a severe reverse. None of us quite realized how besotted he had become with Fräulein Gutenberg, more's the pity. Well, you know yourself how Carey is forever sighing over a pretty face."

"Indeed I do. He tumbles in and out of love as many times as some gentlemen put on their boots," Lady Caroline quipped.

Lord Heatherton nodded, taking the joke in a serious vein. "Aye, but this time he proposed to the lady in question."

Lady Caroline's mouth dropped open. "I do not believe it!"

"I do not wonder at your astonishment, my lady, for I felt the same. In any event, poor Carey was fairly certain that he had begun to fix his interest with the Fräulein. Well, anyone could see that she was beginning to thaw toward him after the dinner party," Lord Heatherton said. He shook his head. "It was deuced odd. Yesterday, when Carey offered for the Fräulein's hand, she told him that she would never consider his suit. Yet not four hours previously he had hinted to me that the Fräulein had freely bestowed upon him a kiss."

Lady Caroline did not reveal to Lord Heatherton her own unpleasant conclusion. She remembered quite clearly that during the afternoon tea Fräulein Gutenberg had steered the conversation onto the subject of English gentlemen. She had wondered at the time that the Fräulein seemed inordinately interested in Mrs. Burlington's somewhat malicious recounting of gossip regarding Lord Trilby's friends, but she had never expected this result.

"It is a pity, indeed. One must feel for poor Carey," she said quietly.

Lord Heatherton nodded sadly. "Aye, but I cannot but wonder whether fate took a hand in it, for Carey has dealt often enough in that same coin. In any event, Lady Caroline, you must see that the truth would not do for Lady Eddington."

"Pray do not be anxious over that point, Nana. I shall say all that is necessary," Lady Caroline said.

There was an impatient shout from somewhere outside the drawing room. "That will be Sinjin. He is in the devil of a mood; no one knows why. Between the pair of them, I shall have a jolly time of it," Lord Heatherton predicted morosely.

Lady Caroline and Lord Heatherton emerged from the drawing room. The viscount stood in the entry hall, slapping his gathered whip against his thigh. The ferocious scowl on his face lessened when his eyes fell on Lord Heatherton. "There you are. Carey is waiting for us." He glanced at Lady Caroline and abruptly smiled. "It has been a damnable visit, but still I am glad to have seen you again, Lady Caroline. You are not in London nearly often enough to leaven the dull functions one is forced to endure."

Lady Caroline laughed and shook hands with him. "Be off with you, Sinjin."

She walked outside with the gentlemen, to discover Lord Trilby conversing with Mr. Underwood next to the phaeton. "My lord, Mr. Underwood. I rode over to confirm the date of the soiree for three days hence, only to discover that our company will be sadly depleted."

Mr. Underwood smiled. There was a look of strain about his eyes and mouth, but none of his previous reserve toward her. "Pray convey my apologies to Lady Eddington. Unavoidable obligations carry me back to London."

"Of course, Carey," Lady Caroline said quietly.

The gentlemen climbed up into the phaeton, again said their good-byes, and then they were off. Lord Trilby and Lady Caroline stood looking after them until the carriage had bowled around the curve and was lost to sight.

"Will you come in for a few minutes, my lady?" Lord Trilby asked.

Lady Caroline heard the entreaty in his lordship's voice. She was not immune to his appeal, and that was what made up her mind. "I think not. I left Lady Eddington with my aunt, who has for several days now taken it upon herself to educate her into her duties as mistress of Berwicke. Lady Eddington cast me a rather wild look as I set out, and I suspect that by now she will be in dire need of rescue," she said with a laugh. She nodded to the waiting groom that she was ready to mount.

The earl waved aside the man and himself tossed her into the saddle. Silently he adjusted the stirrup for her, his hands lingering a little. Then he stepped back a pace, still without having said a word.

Upon meeting his gaze, Lady Caroline rather breathlessly said good-bye and rode away.

28

The soiree at Berwicke Keep threatened to fall sadly flat owing in large part to the departure of the London gentlemen. Lord Eddington remarked regretfully if somewhat tactlessly that he would have enjoyed a few rousing hands of cards played for more than chicken stakes.

The Grandduchess Wilhelmina Hildebrande contemplated the gathering with jaundiced eyes, somewhat in sympathy with Lord Eddington's view. She found the maneuverings of her grandnephew and Lady Caroline particularly tedious. Lady Caroline had allowed her attention to be dominated by Lord Hathaway all the evening, while Lord Trilby pursued conversation with Fräulein Gutenberg. The earl betrayed himself several times, however, by allowing his eyes to stray in Lady Caroline's direction. The grandduchess thought it time to give her grandnephew a determined path.

Lifting her guttural voice, she made an abrupt announcement. "I shall shortly be leaving England." She raised a commanding hand to still the astonished murmurs. "However, I shall carry with me the glad knowledge of my grandnephew's engagement to Lady Caroline Eddington." She smiled knowingly at the sudden stillness that fell over the Earl of Walmesley's expression.

Lord Eddington whooped. He shook hands with Lord Trilby and kissed his sister fondly. "This is glad news indeed! I have always known you and Trilby here would make a match of it."

Lady Eddington pressed Lady Caroline's fingers and said softly in her ear, "I am very glad that you shall not be living too far away for me to call on you, Lady Caroline."

Mrs. Burlington was in high alt. "I have hoped for this happy event for far longer than I wish to recall! Berwicke Keep shall miss you, dear niece, but I assure you that all will be kept just as you like it."

Lady Caroline met Lady Eddington's twinkling eyes. "I am certain that will be so, Amaris."

Of the company, only two greeted the announcement with less than enthusiasm. Fräulein Gutenberg exchanged a long look with the Grandduchess of Schaffenzeits. There was nothing to read in the grandduchess's expression but a faint amusement. Fräulein Gutenberg's gaze dropped to her rigidly clasped hands, but she said not a word.

Lord Hathaway was not so retiring. His mind grappled with the enormity of what he had heard, for he had been confident that it was he who would carry the day with Lady Caroline. "Lady Caroline affianced? To the Earl of Walmesley?" He seemed to choke on the words.

As he dropped heavily into a chair, his expression was seen to be stricken and his reaction served to subdue the glad expressions of most of the others. Mrs. Burlington, however, uttered only an exclamation of impatience. She did not care what gentleman had at last succeeded in capturing her niece's hand. The fact of it was good enough for her.

Lady Caroline had the grace to feel compassion for Lord Hathaway. She had attempted to discourage his lordship for months, but he had not taken her rejections as serious. He had instead continued to insist that she must one day come to her senses and accept his suit.

Though Lord Hathaway had often tried her patience and

on one occasion subjected her to humiliation, she could yet feel sorry for him.

Lord Trilby was silent. He, too, recognized Lord Hathaway's pitiful disorientation, but he was not inclined to commiserate with the gentleman.

As for the grandduchess, she had no patience for fools. This obtuse and arrogant English lord reminded her in part of those of her retainers for whom she reserved contempt. Her glance was therefore pitiless. "That is correct, my lord. It has been known to me for some months, but I withheld my approval until such time as I could meet and judge Lady Caroline for myself. I am happy to say that all my reservations are at an end. I am honored to welcome Lady Caroline as my grandniece." She turned her shoulder on the shattered Lord Hathaway and thereafter ignored him.

Fräulein Gutenberg for the first time revealed emotion. She stared at the Grandduchess of Schaffenzeits as though what she had heard was unbelievable. And so it was, if true, for it meant the entire journey to England had been made on the grandduchess's empty promises.

The grandduchess looked up suddenly, as though aware that she was under scrutiny, and her eyes met the Fräulein's. Suddenly, in the moment before the grandduchess's gaze drifted away, Fräulein Gutenberg looked as if she could feel her advantage slipping away from beneath her like so much sand.

The Fräulein's gaze traveled to the affianced couple. Lady Caroline blushed at something said by Lord Trilby, and a shudder went through the Fräulein, for it was horribly apparent she had rejected an honorable proposal for her hand in favor of the nonexistent chance to become the Earl of Walmesley's bride.

Fräulein Gutenberg's eyes sought Lord Hathaway. For a

long time she unblinkingly regarded his lordship's downcast countenance, while about her the conversation advanced.

"I am well-pleased, Miles. You have at last done as I have instructed. You will now be so good as to enter with me into plans for the wedding. It must be in the spring, naturally. This dreary English winter is not the proper time for a wedding. I shudder to think of it."

"Lady Caroline and I shall address the question of the date in good time," Lord Trilby said easily, but with a hint of steel.

The Grandduchess Wilhelmina Hildebrande stared levelly at her grandnephew. Apparently what she saw satisfied her, for she abruptly nodded. "Good, good. For now, it is enough."

Lady Caroline cast another glance in Lord Hathaway's direction. He seemed to have regained some of his color, but there was still a bewildered look in his eyes.

She had never believed that Lord Hathaway was the least bit in love with her. He had never averred that he was, and certainly, with that one extraordinary exception, his dealings with her had not been in the least loverlike. Yet now, witnessing Lord Hathaway's devastation, she could not but wonder if he had indeed harbored the smallest *tendre* for her.

Lord Hathaway seemed quite unable to pull himself together. Lady Caroline knew that she could not very well offer words that might ease his troubled countenance. It would be unwise to do so, as well as lacking in sensibility. She was the cause of his lordship's distress, after all. Still, she hated to see his lordship sunk so low. Lord Hathaway needed to be distracted, she thought.

Lady Caroline's gaze fell on Fräulein Gutenberg's smooth countenance. As always, the young woman's polite expression revealed only the mildest interest in what was taking place about her. Knowing what she did now about the Fräulein, Lady Caroline wondered what thoughts were hidden behind those beautiful veiled eyes. On the instant, she decided upon what in other circumstances she would have thought to be a reprehensible suggestion.

As coffee was brought in, Lady Caroline seized the opportunity to drift over toward Fräulein Gutenberg. Quietly she said, "Fräulein, I hope that I may rely upon you for a small favor. Lord Hathaway has suffered something of a shock, I think. Perhaps—if you would not mind it—you could speak to him and attempt to give his thoughts a new direction?" Their eyes met and a long unspoken conversation passed between them.

Fräulein Gutenberg gazed at Lady Caroline calmly for a moment longer. Then the young lady's eyes turned in Lord Hathaway's direction. "Certainly, if that is your wish, my lady." She rose from her place, made a formal bow to Lady Caroline, and glided over to seat herself beside Lord Hathaway.

In a very few minutes' time Lord Hathaway appeared to be reviving. It was from the Fräulein's hands that he accepted a cup of coffee, sweetened exactly to his taste.

Lady Caroline watched these encouraging signs with satisfaction, and was startled when she felt warm breath on her ear. She turned quickly. "My lord!"

"Tossing the Fräulein into the breach, are you, Caro? Are you perhaps hoping to make a match of it?" Lord Trilby's voice was low and teasing.

Lady Caroline opened her eyes wide. "Why, no, my lord. Whatever would give you such an odd opinion of my character?" When he but smiled, she said, "It is not such a bad notion, you know. They would deal extremely well together. He is such a worthy, and would treat her with a most tiresome respect, while she is perfectly willing to be coddled for the remainder of her days."

"You have at least provided the Worthy with a way to salvage his pride," Lord Trilby said dryly.

"It is true, his lordship has appeared incapable of meeting my gaze. I suspect that he would gladly forgo addressing me for the remainder of the evening," Lady Caroline said.

"Awkward, indeed, since you are to receive the felicitations of this little gathering," Lord Trilby agreed.

Lady Caroline flashed an appreciative glance up at him. "You are a wretched man."

The earl shrugged, not at all perturbed. "I am not greatly interested in Lord Hathaway one way or the other. In any event, Fräulein Gutenberg appears to be doing the job. Perhaps you may now turn your attention to one much more deserving of your sympathy," he suggested.

Lady Caroline did turn toward him then. She cocked her head to regard him with twinkling eyes. "Indeed, I do seem to detect a certain despondency in your carriage, my lord."

"Do not overlook the care that has been permanently worn into my countenance by this farrago," Lord Trilby said.

"No, indeed I do not! Why, one could believe that you have most recently scraped through a most unpleasant situation, only to become resigned to an ignoble fate," Lady Caroline said.

Lord Trilby laughed at that. He eyed Lady Caroline appreciatively. "That was unkind, Caro."

"Quite unkind," she agreed. "You shall trounce me for it, I daresay, but I think that, at least for now, I am safe enough." She gestured in the direction of the Grandduchess of Schaffenzeits. "Her grace has not yet said exactly when she means to leave England."

"Take care, my lady! You have become emboldened by what

you perceive as your security, but I shall come about, never fear, and teach you a proper respect," Lord Trilby promised.

Lady Caroline cast a glance up at him through an exaggerated flutter of her lashes. "Perceive that I am quaking in my boots, my lord."

"Are you indeed! A poor show you make of it, then." When Lady Caroline laughed, he said, "Come, my lady, make a clean breast of the thing. I have never succeeded in exciting the least emotion in you, have I?"

With one stroke, the props were knocked out from under her. Lady Caroline felt as though she had fallen off the front of the stage, but from long practice she retained hold of her smile.

"Oh, as to that! What can I say that would not insult or embarrass you, my lord? If I agree, surely your ego would be bruised to learn that you had not made an impression upon my stony and indifferent heart. If I disagree, and assure you that indeed my poor heart is sent tripping whenever you enter the room, then you must be horridly discomfited by such maudlin declarations. So you see, my lord, it is best never to delve too deeply for an honest opinion."

The earl laughed again, though there seemed to flicker in his eyes a disappointment. But it as swiftly vanished, and Lady Caroline was unsure that it had ever actually existed.

Her attention was claimed then by Lord Eddington, and she entered with relief into easy banter with her brother. Though it pained her when, after a few moments, Lord Trilby moved away, she was nevertheless glad of it.

"Caroline, are you quite the thing? You appear somewhat pale," Lord Eddington said.

"Do I? It is all the excitement, I suppose," Lady Caroline said. Her brother was satisfied, and finished his conversation with her.

When Lady Caroline slid a glance after Lord Trilby, she saw that the earl was paying gentle compliments to Lady Eddington and politely holding off Mrs. Burlington's attempts to commandeer his attention for herself.

Lady Caroline turned away and walked over to the grandduchess to inquire whether her grace would like to get up a game of whist. This suggestion was met with gracious approval, and Lady Caroline caused card tables to be set up for any who might be similarly inclined.

The Grandduchess of Schaffenzeits proved herself to be a shrewd and ruthless player, bringing cries of admiration from Lord Eddington, who was her partner, and petulant shrugs from Mrs. Burlington, who was enjoined by her grace to pay closer attention to her hand. The evening passed pleasantly enough in such activity and polite conversation.

It was noticed that Lord Hathaway and Fräulein Gutenberg spent an inordinate amount of time removed from everyone else, but nothing much was thought of it, since it was known both had suffered reverses where they had not expected to.

At the stroke of midnight the Grandduchess of Schaffenzeits proclaimed that she was ready to return to Walmesley and thence to her bed. It was counted a signal that the evening had come to an end. However, before the guests had the opportunity to begin gathering their wraps, Lord Hathaway portentously begged the attention of the company for an announcement he intended to make.

After glancing around to be certain that he had gained everyone's attention, Lord Hathaway blew out his cheeks in self-importance. "This evening I have the pleasure to make known to my neighbors and acquaintances that I have decided upon a lady-wife. Allow me to formally present my intended, Fräulein Gutenberg." Fräulein Gutenberg came to stand beside Lord Hathaway, placing her hand in his ready palm. In ceremonious formality, his lordship raised her hand to his lips.

The company was bound by universal astonishment. Fräulein Gutenberg sought and found Lady Caroline's eyes. She smiled faintly before turning her head to look up at her chosen Englishman.

The Grandduchess of Schaffenzeits gave a loud cackle, at which Lord Hathaway visibly bristled. When the grandduchess walked up to the newly affianced couple, she said, "My dear Lord Hathaway, I could not be more pleased. I consider you a most worthy suitor to my young protégée's hand." As Lord Hathaway reddened with surpised gratification, her grace turned her gaze on Fräulein Gutenberg. Amusement deepened her guttural accents. "Marie, my dear. You have more than fulfilled my expectations for you. I shall be glad to carry back news of your marriage to your dear family, who I know will be most pleased to learn of your new station in life."

"Thank you, madam. I should like to send letters by you to all my sisters," the Fräulein said.

The grandduchess cackled again and nodded. "Certainly, my dear. I expect they will be most interested in all you have to convey. Perhaps when I return to England for my grand-nephew's wedding in the spring, I shall bring with me a few members of your family to visit." The Fräulein did not reply except with a small smile.

With the grandduchess's affable acceptance of the match, Lord Hathaway quickly reverted to form. He accepted the felicitations of all present, and by the time he had volunteered to escort the ladies back to Walmesley, he was firmly convinced that Fräulein Gutenberg had been his firm choice from the moment that he had been presented to her.

Lord Trilby urged Lord Hathaway to remain the night at Walmesley, observing the lateness of the hour as well as pointing out the propriety of settling the marriage terms at the Grandduchess of Schaffenzeits' earliest convenience, since her grace undoubtedly intended to shortly take her leave of England.

Lord Hathaway was much taken with the mention of settlements. The Fräulein, who had her own reasons for wishing to have matters swiftly concluded, added her gentle weight in favor of the notion.

As the grandduchess took her leave, she recommended that her grandnephew remain at Berwicke for the weekend. Waiting only for Lord Hathaway and Fräulein Gutenberg to move past her, she said, "I seek to spare Marie's blushes, my lord, for naturally she must feel awkward with the speed at which her affections have been redirected."

Lord Trilby did not think that there was anything at all self-conscious about Fräulein Gutenberg's departing glance, but he wisely did not say so. "Of course, madam. The delicacy of your concern does you much credit. I shall naturally do just as you think best. That is, if Eddington here will have me."

Lord Eddington shrugged in an amiable way. "Of course we will put you up, Trilby. Dashed good notion, actually. I have been meaning to ask your opinion on a certain estate matter that—"

"My lord, do forgive my bold interruption, but do you not believe that this matter might wait for the morrow?" Lord Eddington looked down, startled, at his lady. He easily interpreted the soft expression in her eyes. "That thought did cross my mind," he agreed.

Lord and Lady Eddington said good night and went up the stairs, leaving to an outraged Mrs. Burlington the task of

providing what she considered to be the essential chaperonage for her niece.

Lord Trilby said, "I do not wish to keep you from your
bed, Mrs. Burlington."

"Oh, pray do not give it a thought, my lord. It is always a
pleasure to adjust oneself to the whims of our guests. I hold
myself in readiness to arrange everything to your satisfaction,
though of course with such an old friend as yourself we may
dispense with formality and beg you to make yourself quite at
home," Mrs. Burlington said.

"Then I know that I need not stand on ceremony with you.
I shall see Simpson about my requirements, so you must not
feel any further obligation toward me," Lord Trilby said.

He held open the door, his brows raised suggestively. Mrs.
Burlington flushed. She shot a glance at Lady Caroline, but
far from coming to her rescue, that lady said nothing at all.
Mrs. Burlington swept angrily out of the room.

29

Lord Trilby shut the door.

"That was very bad of you, my lord," Lady Caroline observed. She was very curious why the earl had gone to such lengths to be private with her.

"Yes, it was," Lord Trilby said. His satisfaction was such that it made her laugh.

"Really, Miles!"

Lord Trilby smiled at her, regarding her for a moment as his thoughts sped swiftly backward.

He had found his thoughts strangely taken up with Lady Caroline all evening. When the Grandduchess of Schaffenzeits had made her surprising announcement, he had heard of her departure with more regret than he would have believed possible. His mixed feelings were puzzling. Certainly he was fond of his great-aunt, but she had also represented a problem to him. Yet he had enjoyed her grace's visit. Surely his uppermost emotion must be relief that at last it was to be all over.

He had felt unusually threatened by the presence of Fräulein Gutenberg, who had the granduchess's sanction and had as well proved a formidable factor in her own right. The Fräulein's potency had less to do with her extraordinary beauty than with her unshakable and absolute assumption that he would make her his wife.

The coincidental arrivals of Viscount Weemswood, Mr. Underwood, and Lord Heatherton had meant a radical reshifting in the scheme of things, and to his benefit. Those gentlemen had indeed served admirably to diffuse Fräulein

Gutenberg's single-minded fixation on himself.

He had been by turns irritated and amused by the problems created by the false engagement, but his greatest feeling had been one of gratitude that he had had Lady Caroline to see him through.

Now that the time had come to end the farce, he was strangely reluctant for his relationship with Lady Caroline to return to what it had been before. His consciousness had teased and wondered at it for several days, but up until this evening, when it became certain that there was an end in sight, he had been able to thrust it repeatedly out of his mind.

"Miles? What is it?" Lady Caroline regarded him with her brows raised in inquiry. A faint amusement lit her eyes and curved her lips.

"I discover myself at a crossroads, my lady, and I hope that you might help me to discern my way," he said, guiding her to the settee.

Lady Caroline sat down, keeping her gaze on his face. "Oh, dear. *Not* another coil, Miles?"

The plaintive note in her voice raised a laugh from him. The earl looked at her, the amusement pronounced in his eyes. "Not precisely a coil, but certainly a dilemma of sorts." He paused. "Caro, can you not guess what I wish to convey to you?"

Lady Caroline stared at him for several moments. Finally she said quietly, "Yes, I think that I can. But if I am wrong, I shall look all sorts of fool, so perhaps it would be best for you to tell me."

Lord Trilby smiled. "I suppose that would be for the best," he agreed. "There has been so much subterfuge and so many hidden meanings in our dealings these last few weeks that I, too, have had difficulty discerning what was true and what was not."

He had expected to raise a laugh from Lady Caroline with his witticism, but she simply glanced away from him. There was that about her, in the manner in which she tilted her head and clasped her hands, that betrayed she was under the sway of an uncharacteristic tension.

She looked so vulnerable, yet so proud.

Unaccountably, Lord Trilby felt his easy address desert him.

"Dash it, Caro! You are so lovely it makes a man's bones ache just to look at you," he said harshly.

She looked at him then, true surprise lighting her eyes. "Why, Miles, you've never said such a thing about me before."

"I believe that I feared to," he said slowly, as by degrees that which had been teasing his consciousness for days came into focus and at last he began to comprehend certain things about himself.

"I do not understand," Lady Caroline said. Her voice wobbled and she made an effort to pull herself together. It was just that he had so thoroughly blasted through her defenses. There was something in the earl's eyes, something that almost frightened her. Her heart began to hammer in an oddly disquieting way and she could not seem to catch a proper breath.

"That does not surprise me, my dear, for I have hardly begun to do so myself."

Lord Trilby got up from the settee, restlessly pacing between there and the mantel and back. He stopped to stare down at her, but she was not at all certain that he actually saw her. He appeared to be frowning into a middle distance.

"That Season when I saw you again, seemingly for the first time in my life, I thought I had never beheld a more beautiful girl. I tumbled head over heels without truly recognizing what it was that I felt. I do recall thinking that whenever you were not at a function, it all seemed rather flat."

Lady Caroline's hands had crept to her face, and she

pressed against the sudden warmth in her cheeks. "It was a lovely Season," she said, tears clouding her vision. She dropped her eyes, no longer able to meet his gaze.

There was a long moment of silence.

"Caro, do you recall a fellow by the name of Swallow?"

Lady Caroline was startled. The unexpected harshness of his lordship's voice and the abrupt change in topic threw her into confusion. She understood, however, that the sweet reminiscence was done. Blinking away the foolish tears, she said, "No, I . . . Oh, wait a moment. I seem to vaguely recall . . . He was a friend of yours, was he not? For some reason, I seem to connect the name with some sort of sad tragedy."

"Yes." The earl gave a short laugh. "Swallow was a particular friend of mine at Cambridge, though he was two years my senior. After he left Cambridge and went up to London, I saw little of him, but we managed to keep in touch through a few scattered holidays and letters. In any event, at some point I began to realize that Swallow was unusually melancholy. When next I saw him I taxed him over it, trying to discover the reason behind his odd bursts of emotion, but he insisted all was perfectly well."

Lord Trilby paused, as though remembering again that time. "Months later I had a letter from Swallow in which he told me that he had at last gained the affections of the lady he had loved, quite passionately, for more than a year. Naturally, this satisfied my concern. I thought the rocky courtship was behind Swallow's depression, and thereafter I forgot the matter."

Lady Caroline had been sorting through her own memory as the earl spoke. "I do recall something now, I think. It happened near the end of the Season, as I remember. The young couple took flight for Gretna Green, but there was a ghastly accident of some sort that killed them both."

"No accident occurred, my lady, but murderous violence," Lord Trilby said harshly. He returned to the mantel, and now he was staring into the fire, his expression such that Lady Caroline could have sworn he saw something horrible in the flames.

She stared at the earl. She could not imagine what any of this ancient history had to do with her or with his lordship, but that it was of importance to him was patently obvious.

"Miles, how do you know that? What do you know that you have not yet told me?"

Lord Trilby glanced quickly at her. He sighed wearily. "On the eve of the scandal, I received a missive from Swallow. It was disjointed, incoherent almost, obviously written in the throes of powerful emotion. I gathered finally this his lady had spurned him, and as a result, all of his former love for her had turned to black hatred. Swallow said he meant to have his revenge, however, for he would abduct her that very night and carry her off to Gretna Green."

"My word, did he do so, then?" Lady Caroline asked, appalled and yet fascinated.

The earl nodded. "I did not at first believe that Swallow would do anything of the sort, but as the hours passed, I became more uneasy. I chanced to show the letter to Sinjin, who also knew Swallow, and he suggested that we go around to Swallow's lodgings. Swallow was not at home, and he had not been since early that afternoon. After some debate, we went round to the young lady's home. She was gone as well. Her family was half-crazed with worry. Sinjin and I spoke privately to the father, showing him the letter. He instantly called for his carriage, swearing that when he caught up with Swallow he would horsewhip him to within an inch of his life."

Lady Caroline kept her eyes on the earl's face. "You and Sinjin—you went after Swallow and the young lady."

"Yes. Before we could get a team put to, the girl's father had already gained a good lead on us. But Sinjin was always a better whip than anyone I've ever known. We quickly overtook and passed the irate gentleman."

"Did you come up with them, then?"

The earl nodded. He moved his shoulders in a restless fashion as though to shift an unpleasant weight. There was a grim look about his mouth. "They had stopped at an inn and taken a private parlor. The staff was standing about, listening, as we walked inside. There was a hideous commotion abovestairs, the muffled screams of rage from a man and a woman, and the smashing of crockery. Sinjin and I ran up the stairs. We pounded on the locked door, but to no avail. We had decided to set our shoulders against the door, when a single piercing scream came from inside the room. Sinjin and I stared at one another, quite frozen. Then in a frenzy we attacked the door. The young lady's father arrived while we were at it, and shouted us on, shaking his coiled whip over his head. There was a crashing report, and then utter silence. When we had beaten the door down, we found them, both quite dead. Swallow had stabbed the girl and then shot himself."

"Oh, Miles. How utterly horrible," Lady Caroline whispered, throat tight. She could not dare to begin to imagine the spectacle that must have greeted the horrified eyes of those who had entered the room. How truly horrible for the poor girl's father. For Sinjin, and for Miles.

For Miles, she thought in awful comprehension. "I wondered, that Season, why you seemed changed. Oh, you were still amusing and witty, but somehow grown aloof. I did not understand it. I could not."

"I had seen what lengths a man could be driven to by strong emotion. I had lost one who in some ways had stood for me as a brother. I was struck with horror that I might one day . . ." Breaking off suddenly, Lord Trilby drew a long breath. He managed to summon up a smile, but one that did not quite reach his eyes. "In short, Caroline, I became terrified of my own capacity to feel for others."

"You became frightened of me." Lady Caroline nodded, as though at a quite normal revelation. "Yes, I see. I quite see." There was a blind look in her eyes. She was caught in the grip of an almost intolerable despair. She understood very well. Oh, how well she understood. The earl was attempting to explain to her, as painlessly and gently as was possible, that the hopes she had once harbored had become futile in that very Season she had fallen in love with him.

The long years had passed, but her hopes had remained, banked as coals beneath the ashes perhaps, but still warmed in the friendship that she had retained with the Earl of Walmesley. She could see now that those hopes had been utterly wasted.

Lady Caroline made a curious gesture. "I do not know quite what to say, my lord, except . . . I do understand what you are trying to tell me."

Lord Trilby returned swiftly to sit beside her on the settee. He took her hands, though she resisted at first. She refused to meet his eyes, however. "Do you understand, my lady?" he asked softly.

She gave a jerky nod. "Of course. It is unfortunate that we must wait until the grandduchess is gone from England before I might safely jilt you, but—"

"Caro, I have been the greatest of fools these six years."

Her startled gaze flew to his face. "My lord?"

He smiled somewhat twistedly. "I do not wish to be jilted, my lady."

"Do you not?"

The earl lifted one hand to touch her face. His fingers

trembled. "When I think of the wasted years, Caro . . . Sinjin was right: someone should have married you years ago."

Lady Caroline was held by the expression in the earl's eyes, and the tightness about her heart began to loosen. Suddenly she felt herself to be winging back in time to her first Season. Her pulses tumbled erratically. "Yes, someone really should have."

The earl slowly narrowed the distance between them. His lips touched hers tentatively. He drew back a little. "I have grown attached to our engagement, Lady Caroline."

"Have you indeed, my lord?" she asked breathlessly.

Suddenly she was crushed in his arms. He kissed her thoroughly, with a hunger that had been denied for too long. Lady Caroline returned the earl's passion with fervor, laughing and crying at once.

When he at last released her, her eyes glowed with the blaze of a thousand candles. "What means this ungentlemanly display, my lord?"

Lord Trilby slanted a brow. "I should have known you would demand your pound, my lady." She but laughed and shook her head.

Lady Caroline would have returned to his arms then, but he held her away a bit longer. His voice deep and somber, he said, "I love you most earnestly and with all my heart, my lady. I have used you abominably, I know, and I am unforgivably behindtimes. But despite it all, will you accept my suit?"

"What of your fears, my lord?"

"I fear more your rejection, Caro."

"I could not possibly spurn you, my lord, for I have loved you quite hopelessly for too many years. It is a wretched habit that I shall never be free of, I fear."

The Earl of Walmesley directed a heart-stopping glance at her and caught her up in his arms at last.